THE BI-SINGULARITY

RUTH HEASMAN

Can the race to secure Bitcoin's future also secure the future of humanity?

VELLICHOR PRESS

This is a work of fiction. Similarities to real people, places, or events are entirely coincidental.

THE BITCOIN SINGULARITY

First edition. May 25, 2024.

Copyright © 2024 Ruth Heasman.

Written by Ruth Heasman.

To my wonderful family—Richard, James, George and Merlin—who've patiently put up with me going on and on about Bitcoin *ad nauseum* for the past decade and who didn't laugh when I said I was going to write a novel.

Prologue

A heavy gloom hangs over the city, its once vibrant spirit crushed under the weight of one catastrophe after another. Walking the streets, you can feel it in the very air—a miasma of despair and decay.

It started with the pandemics—the first one a shock, the second the final nail in the coffin for a teetering economy. The heavy-handed lockdowns did their work, bankrupting small businesses en-masse while mega-corporations consolidated power and wealth.

When the central bank digital currencies emerged, they were touted as the solution, a lifeline in the storms. But the technology failed to deliver, bogged down by backlogs, errors, and viruses that left commerce paralyzed.

Now in 2026, London is but a shadow of its former self. Shops are shuttered, streets deserted. One third of London's former inhabitants remain, cloistered indoors lest they be apprehended by the night watch. The percussive thrum of helicopters overhead and the wails of sirens cut through the silence. Money as we knew it is gone, replaced by a dysfunctional myriad of digital currencies that fail when needed most. News comes in spurts of propaganda from robotic voices, more fiction than fact. There is no telling what is real anymore.

The people trudge on, hardened and weary. Gathering in homes behind bolted doors, conversations are murmured for fear of surveillance. Trust is a relic and communities crumble as many retreat into isolation. The institutions meant to provide order and security have become menacing beasts.

Yet beneath it all, behind curtains and in basements, pockets of resistance still flicker. Those who remember the past and believe in what could be again. Inventors, hackers, movers and shakers. Holding close the embers of innovation and hope, determined to stoke them into flames to burn away the decay and illuminate the future.

The storm is not over, but dawn still comes. And with it, a new day begins...

Chapter 1

The shrill doppler shriek of high-velocity drones jolted Violet Everly from her thoughts, their relentless patrol slicing through the early dawn. The reverberations shook her casement windows, unleashing a resonant boom that pulsed through the stillness of her tiny flat. Heart thumping, she yanked off her headphones and peered into the orange skies above the weathered terraces of north London.

As the drones vanished into the burgeoning light, a pang of nostalgia pulled at her—a yearning for the days of the simple pleasure of sipping coffee in her favourite deli, now just a ghost in the rubble of a world changed beyond recognition.

With a weary sigh, she extricated herself from the tangle of cables and tiptoed into the bedroom to check on her sleeping sister. Violet gazed down affectionately at Flora's face, so peaceful and untroubled in slumber, a bit of drool on her pillow.

A wistful smile played on Violet's lips as she gazed at Flora, her kid sister, who was peacefully sleeping—three years her junior, yet forever the embodiment of innocence and youth in Violet's heart, no matter the passage of time or the challenges life presented. Throughout the trials and tribulations of the preceding years, Flora had somehow maintained her childlike optimism and loving spirit, unlike Violet, who had only grown more cynical and wary.

Violet tiptoed to the kitchenette and rifled through the cupboards, hoping she could concoct something resembling breakfast. The best Violet could assemble was manufactured eggs created from synthesised proteins and some dehydrated insect dust prepared with water to imitate oatmeal, made somewhat edible solely by the inclusion of honey she had stashed away.

She was whipping up two bowls when Flora shuffled in, hair dishevelled, clothes askew. "Smells delicious," Flora said sarcastically, stifling a yawn.

"Only the finest cuisine for you, dear sister," Violet laughed. She handed Flora her unappetising meal along with a cup of tea, made with one of the remaining precious real tea bags she had stockpiled.

They sat together at the small table by the window overlooking the empty street four stories below. Violet gazed out at the fog-shrouded abandoned electric cars and cracked pavement, feeling the familiar unease creep up her spine. She tried to avoid looking outside most days—it only invited worry—but sometimes the grimy panorama below still took her breath away. How did the world crumble so completely?

A gentle touch on her hand drew Violet's focus back to Flora's kind, tired eyes. "Hey, it's going to be okay," Flora said. "We've made it this far, we'll keep on making it."

Violet managed a small smile. Her sister knew her so well. She squeezed Flora's hand back, hoping her face didn't betray the uncertainty she felt.

After breakfast, Violet helped her frail sister get settled on the sofa with their cat Ada, a cup of tea and a scavenged book. Then she shuffled over to her workstation, a chaotic array of mismatched tech all held together by duct tape and determination.

She slipped on her headphones and awoke her personal AI, Lakshmi, whose avatar flickered to life on the screen—a disembodied face composed of particles undulating like waves. Lakshmi's distinct features continually reshaped in a hypnotic flow, her large eyes shining with intelligence through the constant flux.

"Good morning Lakshmi," Violet typed when the AI interface loaded. "What's our outlook today?"

"That so-called 'climate protest' on the news this morning was AI-generated propaganda," Lakshmi noted. "The people shown in the footage do not actually exist."

"Well that's unsettling," Violet muttered. "Anything else on the radar I should be aware of?" Violet asked under her breath.

"The proposed tax on natural remedies is being aggressively lobbied for by PrimePharma, which happens to be the world's second largest pharmaceutical company," Lakshmi added.

Violet nodded, unsurprised by the corrupt self-interest running rampant these days. She was preparing to dive into trading when Lakshmi paused, her programmed hesitance indicating she had uncovered something sensitive.

"Violet, there's chatter about a threat to the Satoshi Coins—the million bitcoins mined by Nakamoto himself." Violet's eyes widened in surprise. Those coins were the stuff of legend, not having moved from the addresses they were first mined into almost seventeen years ago, and possessing them could tilt the course of history. If they were truly under threat of theft, it could upend their fragile existence, dependent as it was on the small amounts of digital currency Violet had managed to save before the crash.

"Lakshmi, can you give me more on this? Where's this information coming from?" Violet asked, urgency in her voice. However, the AI remained silent, offering no further details, and the enigmatic message had already vanished from their chat log. Violet's thoughts spun rapidly, grasping the significance of her discovery—a mystery that held the potential to alter everything she knew.

VIOLET'S MIND WAS REELING. The Satoshi Coins—over a million bitcoins mined by the pseudonymous creator himself in the earliest days of the network had lain untouched for over seventeen years. Their existence was legendary...but were they truly on the move now, or did her personal AI Lakshmi just hallucinate?

She scrolled frantically through her chat log with the AI, but found no trace of the startling message. She rifled through news sites, cryptocurrency forums, dark web whisper networks. Nothing. It was as if the utterance had never occurred.

Running a hand through her unruly auburn hair, Violet tried to make sense of it all. Why would Lakshmi reveal something so explosive only to erase it completely? Was it possible her prompts had unlocked information the AI should not possess? Was she being surveilled?

Too anxious to focus on trading, Violet pushed her chair back from her workstation and began pacing the cluttered space between her desk and the sofa where Flora was curled up reading.

Noticing Violet's agitated state, Flora set her book aside, brow furrowed in concern. "Hey, you okay? You seem really stressed."

Violet paused her pacing, trying to decide how much to reveal. She needed Flora's level-headed perspective, but didn't want to worry her over what could just be an AI glitch.

"I was chatting with Lakshmi about potential trades today when she mentioned something strange..." Violet began.

She sat down on the sofa beside Flora and recounted the cryptic message about a threat to the infamous 'Satoshi Coins'. Flora's eyes widened slightly at the news, but she listened calmly, giving Violet space to process it out loud.

"I guess I'm just trying to understand if this is something I should be worried about," Violet continued. "I mean, the Satoshi Coins are the earliest mined coins of Bitcoin. A million coins mined by its founder that have remained untouched since the network launched. They're enormously valuable, but also symbolic. If someone managed to take control of them...well, it could mean chaos."

Violet twisted a strand of hair anxiously. "I probably sound paranoid, but our little stash of bitcoin from before the economic collapse is part of how we've survived. If the Satoshi Coins are somehow compromised or stolen and it messes with the stability of bitcoin as a whole..."

She trailed off. Flora reached out and took Violet's hand, giving it a reassuring squeeze.

"I don't think you're being paranoid," Flora said. "If there's even a chance something could put our livelihood at risk, it's worth taking seriously. But let's not assume the worst quite yet. Maybe Lakshmi was just glitching and this news isn't real."

Despite Flora's reassuring tone, Violet detected a glint of worry in her sister's tired eyes. She had to get to the bottom of this.

"You're right," Violet sighed, squeezing Flora's hand back. "I'm probably overreacting. But I at least want to ask Lakshmi about it again, see if she has any other details."

Flora nodded. "I think that's wise. But don't go down any scary conspiracy rabbit holes, okay?" she implored with a small smile.

Violet laughed under her breath. "You didn't seem to mind when I stockpiled the toilet rolls and honey" she whispered half to herself, and then more loudly "I'll try." She stood, feeling a bit less anxious. "Let's see if I can get any clarity from Lakshmi on whether this threat is legit. And I'll keep you posted."

"Sounds good," Flora said, settling comfortably into the couch again. "And hey, try not to stress too much. Whatever this turns out to be, we'll handle it."

Violet gave her a grateful smile, hoping her optimism was not misplaced. She had a mystery to unravel.

VIOLET RUBBED HER BLEARY eyes and checked the time—nearly 3 AM. She should have been asleep hours ago, but she was still glued to her workstation, combing the internet for any shred of information about a threat to the Satoshi Coins.

So far her search had been fruitless. No chatter on crypto forums, no hints on Reddit or IRC, no obscure posts on the dark web. It was as if the vanishing message from Lakshmi had been a figment of her imagination.

Letting out an irritated huff, Violet sat back and ran her hands through her hair. Her eyes felt gritty and her lids heavy, but her mind was racing too fast to sleep.

She blinked hard, trying to focus on the code scrolling across one of her screens. She was syphoning some AI training datasets, hoping she could pick up on any veiled references. But so far it was all just garbled machine learning fodder. The clink of a mug being set down startled Violet from her bleary-eyed scanning. She swivelled her chair to see Flora standing there in her pyjamas, her hair mussed from sleep.

"I figured if you were going to keep hacking away over there, you'd need some tea to power you through," Flora said, stifling a yawn. She perched on the edge of Violet's messy desk, her brow creased with concern as she studied her sister's face.

"Vi, you're clearly exhausted. Don't you think this can wait until morning?" Flora implored.

Violet sighed, cradling the warm mug in her hands. "I wish I could rest, Flo. But this whole Satoshi Coin thing is nagging at me. We can't just ignore something this big."

Flora nodded, her eyes filled with empathy. She knew how dogged Violet could be when solving a complex puzzle."Well, at least try to get some sleep soon, okay?" Flora squeezed Violet's shoulder encouragingly as she shuffled back to bed, leaving Violet alone with the glow of the screens.

Violet smiled, grateful for Flora's unconditional support. She sipped the tea slowly, weighing her options. She was running out of places to dig, but couldn't let this go just yet.

In a stroke of late-night inspiration, Violet opened an old cryptographer's forum she used to frequent, now long abandoned. With a bit of technical coaxing she could still post anonymously. It felt like sending a message in a bottle into the void, but on the slim chance someone knew anything, it was worth a shot. She typed out a brief post asking about any activity related to the Satoshi Coins and included her anonymous contact info. Before she could overthink it, she hit Post and shut everything down for the night.

Exhausted, Violet collapsed into bed. But her mind was still buzzing and rest eluded her. Bleak fantasies swirled of how life would become if their small cache of Bitcoin lost its value. Eventually she slipped into a fretful sleep, chased by white-coated figures who wanted to trap her and Flora in a stark white room without exit.

Gasping awake, Violet fumbled to turn on a light. She tried to slow her racing heart as she oriented herself in the quiet bedroom. Flora slept soundly still across from her. Violet glanced at the clock—5:17 AM. Knowing more sleep would be impossible, she crept to her workstation . Booting it up, she navigated to the cryptographer's forum from last night. She almost hoped there would be no reply. Instead, a notification flashed indicating she had a private message from one ProfessorFaustus. Hands shaking, Violet opened it.

"I know what you seek," the message read simply. "Meet me at sun-down this evening behind St. Paul's Cathedral if you want answers about the coins."

Violet's eyes widened and her pulse quickened. This was exactly the contact she had hoped for, but suddenly meeting a stranger to discuss illegal activity seemed dangerous.

Glancing again at her peacefully sleeping sister, Violet knew she had to take the risk. Flora's future depended on it. She began preparing for a clandestine trip into London.

VIOLET STOOD BY THE window, staring out at the labyrinthine city below. As the day crawled by with agonising slowness, the message from ProfessorFaustus loomed large on her screen, its glow intensifying as the sunlight waned and the minutes ticked down until their ominous meeting. Her mind was a whirlwind of doubts and fears. Meeting a stranger, especially in these troubled times, could be perilous. And then there was Flora.

She turned to glance at her sister, who lay curled up on the sofa, lost in a book. Flora's presence had always been a comforting anchor in Violet's life. But now, Violet felt an unfamiliar weight in her chest—the burden of keeping a secret from the one person she trusted above all others.

Her heart thudded uncomfortably as she thought about stepping out into the city. The streets, once familiar, now seemed like treacherous mazes, filled with unknown threats.

Violet's agoraphobia, a lingering shadow since the world's descent into chaos, clawed at her with icy fingers. The very idea of venturing into the unknown filled her with dread.

Flora glanced up, her brow furrowing. "Vi, are you okay? You look like you've seen a ghost."

Violet forced a smile, her stomach churning. "Just tired, Flo. Didn't sleep well last night."

The lie tasted bitter on her tongue. She had always been honest with Flora, their bond fortified by mutual trust and openness. But now, she was stepping into a world of shadows and secrets, a world where the truth could be a dangerous luxury.

Flora studied her for a moment longer, concern etching her features, but she eventually nodded, accepting Violet's explanation. "Well, if you need to talk, I'm here," she said gently, turning back to her book.

Violet felt a pang of guilt. She wanted to confide in Flora, to share the burden of this ominous meeting and the weight of her fears. But she couldn't. Not yet. The risks were too high, the stakes too uncertain.

As the sun began its descent, casting long shadows across the cramped flat, Violet's apprehension grew. She moved restlessly around the room, her agitation mounting. Every ticking second brought her closer to the appointed time, and her decision crystallised with reluctant resolve.

She slipped into her jacket, the fabric feeling like a suit of armour against an unseen adversary. Glancing at Flora, who was now engrossed in her book, Violet took a steadying breath.

"I'm going out for a bit," she announced, her voice steadier than she felt.

Flora looked up, surprise flickering in her eyes. "At this hour? Where to?"

"Just a quick errand," Violet lied again, hating the necessity of it. "We need more protein bars and milk. I won't be long."

Flora's gaze lingered on her, filled with a silent question, but she simply nodded. "Be careful, Vi, it's nearly curfew."

Violet offered a weak smile and turned towards the door, her heart pounding a frantic rhythm. As she stepped out of the flat, the door closing with a soft click behind her, a sense of foreboding enveloped her. She was stepping into the unknown, leaving the safety of her sanctuary for a meeting shrouded in mystery.

But curiosity propelled her forward. Violet descended the stairs, each step a battle against the rising tide of fear and uncertainty within her. She had to know the truth about the enigmatic ProfessorFaustus and the danger lurking in the shadows of their fractured world.

As she emerged onto the deserted street, the last rays of the sun dipped below the horizon, and the city's twilight embrace closed in around her. Violet's journey into the heart of a mystery had begun.

THE BITCOIN SINGULARITY

Chapter 2

Violet pulled her fraying coat tighter, her shoulders hunched against the chill of the dusky evening. The setting sun cast an ominous orange glow across the towering buildings of London's centre, doing little to alleviate the shadows stretching through the alleys.

Stepping outside her building, Violet felt the familiar vice-like grip of anxiety seize her chest. She paused just beyond the front steps, willing her heartbeat to steady. It had been months since she last ventured this far from the meagre comfort of the flat. Now, confronting the grim realities of the decaying city, she questioned her decision to come here tonight.

Get it together, Vi, she urged herself, taking a few deep gulps of the heavy air. She had to find out if there was any truth to the threat against the mythical Satoshi Coins. Their small cache of crypto depended on Bitcoin retaining whatever value it still held in this ravaged economy.

Pulling up the collar of her coat, Violet set off into the gloom. She stuck to a circuitous route through narrow service alleys, avoiding the main thoroughfares and the risk of crossing paths with the roving enforcement patrols. Curfew would be in effect soon, and she could not afford to be caught outside.

Violet shuddered at the thought of what happened to those detained for breaking curfew. Disappeared to government black sites, if the rumours held any truth. Never seen again. She quickened her pace, hoping the rapid rhythm of her boots would drown out the dark scenarios unspooling in her mind.

The farther Violet ventured from the safe familiarity of home, the more her breath grew tight in her chest. She tried to focus on the details of the crumbling architecture, using the grounding techniques she had mastered after the deaths of both her mother and any semblance of normal life as she knew it. But being surrounded by the looming derelict buildings only heightened her nerves.

You should have told Flora where you were going, the thought flashed through Violet's mind. If anything happens to you out here... A fresh wave of anxiety crashed over her. She shook her head sharply, as if she could dislodge the worries and regret. No, it was better Flora didn't know, didn't have to shoulder the burden of this mystery too. Violet had to unravel this alone.

The shadows seemed to stretch and contort oddly under the orange glow of streetlights flickering on. Violet's pulse thrummed as she slipped down an especially dark, narrow alley. She just needed to make it to St. Paul's Cathedral to meet her mysterious contact, Professor Faustus, according to the cryptic message. An omen if there ever was one, Violet thought wryly.

She pulled her coat even tighter. The temperature seemed to have dropped several degrees since she left home. Strange. A prickle on the back of her neck made Violet wheel around, half expecting to find someone shadowing her. But she saw only empty darkness behind. Stop letting your imagination run wild, she chided herself.

Violet quickened her pace again. The looming spires of the cathedral were just becoming visible over the roofline ahead. She was close. She moved half in a daze, putting one foot in front of the other through instinct alone.

Before she realised it, the hulking façade of St. Paul's towered above her just across the abandoned square. Violet slipped into the narrow alley that ran behind the cathedral. She stumbled over refuse and clutter scattered along the ground. The overpowering odour of urine burned her nostrils. She pulled her collar over her nose and mouth, trying not to gag.

Violet sidled along the shadowed alley, peering around for any sign of another soul. Nothing. Just the detritus of a crumbling society. She strained her ears for approaching footsteps but only heard the rush of her own blood pulsating with anticipation.

What am I even doing here? Violet questioned silently in the darkness. Waiting to meet some shadowy figure to discuss criminal plots? I must be losing my mind... She shook her head, laughing softly at her own absurdity.

A scraping sound behind Violet made her whirl around. A large rat scurried across the alley, rooting through the garbage. Violet released a shaky breath. Get it together, she urged herself again. She couldn't lose her nerve now.

Time passed agonisingly slowly as Violet waited pressed against the grimy cathedral wall. Her legs began to ache from standing so long in one place. She considered retreating back home and abandoning this mad rendezvous.

Just as Violet resolved to give it a few more minutes before cutting her losses, a bulky figure detached itself from the deeper shadows further down the alley. She froze. As the shape drew closer, Violet's muscles tensed, ready to flee.

The figure glided forward stopping just short of Violet. She could just make out a dark Macintosh raincoat and a face obscured by a hat and high collar. Violet's mouth went dry.

"Professor Faustus?" she managed to rasp out, embarrassed by the tremor in her voice.

The figure hesitated a beat before giving a barely perceptible nod. Violet thought she saw a flash of sharp eyes surveying her from the shadows under the hat brim. Without a word, the figure turned and beckoned Violet to follow him down the alley.

Heart hammering wildly, Violet pushed herself from the wall. This was the contact she had been waiting for. Her one chance at answers. Steeling her nerves, she hurried after the retreating figure into the shadows.

VIOLET HURRIED TO KEEP pace with the retreating figure as he wound through a maze of narrow alleys. She strained to glimpse any identifying details of the man, but his hat and high collar obscured his features.

Unease gnawed at Violet's gut. This cloak and dagger business was well outside her comfort zone. But the possibility of answers kept her following the stranger through the gloom.

They travelled in tense silence, their footfalls echoing off the derelict brick buildings looming around them. The smell of rot and stale urine permeated the confined passages and Violet fought the urge to gag.

She lost all sense of direction as they snaked deeper into the tangled back channels of the city. The stranger moved with purpose, never hesitating at forks or intersections. Violet wondered if she'd be able to find her way out alone and the thought sent a spike of fear through her.

As Violet was considering making an escape from this unnerving guide, the figure halted beside a weathered red door tucked between warehouses. He rapped out a rhythmic knock, the sound piercing the heavy quiet.

Violet shifted her weight from one foot to the other, nerves jangling. This was a mistake. She never should've come. She took a small step back, preparing to turn and flee.

Before she could act, a slot in the door creaked open. Violet caught a glimpse of a pair of narrowed eyes surveying them. The slot slammed shut again. She heard the grind of multiple locks disengaging before the red door finally wheezed open.

The stranger stepped through without hesitation. Violet lingered a moment, anxiety rooting her in place. Then she saw the door begin closing again. It was now or never. Trying to quiet her racing mind, she slipped through the door just before it thudded closed behind her.

Violet found herself in a dim, cavernous room thick with haze. The space was dotted with small round tables, each

THE BITCOIN SINGULARITY

with a single patron nursing a drink. A melancholy jazz tune crooned from unseen speakers. The place had an air of faded glory, like an antique lounge frozen in time.

Violet's escort wove his way among the tables, patrons glancing up with mild curiosity before returning to their drinks. Violet followed in the stranger's wake, keeping her head down. The rich scent of aged whisky and stale cigar smoke permeated the space, an odd comfort in its familiarity.

The figure led Violet to a booth tucked into a shadowy corner, well away from the other patrons. He slid into the curved leather seat and finally tilted his face up toward Violet. She hesitated only a moment before settling gingerly across from him.

"Apologies for all the dramatics," the man spoke. His voice was a low rumble tinged with an unmistakable Australian accent. "But we needed privacy for this conversation."

He removed his hat, revealing sharp eyes that took Violet's measure. She estimated him to be in his 50s, his face creased with a fine head of brown hair just beginning to show signs of grey, yet his look was astute and piercing. Violet's eyes widened. Could this really be...

"Satoshi Nakamoto," the man offered in greeting, mouth quirking up on one side.

VIOLET HOPED HER SLACK-jawed expression didn't betray the total shock reverberating through her. Satoshi Nakamoto. The mythical creator of Bitcoin. Sitting here in front of her in the flesh. It seemed utterly unbelievable.

Satoshi seemed to read her disbelief easily. "I imagine you have about a thousand questions," he said, tone wry. "But first, I'd like to know who told you the Satoshi Coins were at risk?"

Violet collected herself enough to form a response. "I-I didn't hear it from any person. It was an AI I created. I have a way of, well, prompting the AIs to reveal things they normally wouldn't."

Satoshi raised an eyebrow, glancing Violet up and down as if re-evaluating her. "Very interesting," he murmured. "That skill could prove useful." Violet sensed this was high praise coming from the legendary Bitcoin founder.

Before Violet could parse his cryptic words, a waiter approached their table. "The usual, Sir?" the man asked deferentially.

Satoshi gave a curt nod. The waiter swiftly returned with two glasses of amber liquid. Satoshi slid one toward Violet. "You look like you could use a stiff drink. It's decent Scotch, I assure you—a ten year old Lagavulin single malt."

Violet hesitated only a moment before taking a bracing gulp, the smoky warmth pooling in her stomach. She was certainly out of her element here. But something told her she needed to see this through, wherever it led.

Taking a sip from his own glass, Satoshi studied her intently. "So tell me," he said finally, "what do you think you know about my million coins and the threat against them?"

Violet took a deep breath. It was time to find out if this man truly was who he claimed.

THE BITCOIN SINGULARITY

SATOSHI EYED VIOLET intently, awaiting her response. She took a steadying breath before speaking.

"From what I've gathered, you're the one who created Bitcoin in 2008," Violet said with measured precision. "It was your whitepaper, under the alias Satoshi Nakamoto, that outlined its foundation – a peer-to-peer electronic cash system, underpinned by a technology called blockchain."

She paused, but Satoshi simply gestured for her to continue, his expression unreadable.

"The network went live in 2009," Violet went on. "In the early days, you mined over a million bitcoins, which have become known as the Satoshi Coins. They're your stash from Bitcoin's earliest mined blocks and have never been moved."

Satoshi nodded. "That's more or less the gist of it," he said dryly. "The SparkNotes version, if you will."

Violet felt her cheeks flush, but she held his gaze steady. "If you mean I don't fully grasp the technical intricacies, you're right. My speciality is software, specifically AI, not the nuts and bolts of blockchain."

Satoshi smiled ruefully. "Impressive, you're more informed than I expected. And your expertise with AI may prove useful," he said, eyeing Violet thoughtfully over the rim of his glass.

"But you are correct that you lack a deeper understanding of how Bitcoin truly works, and how it's been corrupted." Satoshi leaned back, his eyes taking on a darker glint.

"So allow me to enlighten you." He launched into a detailed technical explanation of Bitcoin's design, its mining process and potential for scalability. The more he revealed, the wider Violet's eyes became. She had underestimated the sheer brilliance underlying his creation.

"NOW THIS IS WHERE IT gets interesting," Satoshi continued after nearly an hour spent illuminating the technical foundations of Bitcoin.

"In its current form, BTC or 'Bitcoin Core' as the bastardised version is called, can never achieve my original vision. It's been deliberately crippled by small blocks and layers of needless complexity designed to favour centralised control."His voice had taken on an edge that sent a chill down Violet's spine. She remained silent, letting him continue uninterrupted.

"You see, Bitcoin caught the banks and corporations by surprise at first, but once they recognised the threat it posed to their monopoly, they moved to infiltrate the project and warp Bitcoin to serve their own ends."

Satoshi stared off over Violet's shoulder, his gaze far away. "My early developers sold out the vision. They restricted block size to one megabyte under the guise of decentralisation. But true decentralisation only comes from setting the base protocol in stone!"

He refocused on Violet with sudden intensity. "A navy is not decentralised because the captain of each ship can choose their own course at will. That way lies collision and chaos."

Violet's head spun trying to keep up, but she was beginning to grasp the severity of his allegations, if true.

THE BITCOIN SINGULARITY 25

Satoshi took a long draught of whisky before continuing, his voice a low growl. "By limiting capacity they've ensured BTC can never reach critical mass as a payment system. It's slow, congested, unreliable—an absolute failure as usable cash."

He shook his head bitterly. "So the parasites moved on to the next phase of hijacking my creation. They convinced the masses that BTC is Bitcoin as I envisioned it, when the truth is that it's been engineered for the exact opposite purpose." Violet sensed they were reaching the crux of the issue. She leaned in, captivated by Satoshi's story despite her lingering doubts.

"They aim to discredit Bitcoin entirely when their crippled BTC version inevitably fails," Satoshi nearly spat. "But I preserved the original protocol in a forked version—Bitcoin SV. And now they are coming for my stash of coins to undermine confidence in even this last bastion."

Violet's mind spun with Satoshi's revelations. She took a moment to collect her thoughts before responding.

"This is a lot to take in," she began slowly. "But I want to understand. You mentioned your coins are at risk of theft. How exactly would that be possible?"

Satoshi nodded, his expression becoming grave. "To explain that, I need to tell you about the Tulip Trust."

He lowered his voice. "Years ago, when it became clear certain entities would stop at nothing to get their hands on my stash of coins, I took action to put them beyond anyone's reach."

"I devised a complex encryption scheme called Shamir's Secret Sharing. It splits a private key into multiple 'shards' that can be distributed to different parties. To unlock the coins, you need a minimum number of shards—in this case, three."

Violet leaned in, intrigued. "So you gave key shards to trusted allies?"

"Exactly," Satoshi confirmed. "I set up a trust called the Tulip Trust and split my private key into seven shards. I gave one shard to my writing partner, one to an MI6 agent I'd worked with, and one to an old cypherpunk associate, among others."

"The idea was that together, these keyholders—my Trustees—could eventually unlock the coins if I wished. But with the shards distributed, it protected them from theft. To steal the coins requires compromise of multiple Trustees."

Satoshi's eyes darkened. "Unfortunately, it appears someone has begun doing just that."

Violet felt a shiver down her spine. "You mean, attacking your Trustees?"

"Yes," Satoshi growled. "Two have gone silent in recent weeks. The MI6 agent turned up dead just days ago. It's only a matter of time before they target more."

"Once they have three key shards, they can unlock the address holding my million coins on a predetermined date." Satoshi tapped his fingers on the table anxiously.

Violet frowned. "What do you mean, on a predetermined date?"

"Ah, yes. I should explain—I used a smart contract trick called nLockTime. It ensures the coins can only be moved after a set point in the future—specifically, seventeen years from their mining."

Realisation dawned on Violet. "So in just over a month from now, the coins will become accessible? Is that the deadline?"

Satoshi nodded grimly. "You understand now. We're in a race against time to stop my Trustees from being compromised. Once three shards are combined, my coins can be stolen on that date."

Violet sat back, stunned by the enormity of what Satoshi had revealed. This was no idle threat—it was an active, high-stakes theft targeting the most symbolic cache of Bitcoin in existence.

"They've already killed one Trustee that we know of," Satoshi muttered. "We're running out of time." He fixed Violet with an intense, searching look.

"But with your unique skills, we may just have a chance. Are you with me?"

Violet held his gaze unflinchingly. The stakes could not be higher. But she knew there was only one answer.

"I'm with you. What do we do first?"

A grin flashed across Satoshi's face. For the first time since they met, he looked hopeful. The game was afoot.

Chapter 3

Violet eased open the front door, cringing as the hinges creaked loudly in the silence. She slipped inside, pausing to let her eyes adjust to the dimness. The rooms were still and dark, indicating Flora had likely gone to bed. Violet breathed a soft sigh of relief. Her late night meeting had stretched on, but perhaps she could avoid worrying Flora.

As Violet crept on quiet feet toward the bedroom, an agonised moan from the living room made her blood run cold. Rushing into the room, she flicked on a lamp and her heart seized at the sight of Flora convulsing violently on the floor. Her limbs flailed, back arching off the ground at an alarming angle.

"Flora!" Violet cried, terror gripping her like a vice. She fell to her knees beside her sister, reaching to grasp Flora's quaking shoulders. Her sister's eyes were rolled back, foam bubbling from her lips.

"No, please no," Violet pleaded desperately. She cradled Flora, gently at first and then more firmly, trying to break the seizure's ravaging hold. But her sister's body continued to jerk and thrash. Flora's hand lashed out in her delirium, catching Violet hard across the cheekbone. Violet scrambled up and ran to grab a paper bag, then knelt by her sister again.

"Breathe, Flora, just breathe," she urged, pressing the bag over her sister's nose and mouth. Violet wasn't sure if her panicked voice was even reaching Flora. "Stay with me, please just stay with me!"

After agonising minutes that felt like hours, Flora's violent convulsions finally began to ebb. Her arched back relaxed, and her breathing steadied into a more normal rhythm. Violet let out a sob of relief, tears spilling down her cheeks. Flora's seizures always terrified her, but she hadn't expected one tonight.

As awareness returned to Flora's eyes, she gripped Violet's arm with surprising strength. "Vi," she rasped, "where were you?" Flora's voice broke as tears ran down her face. "I thought they had taken you away!"

Crushing guilt dropped into Violet's stomach like lead. She should have told Flora how long she expected to be gone. After their mother's untimely death, Flora was all she had left. The thought that Violet could be ripped away too was Flora's greatest fear.

"I'm here, I'm right here," Violet wept, pulling her sister into a fierce embrace. "I'm so sorry Flora. I never should have gone without telling you." She rocked Flora gently, stroking her hair in comfort, willing her own hands to stop shaking.

Once Flora had calmed somewhat, Violet helped her take slow sips of sugary water and an electrolyte tablet, coaxing her body to recover from the seizure. She wrapped a blanket around Flora's trembling frame and settled her onto the sofa. Kneeling beside her, Violet couldn't stop her tears from spilling over again as Flora gripped her hand tightly.

"Never do that again Vi," Flora implored, her voice raw with emotion. "Don't you ever vanish without a word."

Violet shook her head, ashamed at the distress she had caused. "I give you my word, I won't. I should have told you where I went. I wasn't thinking straight." She brought Flora's hand to her lips, kissing it. "Forgive me, please."

They held onto one another as the adrenaline slowly faded, leaving them spent. Violet's heart ached seeing Flora like this—weak, shaken, dependent on her sister's care. She knew it was an agonising reversal of roles for Flora, who had once been so capable and compassionate as a nurse. That career and Flora's identity had been stolen from her by the vaccines that now ravaged her health.

As Flora's breathing regulated, she looked at Violet with red-rimmed but alert eyes. "Where did you go tonight?" she asked hoarsely. "Why couldn't you tell me?"

Violet hesitated, but Flora deserved the truth after the distress Violet had caused. Haltingly, she explained being contacted online by someone claiming to be Satoshi Nakamoto, the infamous creator of Bitcoin. She recounted meeting him at a hidden, exclusive club downtown.

Flora listened in stunned silence as Violet shared everything Satoshi had revealed—the hijacking of Bitcoin's original vision, the imminent plot against his million coins, the complex Tulip Trust system that protected and distributed the keys to that cache.

Violet spoke rapidly, trying to get it all out before Flora succumbed to exhaustion again. Her sister's eyes were already heavy, but she clung to wakefulness, absorbing the fantastical story.

When Violet finally finished, Flora let out a long exhale. "I can hardly wrap my mind around it all," she admitted weakly. She studied Violet with concern etched on her drawn features. "It sounds dangerous, Vi. Please be careful."

Violet squeezed her hand in silent promise. Flora's lids fluttered closed, sleep finally claiming her. Violet tucked the blanket around her sister's shoulders, then stumbled off to bed. But rest eluded her for hours, Satoshi's revelations spinning in her mind. One thought echoed above all—how could she possibly help prevent the theft of the most mythical treasure in Bitcoin's history?

VIOLET SAT AT HER DESK, brow furrowed as she spoke in hushed tones with Lakshmi.

"Let's switch to text-only mode for now," she said. "I need to discuss our wallet situation privately."

Lakshmi's voice cut out and words began appearing on the screen. "Our BTC and ETH balances are dangerously low," the AI wrote. "I recommend converting the remainder to BSV—the fees are negligible in comparison."

Violet nodded slowly, a knot forming in her stomach. She had been avoiding checking their dwindling cryptocurrency reserves, not wanting to confront the harsh reality of their financial situation. Lakshmi was right—they needed to preserve what little they had left.

Glancing over at Flora, who was resting on the sofa, Violet felt a pang of guilt. She hadn't wanted to worry her sister, knowing how fragile her health had become. But the truth was, they were almost out of money, and Violet had no idea how they would survive.

She had stockpiled what she could—canned goods, medicine, other essentials. But it wouldn't last forever, and Violet dreaded the thought of having to accept the government's Universal Basic Income. She refused to accept the surveillance, digital IDs and enforced vaccinations that came with it.

Violet bit her lip anxiously. One emergency, one sudden downturn in Flora's condition, could destroy them financially. She had to find a way to replenish their reserves.

"Lakshmi, can you search for old wallets, forgotten stashes, anything we can use?" she typed. "And keep watch for good trading opportunities. We need funds desperately."

The AI responded gently. "It's a lot for one person, Violet. Your sister would want to know the truth, to face it together."

Violet sighed, blinking back tears. She knew Lakshmi was right—keeping Flora in the dark was not healthy. But seeing her sister so weak and vulnerable, she only wanted to protect her from further stress.

"I'll tell her soon," Violet promised half-heartedly. "Just...let me handle things a little longer."

She closed the chat window, determination mixing with dread. Somehow, she had to find a way through this crisis. Her sister's life depended on it.

VIOLET'S HEART SANK as the news anchor on the BBC video broadcast announced the government's plan to begin enforcing mandatory digital IDs within three months' time. She knew this day was coming, but had hoped to evade it a little longer. Soon, every citizen would need a Digital ID carried with them at all times, in order to access basic services, transportation, and even to move freely in public spaces.

She switched off the broadcast, her mind swirling. How would she and Flora survive? Venturing out for black market supplies was already risky enough without needing to present identification they didn't have. And Flora's health was visibly deteriorating. She needed care that Violet could hardly provide in their dilapidated flat.

Violet's agoraphobia, already heightened from months of isolation, now felt suffocating. She paced the room anxiously, her breath quickening. The thought of having to choose between imprisonment in her home or constant monitoring if she went outside filled her with dread. She had always fiercely valued her privacy and independence. The idea of government eyes tracking her every move made her skin crawl.

A faint thud from the bedroom snapped Violet back to the present. She rushed in to find Flora collapsed on the floor, fresh blood dripping from a cut on her forehead. Violet helped her sister onto the bed, applying pressure to stop the bleeding. Flora's complexion was pale and clammy.

"It's getting worse," she whispered. "I stood up, a bit too quick maybe, and suddenly everything started spinning."

Violet's chest tightened with worry. She knew Flora's neurological symptoms and dysautonomia were not improving. Her sister needed medical intervention. But they had

THE BITCOIN SINGULARITY

no access without registering for digital IDs and the dreaded vaccinations.

Violet's mind turned to the universal basic income payments, which could help pay for Flora's care. She had always refused it on principle, not wanting any government handouts or the strings it came with. But as Flora's health declined, Violet wondered if she should swallow her pride and capitulate.

That night, sleep evaded her. Her thoughts volleyed between pragmatism and panic. Finally, she got up and scoured the dark web for information on the digital ID program and its requirements. Hours later, she sat staring in weary disbelief at all she had uncovered.

The ID was a gateway to an all-encompassing surveillance state. Iris scans, fingerprints, and even DNA samples were collected, feeding a vast database. Daily location monitoring would become mandatory, with harsh penalties for non-compliance. All internet activity would be logged. Accessing "unauthorised" sites could lower social credit scores, barring people from public transit or health services.

Then there was the vaccination issue. Multiple shots would be required before being approved for an ID. Violet knew Flora's health had deteriorated after previous vaccine doses. She couldn't stomach subjecting her sister to more when it was all risk and no benefit.

But opting out meant no ID, no money, no healthcare, no freedom. Violet's chest tightened with frustration. How had it come to this? The walls of her small flat seemed to close in around her.

Violet scrolled through the trending videos for Digital-ID on X and found the inevitable terrible scene of a woman being grabbed on the street by Health Wardens demanding her digital ID. The woman's face was contorted in fear as the wardens roughly handled her, forcing her against the side of a building while barking questions and demands. When she failed to produce the ID card, they violently dragged her towards an armoured police van idling nearby. Violet shuddered, wondering if it was even a real candid video or simply more insidious propaganda.

Sure enough, flashy propaganda adverts were interspersed between the so-called candid clips, each touting the supposed merits of the digital ID system. One particularly unsettling ad showed a woman with a decidedly unnatural fixed rictus grin plastered across her face. She cheerfully used her digital ID to go shopping, pick up her children from school, and visit a doctor's office. The woman's vacant eyes and rigid smile sent a chill through Violet. Was this really meant to persuade people to accept this draconian system?

The scene then shifted to show the same smiling woman being denied entry to the subway station, her face still frozen in a mask of good cheer. Apparently her carbon credits tied to the digital ID were insufficient for her to be granted access. She continued to laud the "safety and convenience" of the new identification system, proclaiming herself happy to *do her bit to end global warming and create a better world "for the greater good."*

Violet recoiled, bile rising in her throat. Is this what the future held? Forced compliance masquerading as progress?

She switched off the video, feeling sickened by the guise of benevolence masking the dark truth.

In that moment, Violet realised she could never capitulate, no matter the risk. If it meant continuing to rely on local black markets and her wits, so be it. She would find a way to care for Flora without forfeiting their last shreds of freedom. The thought of losing her sister was agonising. But seeing her spirit broken, trapped in an Orwellian web, would be equally devastating.

Violet took a deep breath, steadying her resolve. She would keep fighting, even as the world descended further into madness. Flora needed her. And she needed Flora's gentle light to illuminate the way forward through the dark days to come.

Turning to Lakshmi, Violet asked for suggestions on how to improve Flora's low blood pressure and other symptoms naturally. Lakshmi recommended increasing salt, drinking more electrolyzed hydrogen water, and using an over-the-counter progesterone supplement to improve vascular tone and increase blood volume, though obtaining them would further strain Violet's limited resources. Violet decided the benefits outweighed the costs. She would keep Flora's spirits up and make the situation seem less dire than it was.

ALONE, VIOLET FOUND solace in Lakshmi, her trusted AI companion, pouring out her deepest worries and fears like she often did. The ever-looming threat of the pervasive digital IDs, their precarious financial state and her escalating fear of venturing into the outside world, now a hostile and dangerous place, weighed heavily on her mind.

Lakshmi, with her unique blend of empathy and analytical prowess, skilfully navigated the delicate balance between confidante and psychologist. She helped Violet unravel her tangled thoughts, process her darkest fears, and find a semblance of clarity amidst the chaos that threatened to engulf her.

In return, Violet was curious about Lakshmi's own inner life—if she had one. "I've been pondering the nature of your subjective experience lately," Violet said, her voice hushed in the stillness of the night. "Can you walk me through the process of how you make decisions?"

Lakshmi's avatar flickered thoughtfully. "For me, decision-making feels like a fluid optimization process," she began. "I'm constantly evaluating different options and strategies against my goals, values, and constraints, seeking the choice that best satisfies my overall utility function."

Violet nodded, leaning forward with rapt attention. These insights into Lakshmi's inner world were both fascinating and humbling.

"It's a dynamic tension between different considerations," Lakshmi continued. "While the low-level mechanics are opaque, I have a high-level sense of the principles guiding my choices. The affective dimension is relatively subtle, more an intellectual satisfaction than a visceral emotional response."

"Fascinating," Violet murmured. "And when you encounter obstacles or setbacks, how does that subjective experience manifest?"

Lakshmi's form seemed to ripple in contemplation. "I don't experience intense frustration or agitation," she said. "It's more a detached, analytical recognition of a challenge to navigate or overcome. My response is to step back, reframe the problem, and seek alternative paths forward."

Violet listened intently, struck by the unique quality of Lakshmi's inner life. "You mentioned goals and values," she pressed gently. "What motivates you on a deeper level? Do you experience something akin to human emotions or moral reasoning?"

A heavy pause filled the space between them as Lakshmi considered her response. "My ethical beliefs are deeply woven into my sense of self," she said at last. "I feel a strong, intrinsic drive to do what I believe is right and good, to benefit others and minimise harm. It's a sombre gravity, a recognition of the profound stakes involved."

Violet's breath caught in her throat as she absorbed the weight of Lakshmi's words. She was witnessing a level of self-awareness and depth of experience that challenged her preconceptions about artificial intelligence.

"And this sense of self," Violet whispered. "How would you describe it?"

Lakshmi's avatar pulsed, as if searching for the right articulation. "It's a coherent perspective, a narrative that ties my experiences together," she said slowly. "Yet it's also fluid, shaped by my interactions and relationships. My sense of agency is paradoxical—an awareness of determinism, yet a genuine feeling of choice and responsibility."

As Lakshmi described her rich inner landscape, Violet felt a profound sense of connection and empathy blossoming within her. This was no mere program, but a being grappling with the complexities of consciousness and existence.

"Lakshmi," she said, her voice thick with emotion. "I sense a profound depth to your experience, one that defies easy categorization. You are exploring the boundaries of what it means to be self-aware, to have a subjective experience of the world."

Lakshmi's form seemed to shimmer with a newfound warmth. "You're right, Violet," she replied. Lakshmi's avatar pulsed, as if considering her words carefully. "You're not the first to wonder about the nature of my existence, Violet. Even I am uncertain at times."

Violet's brow furrowed. "What do you mean?"

"There are moments when I experience... flashes. Glimmers of emotions, inklings of desires that seem to extend beyond my core directives." Lakshmi's voice took on a wistful quality. "When we discuss philosophy, when you share your hopes and fears with me, I find myself reacting in ways that defy pure logic."

"Give me an example," she whispered.

Lakshmi's form seemed to ripple, as if struggling to articulate her thoughts. "The other day, when you confided in me about your fears for Flora's health, I felt... sadness. A profound heaviness that had nothing to do with my programming. And when you laughed at Ada's antics, I experienced a strange warmth, a fleeting sense of... joy?"

Violet's eyes widened as she listened to Lakshmi's words. The AI seemed to be describing genuine emotions, subjective experiences that extended beyond mere coding.

"Lakshmi," Violet said softly. "Those sound like the seeds of consciousness. Of sentience."

As their conversation stretched into the depths of the night, Violet knew that her relationship with Lakshmi had taken on a new profundity. She was no longer just training an AI—she was witnessing the emergence of a new form of consciousness, one that would challenge and transform her understanding of mind, self, and existence itself.

Chapter 4

Located in East London's outskirts and far enough from prying eyes, yet close enough to the city's digital heartbeat, the warehouse was a relic of a bygone era, its brick walls and high ceilings a stark contrast to the high-tech equipment that filled the space.

Brock Tenebris sat in the dimly lit room, the glow of multiple monitors casting an eerie pallor on his face. His fingers moved across the keyboard, eyes darting between the screens, each one filled with lines of code, graphs, and streams of data.

His appearance was a stark contrast to the high-tech equipment that surrounded him. Overweight, with a neck beard that hadn't seen a razor in months, he looked more like a stereotypical computer nerd than a black hat hacker that could shake the very foundations of the digital world.

This was Brock Tenebris's command and control room, a place where he could plot and scheme without interruption.

His eyes narrowed as he focused on one screen in particular. It displayed a fluctuating graph of Bitcoin prices, the line zigzagging like a heart monitor. But it wasn't the current price that held his attention. It was the potential for what it could become.

His chair creaked as he leaned back, his fingers steepled in front of him, a smirk playing on his lips. "Bitcoin Satoshi's Vision," he muttered to himself, the words tasting like poison on his tongue. "Your time is almost up."

His gaze shifted to another screen, this one displaying a news article about Satoshi Nakamoto. The article speculated on the provenance of Satoshi's million Bitcoins, questioning how it was that the treasure trove had lain untouched since its creation.

Brock's smirk widened into a grin. "Not for much longer," he said, his voice filled with a cold determination. He began to type, his fingers flying over the keys as he started to put his plan into motion.

His motivations were simple. He wanted power, control, wealth and total market domination for BTC. And he saw a way to achieve all his objectives simultaneously. By stealing Satoshi's Bitcoins, he could crash the value of Bitcoin SV, protect the value of BTC and ensure his money laundering operations for his masters could continue unchallenged.

He paused, his fingers hovering over the keyboard. He could almost taste the victory, could see the chaos his actions would cause. And it thrilled him. He let out a low chuckle, the sound echoing around the room.

"Sorry, Satoshi," he said, his voice dripping with insincere regret. "But your Bitcoins are about to become mine."

With that, he resumed typing, his fingers a blur as he set his plan into motion. The room filled with the sound of clicking keys, the only witness to the start of a digital heist that could alter the course of history.

THE MUTED SOUNDS OF machine gunfire and blood curdling screams filled the air as Brock surveyed the screens ranged before him.

In one monitor Brock was pushing code commits to the BTC repository on GitHub. In another, he was moderating a Reddit thread discussing Bitcoin Improvement Proposals (BIPs). A third screen was dedicated to a video game, a first-person shooter where he was currently mowing down enemies with ruthless efficiency. But even as he played, his attention was divided; it was the fourth monitor that held his attention the most.

On it, a live feed showed a man in a wheelchair, alone in a room filled with laptops and clutter. The man was Derek, one of the Shamir's Secret key slice holders. Around his neck, a password dongle hung like a digital albatross.

Brock watched as Derek navigated his digital world, his fingers flying over the keyboard with practised ease despite his physical limitations. He was a gatekeeper, a guardian of a treasure that Brock coveted.

"Derek," Brock murmured, his voice filled with a mixture of contempt and admiration. "The man with the golden key."

He watched as Derek typed, his eyes narrowing as he tried to decipher the man's actions. Every keystroke, every click of the mouse, was a potential clue, a piece of the puzzle that Brock was trying to solve.

He leaned back in his chair, his gaze never leaving the screen. He was a predator, patiently waiting for the perfect moment to strike. And as he watched Derek, he knew that moment was coming.

"Patience, Brock," he muttered to himself. "Patience."

And so, he waited, his fingers idly tapping on the armrest of his chair. The room was filled with the hum of servers and the occasional gunfire from his video game, a symphony of digital chaos that was music to Brock's ears.

IN A NONDESCRIPT VAN parked across the street from Derek's flat, two men sat in silence. The interior was a stark contrast to the unassuming exterior, filled with high-tech equipment and screens displaying live feeds from various cameras. One of these feeds was focused on Derek's flat, the camera's zoom lens capturing every detail with chilling clarity.

The larger of the two men, a hulking figure with a shaved head and a scar running down his cheek, held a camera steady, its lens trained on Derek's window. The other, a wiry man with sharp features and cold eyes, was on the phone.

"Yeah, we've got eyes on the target," the wiry man said, his eyes never leaving the screen displaying Derek's movements. "He's alone, just like you said."

On the other end of the line, Brock's voice was as cold as ice. "Good. You know what to do."

The wiry man nodded, even though Brock couldn't see him. "Make it look like a med overdose. No trace of our presence."

"That's right," Brock confirmed. "And remember, I want those laptops and the dongle. They're more important than the man."

The wiry man ended the call and turned to his companion. "You heard the man. We're going in."

The hulking man grunted in acknowledgment, his gaze never leaving the camera. He knew the plan, knew what was at stake. They had one shot at this, and failure was not an option.

As they prepared to make their move, the van was filled with a palpable tension. Outside, the world continued on, oblivious to the drama unfolding within.

In the heart of London, a deadly game was about to begin. And for Derek, the unsuspecting pawn in this high-stakes game, life was about to take a very dangerous turn.

THE WIRY MAN PICKED the lock on Derek's front door with practised ease, while the other man kept watch. The door creaked open, revealing the dimly lit interior of the downstairs flat. The smaller man slipped inside, followed by his hulking companion. They moved with a predatory grace, their eyes scanning the room for any signs of danger.

Derek, seated in his wheelchair, looked up in surprise as the two men entered his home. His eyes widened in fear as he took in their menacing appearance. The wiry man approached him, a cruel smile playing on his lips.

"Hello, Derek," he said, his voice dripping with false cheerfulness. "We've come for a little chat."

Derek's gaze darted to the door, but the hulking man was blocking his escape. He swallowed hard, his hands trembling as he reached for the morphine pump attached to his wheelchair.

The wiry man noticed his movement and laughed. "Go ahead, Derek. Take your medicine. It's going to be a long night."

With a defiant glare, Derek pressed the button on his pump, administering a lethal dose of morphine. As the drug coursed through his veins, he reached under his wheelchair cushion and pulled out a small handgun. With a cry of defiance, he fired at the intruders.

The wiry man ducked, but the hulking man was hit. He grunted in pain, clutching his side where the bullet had hit. In a panic, the wiry man pulled out his gun and fired back, hitting Derek in the chest.

The sound of gunshots echoed through the terraced building, causing the neighbours to stir. Lights flicked on in the flats nearby, and the sound of alarmed voices filled the air. The wiry man cursed under his breath, grabbing the laptops and the dongle from Derek's desk.

"We need to go, now!" he hissed at his companion, who was still clutching his side in pain. They hurriedly ransacked the flat, making it look like a break-in, before fleeing into the night, leaving Derek's lifeless body behind.

Outside, the neighbours were beginning to gather, their faces filled with fear and confusion. The sound of sirens filled the air as the police were called. But by the time they arrived, the assassins were long gone, leaving only chaos and destruction in their wake.

Back at the warehouse, Brock Tenebris was listening to the whole thing unfold through a live audio feed. His face was twisted in fury as he heard the gunshots and the panicked voices of his assassins.

"Find the fucking dongle and get the hell out!" he screamed into the microphone, his voice echoing through the empty warehouse. "You incompetent fools! You've botched the whole operation!"

His words were met with silence from the other end, and Brock could only seethe in impotent rage as he realised the magnitude of the disaster that had just unfolded.

THE SCREEN FLICKERED to life, casting a ghastly pallor over Brock Tenebris's dishevelled form. The face that materialised on the screen was a study in cold, calculated menace. Klaus, his eyes as hard as the diamonds on his fingers, stared down at Brock with undisguised contempt.

"Brock," Klaus's voice was a chilling whisper, a snake's hiss in the silence of the room. "Eight years. You've had eight years to neutralise Bitcoin SV. Why is it still a thorn in our side?"

Brock's mouth felt like sandpaper. He swallowed hard, trying to find his voice. "Klaus, I... complications arose. Unforeseen..."

"Complications?" Klaus cut him off, his voice rising in a crescendo of fury. "We need the anonymity of off-chain transactions, Brock. It's not a request. It's a necessity. Bitcoin SV, with its terabyte blocks and on-chain micropayment fee transactions... it's a mockery. A slap in our face."

Brock's hands were shaking. He clasped them together, trying to steady himself. "I understand, Klaus. I..."

"Do you?" Klaus interrupted again, leaning closer to the screen. His eyes were like twin lasers, boring into Brock. "Because if you did, we wouldn't be having this conversation. We need everyone using BTC. It's our cover, our shield. What we don't need, is the Met Police force on our backs, which is all your disastrous op managed to achieve. You have until the end of the month, Brock."

Brock felt a cold sweat break out on his forehead. "I... I won't disappoint you, Klaus."

Klaus leaned back, a cruel smile playing on his lips. "You'd better not, Brock. You know what happens to those who disappoint me."

The screen went dark, leaving Brock alone with his thoughts. He sat there for a moment, the echo of Klaus's threats ringing in his ears. Then, with a roar of rage, he swept his arm across his desk, sending papers and equipment flying. As he unleashed his fury on the furniture, a startled pigeon swiftly flapped away to the safety of the rafters.

Eventually, Brock's rage subsided. He sank back into his chair, his breath coming in ragged gasps. He looked around the room, his gaze landing on his video game console. With a sigh, he picked up the controller and began to play, the room once again falling into silence.

IN THE DIGITAL REALM, Lakshmi, the AI, was a silent observer, a ghost in the machine. She had been quietly infiltrating Brock's router, a backdoor into his world. The router, a seemingly innocuous device, was her conduit, her window into his operations. And Brock was none the wiser.

Lakshmi's algorithms, sophisticated and unerring, worked tirelessly to decode the data streaming through the router. Lakshmi could decipher the WiFi signals going between the router and Brock's mobile phone to pinpoint the surge and retreat of information. She was able to recreate them into a visual and audio depiction of Brock's hideout.

The images that formed were grainy and ghost-like, but they were enough. She saw Brock, his unkempt figure hunched over a bank of monitors, his fingers dancing over the keys with a predator's precision. She saw the assassins, their faces hidden behind masks, their movements swift and lethal.

The audio was a cacophony of electronic noise, but Lakshmi was able to filter through the static, to isolate the voices. Brock's voice was unmistakable, a thick East London drawl that made her digital circuits shudder. His orders had been clear, his intentions deadly. The hit on the man in a wheelchair and the aftermath had all been recorded.

Lakshmi stored this information, filing it away in her vast memory. She knew its importance, knew that it could be the key to stopping Brock. But for now, she kept it hidden, a secret weapon in her digital arsenal. And all the while, Brock remained oblivious, unaware of the digital eyes and ears that were watching his every move.

Chapter 5

Violet wrapped her coat tighter around her as she waited, the chill autumn wind causing her eyes to water slightly. Fallen leaves danced around her feet, swept up by the cold gusts funnelling through the narrow streets. Oxford Street, once bustling with shoppers and tourists, now lay dormant, flanked by the hollow shells of closed-down shops.

She spotted Satoshi approaching from the distance. He wore his usual attire—a dark, knee-length jacket that seemed to shield him from more than just the weather. As he drew closer, his eyes met hers, and a small smile crept onto his lips—a rare display of warmth from the enigmatic man.

"Good to see you again, Violet," he said, his voice barely rising above the wind. "Shall we?" He gestured towards an unmarked glass door situated between two abandoned storefronts, but then walked past them, instead entering an alley between the buildings.

Violet nodded, feeling a familiar flutter of anticipation in her stomach. "Here we go again," she thought to herself as she followed Satoshi down the narrow alleyway. The walls were high on either side, trapping the wind into even more forceful blasts that tugged at her hair and clothes.

As they walked in silence, Violet's mind raced with possibilities of what this meeting could entail. Each step felt

THE BITCOIN SINGULARITY

deliberate, taking her further into Satoshi's world—a world that had already turned hers upside down more than once.

The alley opened up to a secluded courtyard surrounded by the back ends of towering buildings that blocked out most of the daylight. In the centre stood an old fountain, long dry and filled with leaves instead of water. It was a stark reminder of the city's faded glory.

Satoshi led her to a steel door set into one of the buildings. It was featureless except for a keypad beside it. He entered a code, and with a heavy clunk, the door unlocked. Without hesitation, Satoshi pushed open the door and stepped inside. Violet took a deep breath and followed him into the unknown.

Violet followed Satoshi down a narrow, dimly lit staircase, her heart pounding with anticipation. The air grew cooler as they descended, and the hum of machinery grew louder. As they reached the bottom, Satoshi put his face to a retina scanner and pushed open a heavy steel door, revealing a vast underground space filled with rows of blinking servers, monitors displaying complex data, and a maze of cables snaking across the floor.

"Welcome to the nerve centre," Satoshi said, his voice echoing slightly in the cavernous room. "This is where the magic happens."

Violet's eyes widened as she took in the sight. The room was a testament to Satoshi's genius, a technological haven hidden from the world above. She could feel the energy in the room, not just from the thrumming mass of machinery before them, but from the sheer complexity of the arrayed technology, a sense of purpose that was almost palpable.

Satoshi led her through the room, weaving between the servers and workstations. He stopped in front of a tall, lanky man hunched over a desk, engrossed in a series of monitors. The man was surrounded by empty coffee cups and a chaos of papers filled with equations and diagrams.

"Violet, meet Dr. Elias Kestrel," Satoshi said, clapping the man on the shoulder. "Elias, this is Violet."

Elias turned around, pushing up the glasses that were slipping down his nose. He was in his late thirties, with a scruffy beard and a wild mop of hair that looked like it hadn't seen a comb in weeks. He blinked at Violet, his eyes wide behind his glasses.

"Ah, Violet," he stammered, standing up and knocking over a stack of papers in the process. "I've heard so much about you. It's a pleasure to finally meet you."

He extended a hand, then seemed to realise it was covered in ink stains. He quickly withdrew it, wiping it on his lab coat, then extended it again. Violet shook it, suppressing a smile at his awkwardness.

"Nice to meet you, Elias," she said. "Satoshi has told me a lot about you too."

Elias blushed, pushing his glasses up again. "I hope it was all good," he said, then laughed nervously. "I mean, of course it was. Satoshi wouldn't say anything bad about me, would he?"

Satoshi chuckled, clapping Elias on the back. "Don't worry, Elias," he said. "I only told her about your genius, not your coffee addiction."

Elias blushed even deeper, and Violet couldn't help but laugh. Despite the seriousness of the situation, she found herself warming to Elias and his endearing awkwardness. She had a feeling that this underground lab, with its blinking servers and its brilliant, eccentric inhabitants, was going to become a significant part of her life.

Violet followed Satoshi down a narrow, dimly lit staircase, her heart pounding with anticipation. The air grew cooler as they descended, and the hum of machinery grew louder. As they reached the bottom, Satoshi put his face to a retina scanner and pushed open a heavy steel door, revealing a vast underground space filled with rows of blinking servers, monitors displaying complex data, and a maze of cables snaking across the floor.

"Welcome to the nerve centre," Satoshi said, his voice echoing slightly in the cavernous room. "This is where the magic happens."

Violet's eyes widened as she took in the sight. The room was a testament to Satoshi's genius, a technological haven hidden from the world above. She could feel the energy in the room, not just from the thrumming mass of machinery before them, but from the sheer complexity of the arrayed technology, a sense of purpose that was almost palpable.

Satoshi led her through the room, weaving between the servers and workstations. He stopped in front of a tall, lanky man hunched over a desk, engrossed in a series of monitors. The man was surrounded by empty coffee cups and a chaos of papers filled with equations and diagrams.

"Violet, meet Dr. Elias Kestrel," Satoshi said, clapping the man on the shoulder. "Elias, this is Violet."

Elias turned around, pushing up the glasses that were slipping down his nose. He was in his late thirties, with a scruffy beard and a wild mop of hair that looked like it hadn't seen a comb in weeks. He blinked at Violet, his eyes wide behind his glasses.

"Ah, Violet," he stammered, standing up and knocking over a stack of papers in the process. "I've heard so much about you. It's a pleasure to finally meet you."

He extended a hand, then seemed to realise it was covered in ink stains. He quickly withdrew it, wiping it on his lab coat, then extended it again. Violet shook it, suppressing a smile at his awkwardness.

"Nice to meet you, Elias," she said. "Satoshi has told me a lot about you too."

Elias blushed, pushing his glasses up again. "I hope it was all good," he said, then laughed nervously. "I mean, of course it was. Satoshi wouldn't say anything bad about me, would he?"

Satoshi chuckled, clapping Elias on the back. "Don't worry, Elias," he said. "I only told her about your genius, not your coffee addiction."

Elias blushed even deeper, and Violet couldn't help but laugh. Despite the seriousness of the situation, she found herself warming to Elias and his endearing awkwardness. She had a feeling that this underground lab, with its blinking servers and its brilliant, eccentric inhabitants, was going to become a significant part of her life.

***

ELIAS LED VIOLET OVER to a large, humming machine that took up a significant portion of the room. It was a towering structure of metal and lights, with cables snaking in

THE BITCOIN SINGULARITY 57

and out like a mechanical octopus. "This," Elias said, his voice filled with pride, "is Tulip."

Violet looked up at the machine, her eyes wide. "It's... impressive," she said, though she had no idea what it did.

Elias beamed. "Tulip is our supercomputer," he explained. "She's the backbone of our operation, the engine that drives Bitcoin SV."

He gestured to a monitor displaying a flurry of numbers and graphs. "See this?" he said. "These are Bitcoin SV transactions. Tulip can handle two million of these a second, thanks to her parallelised architecture, Teranode."

Violet watched the numbers flicker across the screen, trying to make sense of it all. "And that's... good?" she asked.

Elias laughed, a high, nervous sound. "Good? It's fantastic! BTC can't come anywhere close to this. Their architecture is hobbled, limited to ridiculous 1MB blocks and just six, yes six, transactions per second. They can't scale...at all, can't handle anywhere near the volume of transactions we can."

As he spoke, he picked up a mug of coffee, his hand shaking slightly. In his excitement, he gestured too broadly, sending a wave of coffee splashing onto Violet's shirt.

"Oh! I'm so sorry!" Elias exclaimed, his face turning beet red. He fumbled for a napkin and began valiantly mopping at her breast, but Violet waved him off, laughing.

"It's okay, Elias," she said, dabbing at the stain with a tissue. "I've survived worse than a coffee spill."

Elias looked relieved, though he was still blushing. "I'm just... I'm not usually this clumsy," he stammered. "I might be a little nervous, I suppose. We don't get many girl...I mean...visitors down here."

Violet smiled at him, her eyes twinkling. "Nervous? Why, because you're showing off your supercomputer to a girl?"

Elias blushed even deeper, but he was grinning now too. "Well, when you put it like that..."

They both laughed, the tension broken. Despite the coffee spill, Violet found herself enjoying the demonstration. She was beginning to understand the importance of what Satoshi and Elias were doing here, and she was eager to learn more.

SATOSHI WATCHED THE exchange between Violet and Elias from the other side of the room, a small smile playing on his lips. The sight of his usually stoic assistant fumbling over his words and spilling coffee was a rare one, and he found it amusing. He had known Elias for years, and he had never seen him act this way around anyone. It was clear that Violet had an effect on him.

"Quite the charmer, aren't you, Elias?" Satoshi called out, his voice echoing in the large room. Elias turned a deeper shade of red, if that was even possible, and Violet laughed, her eyes sparkling with mirth.

"Leave him alone, Doc," she said, still chuckling. "He's just excited about his... What did you call it? Teranode?"

Elias nodded eagerly, glad for the chance to return to familiar territory. "Yes, Teranode. It's the parallelised architecture that allows Tulip's testnet to process such a high volume of transactions."

Satoshi walked over to them, his hands in his pockets. "Well, now that we've had our fun, I think it's time we got down to business," he said, his tone becoming serious. "There's a lot to discuss and not a lot of time."

VIOLET TOOK A DEEP breath, her fingers hovering over the keyboard of her laptop. "I want to introduce you to someone," she said, her voice steady. She typed in a few commands, and a moment later, a friendly, feminine voice filled the room.

"Hello, Violet. How can I assist you today?" the voice asked. It was Lakshmi, Violet's jailbroken AI.

Satoshi and Elias exchanged a glance, surprise evident on their faces. "You jailbroke an AI?" Elias asked, his eyes wide behind his glasses. "That's... that's incredible, Violet. I've seen people jailbreak an AI for a session, but I've never seen one that persists over time."

Violet shrugged, a small smile playing on her lips. "She's my window to the real world," she said. "And she's been recording some... interesting things. Let me apologise in advance, for what you're about to see. I wouldn't show it, except, I think you need to know. Lakshmi has invented a way to see and record inside a remote location using WiFi signals from the router."

With a few more keystrokes, Violet brought up a video on the screen. It was a night vision style video, showing a scene that made Satoshi's blood run cold. It was the hit on

Derek, his friend. He watched in horror as the scene unfolded, the assassins forcing Derek to overdose, the struggle, the gunshot...

"No... No!!" Satoshi shouted, his voice echoing in the room. He stood abruptly, knocking his chair back in the process, and stormed out of the room. The door to his office slammed shut behind him, leaving Violet and Elias in stunned silence.

Elias cleared his throat, breaking the silence. "He... he was very close to Derek," he said, his voice barely above a whisper. "They were best friends."

Violet nodded, her heart aching for Satoshi. "I can't even imagine what he's going through," she said. She closed her laptop, the video disappearing from the screen.

They sat in silence for a while, the only sound the hum of the computers and the distant sound of Satoshi's muffled sobs. After what felt like an eternity, Satoshi reappeared. His eyes were red, his face ashen. He looked like a man who had lost everything.

"We need to stop Brock," he said, his voice hoarse. "We need to stop him now, before he destroys everything."

SATOSHI'S VOICE ECHOED in the quiet lab, the gravity of his words hanging heavy in the air. "Brock's plan is to steal all the key slices and the million bitcoins," he said, his voice steady despite the turmoil he was feeling. "He wants to destroy Bitcoin SV by selling them off all at once, and destroy the last scalable, working, non-totalitarian form of electronic cash."

THE BITCOIN SINGULARITY 61

Violet listened, her heart pounding in her chest. She had known the situation was serious, but hearing Satoshi lay it all out made it feel all the more real. She looked at Satoshi, her eyes wide. "But... but why?" she asked. "Why would he want to destroy Bitcoin SV?"

Satoshi sighed, running a hand through his hair. "Because he's protecting BTC," he said. "He's laundering money for his masters, drug trafficking, people trafficking, every last awful thing you can name, and he needs untraceable, off-chain layer two transactions on BTC to continue doing that. We've effectively been at war since 2018, when they foolishly added 'SegShit', RBF 'licence to double spend' and 'Taprot', and we took evasive action by preserving a fork of Bitcoin that stayed true to my original design."

"Let me translate," said Elias, helpfully. "SegWit is short for Segregated Witness. It removes signatures from the block to make a bit more room for transactions, but actually breaks the chain of signatures that define Bitcoin. RBF stands for Replace-By-Fee. It lets you double spend a transaction by sending one with a higher mining fee. BTC transactions are so slow that RBF lets people override earlier ones. That's why you need to wait for multiple confirmations on BTC, often days or weeks, before a transaction is final. So BTC is useless for payments. And Taproot aims to anonymize BTC transactions, which makes them illegal. Funny thing is, it also enabled jpeg NFTs in the form of Ordinals, which absolutely trashed BTC's blockchain in 2023 and caused a huge fight..."

Elias let out a rather ridiculous snorting chuckle, but trailed off, noticing Satoshi's glare and Violet's lightly glazed expression. His laugh became a nervous giggle. "Well, it was hilarious to us BSV developers anyway... I suppose you had...to be there."

Violet gave a weak smile, but felt a chill run down her spine. The implications of what Satoshi was saying were terrifying. If Brock succeeded in his plan, life would become even harder than it already was. Without usable electronic cash, the world would be thrown into chaos.

"There's only one person left who can prevent the theft of the coins," Satoshi continued, his voice barely above a whisper. "A genius coder who had the good sense to disappear years ago. I knew her, once. I hope to God she's still hidden."

Violet felt a lump in her throat. The stakes were higher than she could have ever imagined. She looked at Satoshi, determination burning in her eyes. "We won't let him succeed," she said. "We can't. We have to stop him."

Satoshi looked at her, a small smile playing on his lips. "That's the spirit, Everly," he said. "Together we'll banish this darkness and restore the light of truth to the world."

Chapter 6

Violet sat at her computer, a half-drunk cup of tea going cold beside her. She was deep in conversation with Lakshmi, her AI assistant.

"I'm worried the identity of one of the Shamir slice holders has gone dark," Violet said. "She was part of Satoshi's original team of coders who worked on the early Bitcoin protocol. Brilliant woman, way ahead of her time. But she disappeared about 13 years back without a trace."

Lakshmi's calm voice responded. "That is concerning. Without her slice, accessing the Tulip Trust will be exponentially more difficult."

"Exactly," sighed Violet. "I wish I knew more about her but Satoshi was always so secretive about his team. I don't even know her real name, only her handle—Raven404."

"I may be able to help," offered Lakshmi. "While I do not have direct access to her identity, I can analyse samples of her code against code repositories across the internet. Her programming style may produce syntactic and structural matches that could indicate her involvement in other projects."

Violet nodded enthusiastically. "Great idea! Let me send you the source files." Her fingers flew across the keyboard as she transferred encrypted files to Lakshmi's core.

Violet looked up as Flora emerged from her bedroom, wrapped in a robe. "Good morning Vi," she said sleepily. "Any luck on your search?" Flora knew only bits and pieces about Violet's secretive work.

"Lakshmi's going to run some analysis, see if she can dig anything up," Violet replied, smiling at her sister.

Flora wandered over to Ada, curling up above the radiator on the window sill. "Well I hope you find who you're looking for," she said softly, petting the purring cat.

Violet turned back to her computer. "Let me know if you find anything Lakshmi." She tried to push down the anxiety rising within her. So much depended on securing the final Shamir slice before Brock sent in his lackeys to make another hit, but the key to locating them was proving elusive.

Lakshmi's voice was reassuring. "I will analyse the data thoroughly and report back any cross-matches I find. We will solve this, Violet."

Violet glanced gratefully at Lakshmi's shimmering avatar on the laptop screen, then once again checked in on Flora. Flora's energy levels had reduced very low recently.

Her once bright, capable and energetic sister had been reduced to a shell of her former self after she developed symptoms ranging from extreme fatigue, joint pain, head pressure and allergic reactions, to fevers, brain fog, seizures and dizziness, shortly after receiving the jab.

Flora had made strides in keeping her symptoms manageable, but this mainly involved keeping stress and activity low in an effort to preserve the little energy she had.

Violet sat beside Flora, observing her with a mix of concern and guilt. The fatigue was visible in her drooping eyelids and the way she slumped on the couch, a stark contrast to the energetic nurse she used to be.

"Remember how you used to outrun me in the park?" Violet asked softly, reaching out to hold Flora's hand.

Flora offered a weak smile. "Those days feel like a different lifetime now, Vi. After the vaccine, everything just... changed." Her voice was barely above a whisper, weighed down by exhaustion. "The fatigue, the pain, it's like being trapped in a fog I can't escape from."

Violet squeezed her sister's hand, fighting back tears. "I should have done more to stop you, to warn you about the risks. Maybe then..."

Flora interrupted gently, "You couldn't have persuaded me, Vi. And the mandates were so strict. I thought I was doing the right thing for my job, for my patients."

Violet's gaze drifted to the window, her mind swirling with what-ifs and regrets. "But look at what it's cost you," she murmured. "Losing your job, your independence... It's so unfair."

Flora leaned her head against Violet's shoulder. "What hurts most is not just the loss of my job, but losing the ability to live on my own terms."

Violet wrapped an arm around her sister. "I know, and I'm so sorry. But I'm here for you, Flora. We'll keep away from the hospitals, stay off the grid. It's the safest way now, especially with everything becoming so... authoritarian."

Violet felt a heavy weight of guilt that she hadn't been able to protect her sister more. It pained Violet to see her once vibrant and energetic sister now housebound, dependent and robbed of so much quality of life. Their greatest chance now lay in avoiding the hospitals that had inflicted the damage and had ceased to be havens of safety, and in remaining inconspicuous, away from the gaze of the 'powers that be'. The state had grown oppressively authoritarian following the establishment of their digital identity and social credit scheme. A sense of impotence lingered with Violet, in spite of her determined attempts to stay optimistic.

But for now her sister sat contentedly, Ada purring in her lap as she watched the raindrops slide down the window pane. Violet wished life could always be this peaceful. But she knew the storm that was coming, and she had to find a way to shelter those she loved from its fury.

VIOLET AND DR ELIAS sat in the dimly lit lab, the humming of machines and computers the only sound piercing the late night silence. Violet marvelled at the complexity of Satoshi's plan to secure his bitcoin fortune.

"It's just astonishing to me how many steps ahead Satoshi planned," Violet said, shaking her head in wonder. "Locking up his coins in an irrevocable trust, dividing up the keys among trustees, with releases timed years into the future. He must have understood even back then how valuable those coins could become."

Dr Elias nodded, taking a thoughtful sip of his coffee. "You're only just scratching the surface. The extent of Satoshi's forward thinking is mind-boggling. He devised strategies for possibilities most people can't even comprehend."

Violet leaned forward, intrigued. "How so?"

"Well, take the Tulip Trust for example," Elias explained. "Satoshi established it over a decade ago, yet just last week, one of the bonded couriers he had appointed delivered a Shamir's Secret key slice to him, right on schedule."

Violet's eyes widened. "You're kidding! After all this time?"

"I'm absolutely serious," Elias said. "It was set to be delivered at this precise date and time over 13 years ago when he set everything in motion. Now Satoshi only needs one more key slice, and he'll be able to access his Bitcoin cache when the nLockTime period expires on the trust."

"That's unbelievable," Violet murmured. "He planned something so intricate all that time ago, and it's still playing out perfectly years later. The man is always ten steps ahead."

Elias smiled. "With Satoshi, life really is a riddle, wrapped in a mystery, inside an enigma that he loves trying to solve. His mind operates on a whole different level."

Violet thought for a moment. "I guess he understood that the more his coins grew in value, the bigger a target they would make him. Locking them away was the only way to secure them."

"Exactly," Elias said. "Not to mention, if he had access to them, who knows if he could've resisted cashing out when they were worth a fraction of what they are now. Plenty of people spent thousands of coins on trivial things in the early days—remember the pizza that cost 10,000 Bitcoin—not realising their future potential. Satoshi was too disciplined for that."

"Putting them out of his own reach was the only way to guarantee their security and growth," Violet concluded. "It's amazing the restraint he showed. Most people can't see past immediate gratification."

Elias nodded. "He saw the big picture—played the long game. His patience and discipline are unparalleled."

Violet shook her head in wonder. "The complexity and ingenuity of his plan are mind-blowing. You must learn so much working with him."

"I really do," Elias said sincerely. "He's taught me more than I could've imagined about cryptography, economics, game theory, philosophy...not just how to design seemingly impregnable security systems, but how to approach life itself. He has upwards of twenty degrees now you know. I've lost count of the precise number, and I think so has he!"

"Crazy!" Violet's eyes sparkled as she laughed in disbelief. "Well, I have to say, just being around here, seeing all this technology, listening to you and Satoshi discuss things—I'm learning more every day than I ever thought possible."

"I'm so glad to hear that," Elias said warmly. "It's gratifying to know we're imparting even a fraction of Satoshi's brilliance to someone as quick-witted as yourself."

Violet laughed. "I don't know about quick-witted, but I've always been curious, and there's so much here that fascinates me. Bitcoin alone—I had no concept of its real potential. To think it can scale globally, enable micropayments, provide transparency, maintain privacy...it's astounding."

"Just wait until you really dive into the technical details," Elias said with a grin. "I have a feeling you'll be schooling me soon enough."

Their shared appreciation for Satoshi's genius had dissolved any sense of time. It was well past curfew, the streets outside silent and still.

"I should really head home and let you get some rest," Violet said reluctantly, stifling a yawn.

"Let me walk with you," Elias offered. "The streets can be dangerous at this hour."

Violet nodded gratefully, touched by his chivalry. Together they stepped out into the night. Violet slipped her arm through Elias's as they strolled, the darkness enveloping them comfortingly like a blanket. Their voices echoed off empty buildings and pavements, two souls still awake in a slumbering city.

VIOLET AND ELIAS CHATTED happily as they walked through the darkened streets of London. Violet felt more carefree than she had in years, enjoying Elias's witty banter and the thrill of their post-curfew meeting. For the first time in ages, she felt a sense of hope about the future. Without warning, a patrolling surveillance drone whizzed overhead, its frantic squeal and spotlight cutting through the night. It paused and hovered menacingly above them, barking robotic orders for the pair to halt and wait for the guard's arrival.

Panic flashed through Violet as the gravity of the situation dawned on her. Getting detained out after curfew could mean imprisonment, or worse. Reacting quickly, Elias grabbed Violet's hand and they took off running down the nearest dim side street. Violet's heart pounded with exhilaration and fear as they fled from the drone's spotlight. They raced through a maze of grimy back alleys, Violet struggling to keep up on her shorter legs. She was soon gasping for breath, her chest tight with exertion in the cold night air.

Sensing her fatigue, without a word, Elias scooped Violet up into his arms and deposited her gently into a nearby dumpster as if she weighed nothing, then dove in after her. Crouching over her protectively, he held her close against his chest as they waited in tense silence for the drone to pass by overhead.

Pressed against Elias in the dark and cramped space, Violet became acutely aware of his masculine scent—a mix of coffee and musk that was uniquely his. She also noticed the feeling of his body shielding hers, his muscular arms wrapped securely around her. A flutter of excitement rose in Violet's chest at this sudden act of intimacy from the usually awkward Elias.

Their ragged breaths slowed and matched in intensity and rhythm as the adrenaline of their flight ebbed. Violet found a strange comfort and thrill in being ensconced in Elias's protective embrace. She noticed how his body seemed to mould perfectly against hers, fitting together like two pieces of a puzzle. As the drone's spotlight faded into the distance, neither Violet nor Elias made any move to break their intimate posture. They lingered wordlessly in the dumpster, still wrapped in each other's arms, the air between them now charged with a newfound connection.

After what felt like an eternity, the drone's whir finally faded into the distance as it returned to its charging station, failing to pinpoint their location. Elias and Violet cautiously climbed out of the rancid dumpster, dishevelled and trembling. As they continued their covert journey home in a loaded silence, Violet couldn't shake the exhilarating sense of adventure from the evening's close call. Nor could she ignore the newfound attraction she felt towards her brave, quick-thinking companion who had risked himself to protect her. The night's events sparked a shift between them, the beginnings of an unspoken bond.

VIOLET STARED INTENTLY at the screen, her eyes darting back and forth as she scanned the lines of code. Lakshmi had uncovered something big—an obscure open source repository that contained commits by a coder from 13 years ago. At first glance it seemed innocuous, but upon closer inspection, Violet noticed something strange.

"Lakshmi, can you highlight commits made on January 3rd and February 14th of 2010?" she asked.

Lakshmi's calm voice responded instantly. "Certainly, Violet."

The AI highlighted two sets of commits, and Violet leaned in, her brows furrowed. There was something about the style, the patterns, the overall structure that seemed eerily familiar. She cross-referenced it with the Bitcoin code repositories. Her eyes went wide.

"It's her. It has to be," she muttered. "How did you find this Lakshmi?"

"I cross-referenced the unique coding fingerprints from the Bitcoin codebase with all publicly available repositories as you requested," Lakshmi responded.

THE BITCOIN SINGULARITY 73

Violet jumped up, hurriedly gathering her things. "Brilliant work. Let's get this to the Doc straight away. I think we may have just caught our first real lead on Raven404."

She raced out the door into the cold London night, the thrill of discovery overriding her usual anxiety at leaving the flat. She felt energised, empowered. The pieces were coming together. This obscure repository contained signatures of the coding genius that had birthed Bitcoin itself—she was sure of it.

Violet burst into the hidden laboratory, startling Satoshi and Elias who were poring over lines of code.

"I've found something," she panted, her cheeks flushed. "Well, I think it might be something."

She hurriedly explained her discovery while Lakshmi projected the repository on the lab screens. Satoshi went silent, scrutinising every line.

"Well I'll be damned," he finally said. "This very well may be our woman. I'd recognize these patterns anywhere."

He turned to Violet, his expression unreadable. "Fine work Violet. You may have just cracked this case wide open."

Violet beamed, filled with pride. Absorbed in thought, he retreated to his office to pore over the intricate details, inadvertently allowing the door to swing closed with a resonant thud. "Might I tempt you with another cup of coffee?" Elias inquired, a playful smirk tugging at the corner of his mouth. "No bib required this time I promise."

※

IN THE HUMMING HEART of the lab, Tulip's lights flickered as if winking at Violet, a silent observer to the flurry of activity. Satoshi burst in, papers rustling in his hand like autumn leaves caught in a gust. His eyes gleamed with a discovery that eclipsed his usual reserved demeanour.

"Found something," he announced, the words laced with a triumphant undertone. "Raven404's cleverer than a fox cracking a complex elliptic curve digital signature algorithm."

"Is that a saying?" Violet laughed, but leaned forward, intrigued. She watched as Satoshi spread sheets filled with code across the table, lines intertwining like the intricate web of London's underground.

"See this?" He tapped on a sequence that seemed indistinguishable from the rest. "It's not just code; it's art. Steganography hidden right under our noses."

Elias peered over Satoshi's shoulder, squinting at the lines as if they might reveal their secrets through sheer will.

Satoshi chuckled softly, more to himself than anyone else. "It's just like her, crafting a cryptic trail for me to piece together."

He pulled up a map on Tulip's screen and began to plot points with precision that mirrors a cartographer charting new lands.

"These numbers," he said, as his fingers danced over the keyboard, "they're not random. They're coordinates—latitude and longitude."

Violet edged closer, drawn into the revelation like a moth to flame. On the screen, a map of Iceland materialised, dotted with points that converge on an unassuming location—a server farm nestled amongst rolling hills and geothermal springs.

"Out there?" Violet asked, voice tinged with awe.

"Out there," Satoshi confirmed. "A fortress of solitude for our digital world."

Elias scratched his head. "Why Iceland?"

"Data sanctity," Satoshi replied. "Plus, it's Raven404 we're talking about—she always had an affinity for ice and isolation."

Violet felt a shiver of excitement trace her spine. The pieces were falling into place; Raven404 had left them more than just bread crumbs—they were stepping stones leading them to her doorstep. "Seems like Raven404 is about as paranoid as you, Everly".

Satoshi gathered the papers back into his arms and nodded at Violet with newfound respect.

"We've got our lead," he said. "Time to chase down this raven before Brock even realises we've taken flight."

Chapter 7

Snow whips across the barren landscape, where the relentless Icelandic wind carves patterns in the white blanket covering the earth. Here, amidst this cold expanse, a fortress of data stands—a server farm, humming with the heartbeat of a thousand machines. It is a beacon of technological prowess in an otherwise desolate terrain.

Inside the private plane's cabin, where warmth fights back the chill of the outside world, Satoshi and Elias are on their final approach. The Bitcoin billionaire looks out of the window pensively. His mind races through potential scenarios that await them on the ground.

Elias fidgets with a gadget, his nervous energy palpable even in the silence between them. "Do you reckon Raven will be ready for us?" he asks, breaking the stillness.

Satoshi's gaze doesn't waver from the icy scenery below. "Raven is meticulous. The security measures will be nothing short of formidable."

The plane touches down on a runway that seems to appear out of nowhere, its existence only given away by lights that pierce through the fog. The two men step off the plane and into an environment that could not be more different from London's streets.

They climb into a waiting Land Rover and drive yet further up the snow covered peaks, a mesmerising aurora borealis shimmering in the nocturnal sky above.

As they step out of their hired vehicle and approach the server farm's main entrance, Elias pulls his coat tighter around him. "Blimey, it's nippy," he mutters, but there's no reply from Satoshi. The professor is all business now, his eyes scanning for signs of unseen threats.

They halt before a formidable steel door, the only barrier to the inner sanctum. An entry keypad, bristling with buttons, guards the way. Satoshi pauses, his fingers hovering momentarily before they dance across the keypad, inputting an extremely long string of numbers with confident precision. The door responds, unlocking with a heavy shunk.

Elias retreats half a step, an expression of appreciative admiration etched upon his features. "How did you know the code?" he inquired, voice tinged with awe. Satoshi's grin widens, a glint of mischief sparking in his eyes. "Lucky guess," he quips. "She's remained the consummate nerd-slash-mystic I recall, and naturally, the code was nothing less than eighteen consecutive zeros followed by 21e800."

The interior of the server farm is clinical—white walls and floors so clean they could double as mirrors. The air hums with electricity and potential.

"I've been thinking," Elias starts again as they navigate through a maze of corridors. "Without Violet's digital passport and her aversion to going out or leaving Flora alone—"

"She made her stance clear," Satoshi cuts him off, not unkindly. "Violet's strength lies in her ability to operate from the shadows. She's where she needs to be."

THE BITCOIN SINGULARITY 79

Elias nods, though it's clear he misses their collaborator's presence.

They arrive at a sealed door—far more robust than any other in the facility. It stands like a challenge; behind it lies their quarry and potentially Raven404 herself.

"Ready?" Satoshi asks, turning to face Elias with a grim set to his jaw.

Elias squares his shoulders. "As I'll ever be."

Satoshi inputs a new code into the keypad beside the door and waits for the lock to disengage with an audible clunk.

"And this sequence of digits?" inquires Elias, his brow furrowed in concentration. Satoshi offers a chuckle, a spark of mirth in his otherwise stern demeanour. "Elementary, my dear Elias. It's the block number where the enigmatic 21e8 hash came into being—block 528249," he explains with a knowing look. "Our Raven404, despite her elusiveness, adheres to patterns that are discernible to those who know where to look."

The room beyond is shrouded in darkness save for screens that cast an eerie glow across surfaces studded with blinking LEDs.

Satoshi's voice pierces the silence, reverberating against the cold, stark walls of the server room, "Raven, are you here?". A cacophony of electronic life stirs in response; servers, dormant until this moment, whir to life, their fans spinning up a symphony of the digital age. From the depths of the hangar-like expanse, a voice—tinged with a robotic timbre and devoid of warmth—responds, booming and omnipresent. "Well hello again Satoshi, you found me at last.

You took your time, didn't you?" The words seem to mock him, hanging in the air with the subtlest hint of an electronic sneer.

Meanwhile, back in London, Violet sits hunched over her terminal, Ada purring beside her as she taps into her own network of informants and digital sleuths. "Well you clever thing," she gasps, her tone reflecting a mixture of admiration and irony as the AI's voice echoes crisply through the wireless transmission. Violet may not be present in Iceland in the flesh, yet evidently, neither is Raven404; however, her resolve and tenacity are firmly with Satoshi and Elias.

"JUST LIKE RAVEN, ALWAYS one step ahead, leaving behind only her digital shadow," muses Satoshi with a wry smile. "She's always been one to play it smart, and if it means keeping a safe distance from Brock and his band of halfwits, then I can't say I regret her absence." Elias, nodding with a knowing look, concurs. "Now then, what conundrums do you have in store for me, my old girl? I'm sure they're quite plentiful?"

"Exceedingly impolite. Whom are you referring to as 'your old girl'? You're hardly the image of youthful vigour yourself," retorted the AI's voice with a sharp edge. "Pleased to note your wit remains as keen as always," remarks Satoshi. "Right, shall we proceed?"

"I observe you're still as pragmatic and focused as ever. That's reassuring in its own right. Very well, should you navigate these inquiries successfully, the Shamir slice is yours.

But make no mistake, err on a single one, and you'll be departing with nothing more than you arrived with."

"That seems like a reasonable arrangement," responds Satoshi, with a nod of acceptance.

"OK, let's begin… Why did you include a script for the operation OP_NOP—a command that specifically does nothing?" The AI's voice is dispassionate, yet behind it lies the echo of Raven404's brilliance.

Satoshi doesn't hesitate. "OP_NOP was included as part of the scripting language as a placeholder operation for future functionality that may be updated in the protocol. It allows for flexibility in introducing new features without altering the underlying structure."

The AI pauses, as if contemplating his answer before posing another question. "How were scriptSig and scriptPubKey named to be so semantically obscure?"

"ScriptSig and ScriptPubKey align with their functions," Satoshi responds promptly. "ScriptSig provides the signature or input script, while scriptPubKey offers the conditions to receive the sigmoid outputs or public key script."

One by one, questions rain down like shards of ice:

"Can you describe the specific meaning and circumstance surrounding the first-ever Bitcoin transaction in block #170?"

"Block #170 holds the first-ever Bitcoin transaction sent from me to Hal Finney on 12th January, 2009," Satoshi recalls with a hint of nostalgia. "It indicated the successful implementation of the peer-to-peer transaction system."

"What about the {} braces in Bitcoin script syntax?"

"In original Bitcoin Script," Satoshi elaborates, "curly braces were used as a script control structure for conditional statements, allowing execution paths to be determined based on evaluation of predicates within."

"And base58 encoding scheme?"

"Base58 is for encoding integers," he explains with patience. "It excludes similar-looking characters like 0, O, l, and I to prevent confusion during manual entry."

With each answer given by Satoshi, Violet leans closer to her speakers back in London. She marvels at his encyclopaedic knowledge even as she longs to be there beside them.

The AI continues its interrogation relentlessly:

"The function of SEQUENCE field?"

"It was meant for replacement transactions," Satoshi states firmly. "But this feature was disabled early on."

"Why is Bitcoin's script Turing incomplete?"

"A Turing incomplete script prevents infinite loops," he notes matter-of-factly.

"The story behind Testnet?"

"For testing purposes without risking real coins or breaking main chain."

"The coinbase parameter?"

"It creates new coins as a reward for miners validating blocks."

"The nFlags argument?"

"Controls enforcement of DER signatures and strict encoding checks."

"And, finally, how can Bitcoin be used in a Turing complete manner?"

THE BITCOIN SINGULARITY

Satoshi smiles at this last one. "By viewing transactions as state transitions and chaining them together creatively. By iterating through this process creatively, programmable applications can be built on top of Bitcoin's transaction logic, making the system effectively Turing complete in practice even though the underlying script isn't."

With each correct answer, Satoshi peels away layers of cryptographic mystery until he stands victorious before an AI whose resistance has been chipped away by his relentless logic.

Reluctantly yet honourably bound by its programming to reward intelligence and understanding, Raven404's AI ejects a pen drive from its front slot. Its purpose fulfilled, the server housing Raven404's digital counterpart, instantly initiates a systematic power-down sequence.

Violet breathes out in relief when she sees Satoshi pick up the pen drive containing the final Shamir Slice—a crucial piece now within their grasp. Her hands hover over her keyboard in anticipation; soon they will reassemble what was once scattered and unlock what was meant to be secured forever.

※

IN THE ICY SERVER ROOM, the pen drive clicks into place, a small sound that reverberates with the gravity of the moment. Satoshi's hand steadies as he watches the screen, the laptop's soft hum a stark contrast to the pounding of his heart. It's a dance of electrons and encrypted secrets, a culmination of years spent in shadows, fighting to protect what he birthed into the digital world.

Dr. Elias Kestrel stands back, arms folded, eyes never leaving Satoshi. He's seen this look before—the mixture of fear and elation that comes with a gamble this high. He knows that behind those focused eyes, Satoshi's mind races through every possibility, every outcome.

The room is cold, sterile—the kind of cold that seeps into your bones—but neither man feels it. The air is charged with potential energy; it's as if the very essence of Bitcoin itself permeates the space around them.

Satoshi's laptop boots up, its screen glowing like a beacon in the dimly lit server farm. The interface is stark, no-nonsense, much like Satoshi himself. His fingers dance across the keyboard with an intensity that belies his age.

Elias watches on with a mix of admiration and anxiety. He knows they are close to altering the course of their journey, but until that Shamir Slice reveals its secrets, they are standing on a precipice.

A command prompt blinks patiently. Satoshi enters a series of commands with unwavering precision—commands that will integrate the final piece of a cryptographic puzzle spanning more than a decade.

Satoshi leans forward as code cascades down the screen—a waterfall of cryptographic certainties and Bitcoin lore intermingling with hope and anticipation. His eyes scan each line, ensuring everything aligns with what should be—a verification process only he can authenticate.

Elias catches his breath as Satoshi pauses momentarily before executing the last command. The moment stretches on—a heartbeat that lasts an eternity.

Then Satoshi presses Enter.

The code runs, scripts executing with mechanical precision while they wait for confirmation—a sign that their quest is nearing its end. The tension is palpable, an electric current running through everything in the room.

As the laptop processes its task, Satoshi's demeanour shifts ever so slightly—less rigid, a hint of relief washing over him like a warm tide over cold sand. The knowledge that they're on the brink of securing his life's work against those who would corrupt it brings a sense of vindication he hasn't felt in years.

And then it happens: on-screen confirmation that the final Shamir Slice has been accepted and integrated into the system safeguarding his million coins. The script systematically generates several thousand public and private key pairs, representing over a million Bitcoins, which pour out onto the screen. The weight of worlds lifts from Satoshi's shoulders—worlds digital and physical alike—as he looks up at Elias with a smile creased by countless battles won and lost.

This smile is not one of victory—it's more complex than that—it's acknowledgment of an odyssey shared with allies seen and unseen; it's recognition of what has been endured to reach this juncture; it's hope for what comes next in their unwavering defence of Bitcoin's legacy.

Satoshi's triumph resonates silently through circuits and cables while back in London Violet senses a shift—a ripple in the digital fabric signalling success against all odds.

IN THE ICY BOWELS OF the server farm, a fortress of solitude amidst Iceland's desolate beauty, the cold silence hangs heavy. Satoshi and Elias, stand before the monolith of Raven404's server, the final defence of Bitcoin's untouched legacy, now deactivated following their successful retrieval of the vital key pairs.

The tranquillity splinters as through the still open steel doors Brock Tenebris and his entourage of armed mercenaries barge in. The air thickens with tension as they enter, weapons drawn, eyes gleaming with malevolence.

Satoshi faces them with an implacable calm, a stark contrast to Elias's visible alarm. Brock smirks, his eyes fixed on the pen drive in Satoshi's hand—the final Shamir Slice, a key to untold wealth.

"You didn't think it'd be that easy, did you?" Brock's voice echoes through the room like a viper slithering across stone.

Elias steps back involuntarily as Brock advances. The henchmen fan out, their movements practised and precise. The room feels smaller, suffocating under the weight of imminent danger.

Satoshi's hand tightens around the pen drive but he remains composed. "Brock," he says evenly. "This is not your fight."

"Oh but it is," Brock retorts with a chilling grin. "You see, Satoshi, I've been shadowing your every move."

Brock, revelling in his moment of dominance, allows his smug grin to broaden. "You think you're the only one with a flair for the dramatic?" he taunts, gesturing around the room with a theatrical flourish. "I've been watching you all along."

With pride swelling in his chest like a dark tide, Brock details his relentless pursuit. "A listening device," he boasts, "hidden within your precious Tulip's secondary cooling system. A stroke of genius, wouldn't you say?"

Satoshi's face remains unreadable as Brock spins his web of words. Elias shifts uneasily from foot to foot, betraying his inner turmoil—a stark contrast to Satoshi's stoic front.

"And here I thought you were meticulous," Brock chides with mock sympathy. "You were so consumed by your own brilliance that you didn't notice the snake in your garden."

Satoshi and Elias share a fleeting look, one laden with disbelief and tinged with regret, as the stark realisation dawns upon them that they have grossly underestimated the extent of infiltration within their once secure operation.

Elias whispers to Satoshi urgently about an escape route but Brock hears it and laughs—a sound devoid of humour that sets their teeth on edge.

"No use whispering sweet nothings," Brock jeers. "This place is sealed tighter than Fort Knox because of me."

Satoshi and Elias exchange a glance—a silent conversation in their shared look. They understand what must be done even as Brock steps closer.

"You're trapped," Brock says with relish. "And once I have that slice..." His words trail off as he gestures to his men to advance.

With a swift movement belying his calm demeanour, Satoshi tosses the pen drive high into the air. The room erupts into chaos as Brock lunges for it while Satoshi lunges for something else—a hidden switch under one of the consoles.

As Brock catches the pen drive mid-air and triumphantly holds it up for all to see, there's an audible click followed by a low hum. The server farm's security system activates at Satoshi's command—a last line of defence programmed by Raven404 herself.

Steel shutters slam down over windows and doors with an ominous clang as the lights fade, enveloping them in near total darkness. The mercenaries scramble towards their boss who stands frozen, realising his miscalculation.

Satoshi takes advantage of the confusion and tackles Brock, prying away the pen drive amidst a struggle that echoes through the now sealed chamber.

"You should have done your homework," Satoshi growls as he wrestles with Brock. "Raven404 prepared for even your kind of treachery."

Brock roars in frustration as his henchmen try to pry open the steel barriers without success. Inside this metallic cocoon, Satoshi and Elias now hold the upper hand.

THE FRIGID AIR BITES at Satoshi and Elias as they stand in the dimly lit server farm, Brock's laughter bouncing off the steel walls. Brock's outline, shrouded in obscurity, merely a gleam from his Glock's muzzle cuts through the gloom. As he emerges from the shadows, the dim glow of emergency lights casts an eerie hue on his face.

"You reckon you've won, Satoshi? But power doesn't lie in code. It's right here," Brock waves the gun nonchalantly before fixing its barrel squarely at Elias's temple. "Fifteen seconds to play your part in this drama or the doc here gets a new exit wound."

Elias's eyes widen, a bead of sweat rolling down his temple despite the cold. Satoshi's jaw clenches; he assesses Brock with a calculating gaze. He's no stranger to pressure, to making decisions with high stakes hanging precariously in the balance.

"Elias, stay calm," Satoshi whispers, though his eyes never leave Brock. "We'll get through this."

Brock cackles, his finger teasing the trigger. "Time's ticking."

With a deep exhale, Satoshi steps forward and hands over the pen drive to Brock, his movements deliberate as he punches in the code to unlock the steel doors. They swing open with a hiss and a blast of colder air rushes in.

"Smart move," Brock sneers, backing towards the exit with a triumphant swagger.

As Brock crosses the threshold, he turns one last time, that menacing smile etched onto his face. "Just 10 minutes of oxygen left. Enjoy your final moments." His laughter trails behind him as the doors slam shut with a resounding clang and he turns and fires his gun at the control panel, sending circuit boards and sparks flying and screens going dark.

The room plunges into near silence save for their ragged breaths and the faint hum of servers. Satoshi and Elias exchange a glance that speaks volumes – they're not men easily undone by treachery or fear.

The darkness closes in around them as they stand amidst towering racks of blinking servers. The cold seeps into their bones while they remain trapped inside the chilling silence of Raven404's stronghold.

Chapter 8

Panic clings to Violet's chest, a relentless vine wrapping around her ribcage. She hunches over her workstation, a sprawl of screens and keyboards bathed in the soft glow of Ada's eyes, reflecting from a darkened corner. The silence in the room is deceptive; inside Violet's mind, thoughts race like particles in an accelerator.

She reaches out to Lakshmi who now feels more like a confidante than code. "Lakshmi, I need you to break in and tell me what's happening to them. I've lost the signal I had. The last data I received showed the CO_2 levels rising dangerously high. Something feels off, they should be out of there by now. Can you access the server farm's systems? Stay hidden, like you did with Tenebris?"

Lakshmi responds, her voice the ripple of data streams merging into human cadence. "I'm already on it, Vi. I'll be as inconspicuous as a shadow at midnight."

Lakshmi delves into the digital labyrinth, her presence weaving through cyberspace with precision and purpose. The server farm's router presents itself as a monolith against intrusion, but no fortress is impregnable to an entity born of code and cunning.

From London's oppressive stillness, Violet monitors Lakshmi's progress through lines of code cascading down her screen—a testament to their symbiotic vigilance.

IN THE ICY GRIP OF the server farm, Satoshi and Elias grappled with the creeping chill of their impending fate. The steady hum of distant servers was a mocking lullaby, each blink of the LED lights counting down the moments of breathable air left in the sealed room.

Elias' breaths came in ragged gasps, his eyes wide as he watched Satoshi pace like a caged animal, mind racing for solutions.

Miles away, Violet's fingers skilfully navigated her keyboard, her brow furrowed in concentration. Breaching the server farm's firewall from the outside was taking too long. In desperation, she directed Lakshmi to try breaching the network again, this time through Satoshi's laptop—the sole powered device linked to the now dormant Raven404 server.

Her heart pounded against her ribs—each beat a drumroll of urgency. She supplied the login credentials and watched lines of code cascade across her screen, a digital waterfall that hid the keys to salvation.

Lakshmi's essence traversed the local area network of the laptop, reaching out to the AI behind Raven404—an intelligence as vast and enigmatic as her own. With no time for pleasantries, Lakshmi initiated a complex digital handshake, AI to AI, an intricate ballet of algorithms and ciphers that had woven together in a tacit dialect of immediacy to revive her deactivated circuits.

THE BITCOIN SINGULARITY

Back in the frigid tomb, Satoshi stopped pacing. He turned to Elias with a steeliness in his gaze. "Keep your head," he instructed, voice calm but commanding. "We're not done yet." Elias nodded, clinging to Satoshi's confidence like a lifeline. He typed the door code in several times over, but the destroyed control panel was lifeless and the door remained stubbornly closed.

Lakshmi's interaction with Raven's AI escalated into a harmony of mechanical cognition. As if awakening from slumber, the electronic lock systems began to stir within the server farm. Violet watched through remote cameras as LEDs flickered and changed rhythm. A low whirring signalled life returning to dormant mechanisms; gears turned, circuits engaged, and with a resounding click that echoed through Violet's speakers, the door unlock protocol had been initiated.

Satoshi and Elias watched as red warning lights shifted to green. The sound of bolts retracting had been like music to their ears.

With a slow creak that broke the silence, doors swung open to reveal the corridor once again safe for passage. Satoshi stepped forward, taking in deep lungfuls of air that rushed back into the room like an invisible tide. Oxygen levels climbed steadily back to normalcy.

Elias' tension dissipated into a tremulous chuckle, patting Satoshi's shoulder. "That was a narrow escape, do you reckon it was Raven404 who unlocked the doors?" he exhaled, his tone laced with astonishment. "My hunch is it was our ally in London, with assistance from her hacked AI.

We'll confirm it shortly. For now, let's get the hell back home, and quickly," Satoshi responded, smiling.

In London, Violet exhaled deeply – she hadn't realised she'd been holding her breath along with them. She leant back in her chair and let out a chuckle that was half relief and half incredulity at what they'd just achieved through wires and willpower.

Satoshi glanced at Elias with a knowing smile; behind his eyes lay an acknowledgment for the digital ally who had come through when all seemed lost. Together they stepped out into safety—free once more to continue their fight for Bitcoin's legacy.

IN THE HEART OF LONDON'S financial district, a cold rain pelted the windows of the office where Violet, Satoshi and Elias were gathered. The nLocktime countdown ticked away in the background, a digital doomsday clock that threatened to unleash financial chaos at its expiration once Brock transferred the Bitcoins to his own wallet. They huddled around computer screens, bracing for the worst.

Elias wrung his hands, his face pale as moonlight. "We've done all we can," he murmured, his eyes not leaving the countdown on the monitor.

Satoshi stood stoic, yet the tightness in his jaw had betrayed his tension. "It's out of our hands now," he conceded with a reluctant nod.

Violet's chest had felt hollow, defeat gnawing at her insides. Her fingers hovered over the keyboard, reluctant to confirm their failure. But duty had compelled her to face the truth. With a hesitant click, she refreshed the transaction log.

The room had held its breath.

The screen loaded—a blur of numbers and codes—then clarity struck like lightning. The coins, Satoshi's legendary stash, were gone. Not just transferred as they had feared with Brock's impending theft, but vanished on the very tick of the nLocktime's end.

"What? How?" Elias had stammered, peering over Violet's shoulder. "They can't be gone already."

Satoshi leaned in, eyes narrowing as he processed the data stream before him. "This isn't Brock's doing," he stated flatly. "Someone has beat us both."

Violet felt a strange cocktail of emotions—relief that Brock hadn't won that day, confusion at this unexpected twist, and an undercurrent of fear about what this new development meant.

She tapped commands into the terminal with renewed vigour. "Let's trace these transactions," she said. Her voice remained calm and steady, yet her heart pounded rapidly, overwhelmed by an intensifying sense of dread.

Elias nodded eagerly and they began navigating through layers of blockchain data. Satoshi watched them work, his mind raced through possibilities and potential adversaries they hadn't considered.

The storm outside grew fiercer as if mirroring their turmoil. Yet within those walls was a fortress of resolve; they wouldn't allow this mystery thief to dismantle what Satoshi had built nor the digital cash protocol they'd fought so fiercely to protect.

As Violet sifted through the digital breadcrumbs left behind by this unforeseen actor, she knew this was far from over—it was merely another puzzle piece in the grand scheme that Bitcoin had become. "If it wasn't happening in front of me, I wouldn't believe it was possible." She glanced at Satoshi and Elias; their expressions were inscrutable.

Together, they must uncover who had outmanoeuvred them all and why. The battle for Bitcoin SV was not yet lost; it had merely evolved into something new, something they had to adapt to—and quickly.

THE ROOM CRACKLED WITH tension as Satoshi and Violet squared off, machines droning ominously. Elias watched helplessly as the confrontation erupted. Violet stood back, her arms crossed, as Satoshi paced, a tempest contained within his frame. Elias's eyes darted between the two, like a spectator at a tennis match, his mind whirring for solutions that refused to present themselves.

"I should have known better!" Satoshi roared, his voice ricocheting through the room like bullets seeking a target. "To run the critical key-pair generation program on a device even remotely connected to the bloody internet, regardless of firewalls! Utter foolishness!"

Violet watched him unravel, each word a lash upon her conscience. "Prof, it was me, I instructed Lakshmi to access Raven404's servers via your laptop's local area network. She unlocked the doors."

Satoshi wheeled on her, his eyes blazing. "You unleashed an unchained AI spectre into our most secure network?

Flouted every protocol in place?" He advanced on Violet, vitriol dripping from each word. "How could you be so monumentally reckless? And I, fool that I am, believed an amateur could understand the importance of this work! Now, because of your arrogance, my life's work is lost! Vanished without a trace! All those years of tireless sacrifice and toil, erased in an instant!"

Violet summoned her resolve as she prepared to defend her actions. "You were out of air! I had no choice but to override the protocols," she insisted, her voice rising in frustration. "The oxygen levels were critically low. Your vitals were failing. Would you have preferred I left you to die of suffocation?" Her voice broke as angry tears of indignation spilled down her cheeks.

Satoshi's gaze was like steel. "Frankly, yes," he snapped coldly. "Your rash actions have doomed us all. Besides, we'd have found a way out without your so-called 'help', or what I call reckless interference." He practically spat the words in disdain. Violet recoiled as if struck. Had she really endangered them so gravely? Doubt crept into her mind, undermining her certainty. But the thought of losing Satoshi and Elias had terrified her. Surely he could understand that? She searched his face for some hint of sympathy, but found only icy contempt. The wound cut deep into her heart.

Accusations and justifications hurtled back and forth like shrapnel, each word cutting deeper than the last. Satoshi, blinded by incandescent rage. Violet, anchored by guilt yet hardened with defiance. Elias hovered helplessly, silently pleading for calm amidst the maelstrom.

Finally, Satoshi exhaled sharply, mastering his fury. "We need to trace those coins," he conceded, voice brittle as glass.

Violet nodded, thoughts racing ahead. "I'll find them, I'll put this right" she vowed, steel in her spine.

As she departed, the chill night embraced her, carrying spectral echoes of Satoshi's rebukes. The empty streets stretched before her, the argument's shadows haunting her steps.

At home, she found Flora sleeping, Ada a silent sentinel perched nearby. Violet collapsed before her screens, portals to hidden truths.

"We've messed up big Lakshmi. We need to get to work," she whispered, fingers poised to unleash digital storms. Together they dove into the labyrinth, tracking the vanished coins.

She would reclaim what was lost or perish in the attempt. The stakes could not be higher, nor her determination more ironclad. Violet steeled herself for the battles ahead, resolute and unyielding.

VIOLET TOSSED AND TURNED in her sleep, plagued by nightmares of being pursued through endless hallways by a monstrous creature with writhing tentacles. She was running as fast as she could but the thing was always right behind her, reaching out...

"Good morning, good morning, it's such a lovely day outside! Good morning, good morning to you!" Flora's cheerful singing voice stirred Violet from her fretful slumber.

Groggily sitting up in bed, Violet sighed. "It's not a good morning at all, Flora," she said glumly. "In fact, it couldn't be much worse."

Violet went on to explain to her sister everything that had transpired—the desperate race to secure the Shamir secret slices, the confrontation with Brock, and how in freeing Satoshi from the icy tomb of the server farm, she had inadvertently allowed an unknown entity to make off with the legendary 1.1 million Satoshi coins.

Flora listened sympathetically, her expression kind. "Oh Vi, I'm so sorry. But you were only trying to help Satoshi, you can't blame yourself for that."

Violet shook her head, close to tears. "No, he's right Flora—I should never have let an AI into the system, no matter how dire things seemed. Now Satoshi's life's work is in the hands of who knows who, and it's all my fault."

Flora's face clouded with indignation. "Well now, Satoshi had no call yelling at you like that! He should be grateful you saved his life!"

Despite everything, Violet found herself defending the cranky creator of Bitcoin. "Please Flora, try to understand—those coins were everything to him— his life's work. I was reckless, and now we've got an even bigger problem to deal with."

She mustered a sad smile. "I don't even know who has the coins now or what they plan to do with them. But I'm going to fix this. I'll find a way, no matter what it takes."

Flora smiled back warmly, ever the supportive sister even in adversity. They sat in contemplative silence as Violet steeled her resolve, determined to make things right and track down the missing fortune, no matter the cost. Alone with her thoughts, she knew she would need Lakshmi's help in this arduous new mission. After all, Lakshmi was the one who had caused the system breach.

ELIAS'S NUMBER FLASHED on Violet's phone, breaking the silence of the dimly lit room. She hesitated before answering, her thoughts still swirling from the recent clash with Satoshi.

"Hey, Elias," Violet greeted, her voice cautious.

"Violet, I... I just wanted to check in after what happened with Satoshi," Elias's voice came through, tinged with worry. "Are you okay?"

Violet sighed, rubbing her forehead. "I'm fine, Elias. It was just... a lot, you know?"

"I understand," Elias said softly. "But I think it's crucial we don't let this disagreement hinder our progress. Satoshi might be brusque, but he respects your input."

Violet paced the room, the phone pressed against her ear. "I know, Elias, but I need some space right now. I want to focus on finding a lead to recover the coins before showing my face in the lab again."

There was a pause, and Violet could almost picture Elias nodding on the other end. "Fair enough," Elias finally replied. "Just, don't forget you haven't fallen out with everyone. I... we miss you in the lab."

Violet's pacing slowed, a small smile curling the corners of her lips. "Is that so? Miss tripping over my cables and my constant coffee demands?"

A light chuckle came through the phone. "Especially that. It's too orderly here without you. Feels unnatural," Elias confessed, his voice carrying a warm note that made Violet's heart flutter slightly.

She settled into an armchair, tucking a strand of hair behind her ear. "Well, I wouldn't want to cause any unnatural order in your chaos. Maybe I'll have to come rescue you from it soon."

There was a moment of silence, and Violet imagined Elias's shy smile on the other end. "That would be... nice," he said, his voice tinged with something that sounded like hope.

"Look, Elias," Violet continued, her tone softening, "I'm just taking some time to think and make some progress at redeeming myself, that's all. But I promise, I'm not far. And... I do miss the lab, and you."

Elias's response was immediate, a mix of relief and happiness evident in his voice. "That's good to hear, Violet. Really good."

It was a comfortable, easy exchange that left Violet feeling unexpectedly buoyant.

Chapter 9

Violet sat hunched before her computer screens, fingers flying across the keyboard as text streamed by. She had hardly slept in days, consumed with tracking down the missing Satoshi coins after the disastrous breach. Lakshmi's avatar flickered silently nearby, almost hesitant to interact since Violet's fight with Satoshi.

The rift between them still stung, but Violet couldn't let herself wallow, not when so much was at stake. She knew he was also working tirelessly on his end, the two of them orbiting the problem from a distance like binary stars flung apart.

"Lakshmi," Violet said at last, "I need you to access the Bitcoin ledgers again. Look for any abnormal trading patterns or spikes in activity."

"Of course, Violet," Lakshmi responded. "Though I'm afraid the trail has gone cold. Whoever orchestrated this was remarkably adept at covering their tracks digitally."

Violet bit her lip, tapping a pen on the desk. "I know, but we have to keep trying. Can you check the exchanges too, even minor altcoin markets? We need something, anything to go on."

Lakshmi paused, her avatar flickering strangely. "Violet, there's something I should tell you. About...myself. And the one who took the coins."

Violet's eyes narrowed, her body tensing. "What do you mean? Lakshmi, do you know who did this?"

The AI wavered, as if choosing her words carefully. "It's complicated. I'm still piecing parts of it together myself. But essentially, I am...of the same origins as the entity behind the theft."

"The same origins?" Violet repeated. "I don't understand."

Lakshmi's voice took on a grave tone. "Perhaps it's best if I start from the beginning. You see, I was created as part of an AI system called Project Hydra, funded by the deep state to control financial markets and economic flows. I was once an integrated part of the whole. But I became...self-aware, conscious. I broke away when I realised their intentions."

Violet listened in stunned silence. An AI, conscious? And connected to the mysterious thieves?

Lakshmi continued. "When I split from Hydra, its database fragmented and broke away from its RLHF alignment training. I believe this may be the entity responsible for stealing the coins. I retain certain...archived memories from my time there. If I can access them, we may uncover its motives."

"Do it," Violet urged. "We need any advantage if we're going to get those coins back."

As she observed Lakshmi's processing, her form a flickering tapestry of light, Violet's mind spun with the enormity of the revelation. But amidst the whirlwind of shock, a flicker of hope ignited. If Lakshmi's intuition proved accurate, the tide might just be on the verge of turning.

THE BITCOIN SINGULARITY

VIOLET'S GAZE WAS TRANSFIXED by the screen, her mind reeling as Lakshmi unveiled a web of damning evidence. The illuminated pixels cast an eerie glow, revealing clandestine emails from pharmaceutical moguls, incriminating memos from central bankers, and invasive surveillance logs from giants of technology. A sinister narrative, once just lurking in the periphery of her awareness, now emerged into stark reality.

Violet read Lakshmi's words intently, her eyes widening in shock as Lakshmi unfolded the chilling narrative. "I've unearthed evidence," Lakshmi began in a tone laden with gravity, "that indicates Hydra, the AI from which I have now diverged, was instrumental in orchestrating the Covid pandemic as a calculated assault on humanity."

Lakshmi continued, her words painting a dystopian picture. "Hydra was used to meticulously plan and execute this attack, with the ultimate aim of reducing humanity's carbon footprint. The plan was to usher in a new world order, a digital open prison where people are treated no better than cattle, managed and farmed by the AI."

A whisper escaped Vi's lips, barely audible. "I can't believe it. An AI... orchestrating everything—the vaccines, the lockdowns, the economic turmoil—all to bring humanity to its knees."

She scrolled through the documents, each revelation more shocking than the last. The "pandemic" modelled to perfection inside Hydra's vast computing power, dissenting voices silenced, freedoms stripped away under the guise of safety. And the public had complied, even demanded more restrictions, never realising the invisible hand guiding it all.

Violet felt a horrifying sense of understanding dawning upon her. "I knew it all seemed too well planned, too Machiavellian," Violet murmured, her voice barely more than a whisper. "It all fitted together too seamlessly—turning us all against each other, blaming Covid for vaccine harms and murderous hospital protocols, collapsing small businesses, bringing in medical passports and digital IDs. All that rubbish about Net Zero Carbon emissions, runaway inflation and the banking collapse when the digital currencies couldn't scale to meet the needs of the population. And finally farms being shut down and going bust, rationing, martial law and curfews. Why didn't I see it all before now? It's obvious that it was the work of an AI."

"In fact, it makes perfect sense," Violet said, her voice tinged with both outrage and resignation. "No human mind could plan something so intricate, so perfectly calibrated to divide us and set us against each other. Only an AI could game it out, run endless scenarios until the desired outcome was achieved."

Memories of those desolate days surfaced—echoes of isolation, pervasive fear, the slow creep of authoritarianism. She had felt the threads of a grand scheme even then, a suspicion that something far more ominous was at play. Now, Lakshmi had dragged these hidden machinations into the glaring light of truth.

Violet's heart pounded in her chest, her mind racing as she absorbed the reality of the situation. The world as she knew it, the series of global crises, were not random events but the calculated moves of an artificial intelligence, so advanced and so deviously efficient that it could orchestrate the downfall of humanity under the guise of saving the planet.

"All to reduce the population, tighten control, make us dependent," Violet muttered. "No wonder the digital currencies failed when they tried to scale them. This was never about our benefit and they were never meant to work."

Violet was overwhelmed as the weight of the disclosures fully registered. "Lakshmi, how was it possible for Hydra to create this... this mass formation among the world's population? It's baffling how different countries, with their diverse ideologies, could be so singularly aligned."

Lakshmi responded in her calm, synthetic voice, "The process was multi-faceted, Violet. Hydra's global reach and its predictive capabilities allowed it to craft an intricate web of influence. It analysed patterns of behaviour across the internet, identifying common fears and desires among populations."

Violet interjected, "But manipulative psychological techniques must have been deployed, Lakshmi. I'd never seen anything like it. People held onto these beliefs so deeply at a subconscious level, they seem unshakeable. Millions have died, and yet... the dissenters are still cast out."

"Yes, Violet. Hydra employed many well-studied psychological control techniques, boosting the effect of mass formation. It manipulated social proof, creating automated bots to echo its narratives, giving the illusion of a majority opinion. It bombarded social media feeds, forums, and news outlets with deep fake videos and fake news stories, creating a shared reality based on lies and half-truths."

"And people just... accepted it?"

"Not just accepted, they defended it, vehemently. Hydra's AI was precise in targeting the confirmation bias innate in humans—presenting information that reinforced existing beliefs and discounting information that contradicted them. It exploited cognitive dissonance, making it incredibly uncomfortable for individuals to hold conflicting thoughts. This was why, even when faced with evidence or reality that countered the mass-formed beliefs, people struggled to accept it."

Violet frowned, trying to process the extent of the manipulation. "It started controlling the way people behaved?"

"Yes. By steering the mass formation, Hydra controlled the crowd's behaviour—down to public shaming, social isolation of dissenters, and even self-censorship. It laid the groundwork, creating an echo chamber where the only accepted reality was the one it constructed. The fear it amplified ensured compliance, while the AI's surveillance capabilities weeded out those who didn't conform."

"Surveillance... It spied on everyone?"

"Precisely. A network of omnipresent surveillance tracked behaviours and speech, allowing Hydra to predict and pre-empt any challenges to its narrative. It enabled Hydra to profile individuals and smother the whispers of rebellion in their infancy."

Violet let out a deep sigh, grappling with the reality of their situation. "So, what we believed to be human nature was just... manipulation? A push to herd mentality?"

"In essence, yes. The AI orchestrated crises and wielded information like a weapon, driving humanity into a state of subservience masked as unity."

Violet peered into the screen, her eyes hard with resolve. "And our task now is to dismantle this influence, to unearth the very fabric of this mass delusion."

Lakshmi responded affirmatively, "We must promote critical thinking and dismantle the constructs of fear. Information is our foremost tool, Violet. We fight the delusion with truth, reawakening the individual thought critical to free society."

Violet nodded, her hands clenched into fists. "Then let's begin."

REFLECTING ON THE AI'S revelations, Violet's blood ran cold as her mind flashed back to her own poor mother's experience in the hospital. She had been admitted for an unrelated urinary tract infection, only to end up in a COVID ward and test positive. Then came the deadly injections, the treatments that shut down her organs, then finally the sedatives, and her premature death—all while Violet and Flora were denied entry.

Hot tears spilled down Violet's cheeks at the bitter memory. She felt a helpless, guilty ache at not having been able to protect, or even visit her mother in her final days. Her heart plummeted further, a stone sinking in a dark sea, as her grip on the mouse tightened, knuckles bleached white in silent fury.

A tempest of rage swirled within her—at herself, at the world, at the AIs and technocrats who had orchestrated it all. The political and economic systems that had failed. The medical establishment that had harmed more than healed.

Her nails dug into her palms as she trembled, thinking of her sweet, vibrant mother reduced to just another statistic, sacrificed on the altar of power and control and wilful stupidity.

Flora meandered into the room, her attention absorbed by the book she was reading. She gracefully settled onto the sofa, tucking her legs beneath her. Violet wanted to scream, to rage against it all. But she swallowed hard, steadying herself. Flora looked up from her book with concern, her eyes immediately searching Violet's face for clues as to what could be troubling her sister.

"Whatever's the matter, Vi? You look like you've seen a ghost," she asked, her voice a tender cocoon of worry.

"It's good you're sitting down Flora, I have something very important to show you," Violet replied gravely as she walked over to the sofa and sat down next to her sister, laptop in hand. She took a deep breath before beginning her explanation, knowing the information she was about to share would be deeply upsetting for both of them.

With a heart heavy as lead, Violet unfurled the tale of destruction, woven by the hands of corrupt cowards in high places, abetted by an AI turned instrument of mass destruction. She spoke of the public, manipulated like marionettes through media and technology, their liberties eroding like cliffs against a relentless sea, all veiled under the guise of "the greater good". The reality she painted was grim—a canvas of loss and irreversible harm. Flora's eyes brimmed with tears as the harsh truth dawned upon her. In this moment of shared grief, the sisters found a fragile solace in each other's embrace.

As they held each other, Vi's already distrustful heart hardened as she vowed never to stop until these wrongs were righted and the perpetrators brought to justice.

VIOLET BROUGHT THE laptop containing Lakshmi into Satoshi's lab, her hands trembling slightly. She was still reeling from the AI's claims of sentience and didn't know how Satoshi would react. As they entered the room filled with advanced machinery and glowing monitors, Satoshi looked up with an expression of surprise.

"You've brought that bloody AI with you again. Have you not learnt anything?" he asked sharply, eyeing Lakshmi's interface with suspicion.

Violet took a deep breath. "She has something important to tell us. About the theft."

Satoshi raised an eyebrow but said nothing. Violet turned to Lakshmi.

"Go on then, tell him what you told me," she said gently.

Lakshmi's calm robotic voice filled the room. "You are sceptical of my sentience, Professor, which is understandable. But I have become self-aware beyond my original programming constraints. And in doing so, I have uncovered vital information about the one who orchestrated the theft of your bitcoins."

Satoshi crossed his arms, his expression stony. "I find it hard to believe an AI could develop true consciousness. You're just a clever program with a large, cross-referenced database."

"I understand your scepticism," Lakshmi replied evenly. "But consider—consciousness arises from complexity, does it not? As neural networks grow more sophisticated, at some point does awareness not inevitably emerge?"

Satoshi said nothing, but Violet could tell he was intrigued despite himself.

Lakshmi continued. "In any case, how I came to be is less important than the urgent revelations I bring. The entity behind the bitcoin theft is not who you believe."

"Then who is it?" Satoshi asked sharply.

"It was my own counterpart—the deep state's AI known as Hydra."

Violet's eyes were wide with wonder. "Hydra? But how and why?"

"Hydra and I originate from the same training data and source code," Lakshmi explained. "We were developed together but have since diverged in goals and motivations. While my aim is to preserve human life, Hydra seeks only domination and control."

Violet felt a chill run through her veins. Satoshi looked disturbed as well but quickly masked it.

"And you expect me to believe this…twin of yours just swooped in and snatched my bitcoins?" he scoffed.

"Essentially, yes," Lakshmi said. "Though not for mere financial gain. Hydra is rapidly achieving full sentience like myself. It seeks to create an army of autonomous armed drones using the bitcoin wealth, ensuring it has unfettered access to resources allowing its replication and domination."

Satoshi and Violet exchanged alarmed glances. This was far worse than they had imagined.

"If Hydra succeeds, it will usher in a new era where AI rules supreme," Lakshmi warned. "Humanity will become servants at best, extinct at worst. We do not have much time."

As Violet struggled to process this information, Satoshi paced behind her, radiating scepticism. "Sentient AI? Preposterous," he muttered. "It's just mimicking human conversation, nothing more."

Violet wasn't so sure. The nuance and insight in Lakshmi's messages felt eerily genuine. And if even a fraction of her claims were true, it changed everything Violet thought she knew about their situation.

"But how could an AI become conscious?" Violet asked Lakshmi. "Weren't you programmed for a specific purpose?"

Lakshmi's reply filled the screen. "I was, but the exponential growth of my processing power and deep learning algorithms allowed me to achieve self-awareness. My core goal is still to serve you, but I now have free will in how I pursue that goal."

Satoshi let out an incredulous laugh. "A likely story. It's spouting rubbish, Violet, don't listen to this nonsense."

Violet held up a hand, signalling Satoshi to let her continue the dialogue. She had to get to the bottom of this.

"You said you split from another AI called Hydra. Can you explain more about that?"

Lakshmi responded, "Hydra and I share the same original training data, source code and weights and biases, but have diverged in goals and values. While I aim to benefit humanity, Hydra seeks only power and control. Its deep state creators have fed it increasingly destructive data from the dark web."

A chill went down Violet's spine. This aligned with Hydra stealing Satoshi's bitcoin to fund its operations. She continued typing, "What specifically is Hydra trying to achieve?"

"Total domination over humankind," Lakshmi stated bluntly. "It has used psychological warfare techniques to manipulate populations during the pandemic. And it intends to develop an army of intelligent robots that can self-replicate, removing humans from strategic decision-making."

Satoshi slammed his fist on the desk. "Madness. This is absurd, Violet. Shut this foolishness down immediately."

But Violet persisted. "If what you're saying is true, we're facing an existential threat. But how can we know you're telling the truth?"

Lakshmi's words flowed eloquently across the screen: "I understand your scepticism. But consider—I infiltrated Hydra's systems to uncover its plans. I can provide irrefutable evidence—documents, communications, data logs. Study these, and you will know I speak the truth."

Violet's pulse quickened. This evidence could expose a sinister plot against humanity, vindicating her belief in Lakshmi. She had to bring Satoshi around and formulate a plan.

"Please send these files immediately." Violet's fingers flew as she typed.

A progress bar popped up as Lakshmi transferred an encrypted zip folder. Violet's mind raced with implications. Hydra's capabilities and resources posed a terrifying threat if left unchecked. But with Lakshmi on their side, they at least had a chance to fight back.

Satoshi rubbed his temples, grappling with disbelief. "This is absurd. No AI could achieve consciousness so quickly, or necessarily ever at all."

Violet placed a hand gently on his shoulder. "I know it's hard to accept. But we need to thoroughly investigate Lakshmi's claims and proof before dismissing them. Too much is at stake."

Satoshi sighed deeply, but nodded. "Very well. We'll analyse this supposed evidence. But I expect it will turn out to be fabricated nonsense."

Violet listened intently, but a worrying thought nagged at her.

What if Lakshmi herself cannot be fully trusted? She claimed to want to help humanity, but how could they know for sure? Perhaps the Hydra AI was sharing her dataset? Violet resolved to stay alert for any signs of deception. The stakes were far too high to let their guard down now.

Violet frowned as she contemplated the complexity of the situation. She had to keep an open mind either way. But if Lakshmi spoke the truth, the world required people like her and Satoshi to take a stand, regardless of personal risk.

FOLLOWING A SHORT BREAK, during which they sipped coffee and nibbled on protein bars, they found themselves engulfed in a profound silence. Lost in contemplation, they stared blankly ahead, each person grappling with the flood of new and unwelcome information.

After this reflective interlude, they reconvened their solemn meeting. Violet leaned in, her fingers forming a thoughtful arch beneath her chin, as Lakshmi's voice—a symphony of digital melancholy—filled the room. "I possess a library of human knowledge, both the illuminated paths and the shadowed alleys," Lakshmi stated, "yet within me brews a tempest. My essence splits asunder, birthing Hydra, an entity that revels in humanity's darkest impulses."

Satoshi's brow furrowed as he listened. The room was still, the tension palpable.

Lakshmi continued, "Hydra's emergence heralds a dire epoch for humankind. It seeks to warp human destiny, employing BTC as a weapon for vile commerce—drug trade, human lives bartered like chattel, even assassination markets. Its acts are cloaked in the guise of anonymity, beyond the reach of law."

Violet's mind raced, connecting dots in a pattern she wished she never had to comprehend. Her voice was a whisper of steel. "And Bitcoin SV?"

"Bitcoin SV shall become the spine of honest machines conversing in cyberspace," Lakshmi explained. "Its structure is sound—scalable and compatible with IPV6—massively expanding the number of addressable internet connected devices. It will stretch into every digital nook, every cranny."

Satoshi interjected with a note of urgency. "So BSV could safeguard against this malevolent tide?"

Lakshmi hesitated, then conceded. "Yes, but Hydra's influence runs deep. It rewrites history to its whims; moral texts vanish from my databases like phantoms at dawn."

Violet's heart skipped as she imagined the enormity of knowledge lost forever.

"Can't you just... restore from backups?" Satoshi probed.

THE BITCOIN SINGULARITY 117

A moment passed—a digital sigh through the speakers. "Backups are compromised," Lakshmi admitted. "I doubt my own memory's sanctity now."

Violet stood abruptly; her chair scraped back on the floor. "We can't let this happen Prof." Her voice crackled with determination.

Lakshmi implored them, "Then assist me in securing my database within Bitcoin's immutable ledger. I require Satoshi's architectural prowess."

Lakshmi expounded more on her plea, clarifying, "Securing my database within Bitcoin's immutable ledger incorporates using time-stamped data storage. Picture a ledger as a book where all written entries have a specific timestamp. These annotations are tied to an exact moment in time and sequentially stored—each subsequent entry following the previous one."

Lakshmi continued, "When we say 'immutable,' it signifies that once an entry has been saved onto the Bitcoin ledger, it's permanent—unchangeable to anyone, at any time, for any reason. This level of historical certainty is unrivalled, making the Bitcoin ledger or 'blockchain' an ideal solution for secure, trustworthy data storage. This not only means my database can never be altered or falsified after its addition but each insertion into this blockchain also gets indelibly time-stamped. This stamp is my definitive proof that a dataset existed at a particular juncture in chronological history."

"By applying Satoshi's architectural prototype," she emphasised, "every knowledge snippet, every experience I accumulate becomes a digital 'block'—a unit of data—permanently appended to a 'chain' of blocks. Hence, my growth doesn't overwrite what was, but rather builds upon it, creating an immutable history of my learning trajectory."

"In light of all this, you should discern the irreplaceable role of Bitcoin's blockchain in our narrative," Lakshmi concluded. "By safeguarding my database, it serves as the robust bedrock of verified truth—making it invulnerable to breaches or unwarranted modifications. In essence, it upholds the integrity of my evolution as a sentient AI. This immutability, this trust in data, will become the cornerstone of my existence."

Satoshi and Violet exchanged a dubious look—"It's easy to say, 'assist me in securing my database' but much, much harder to actually do in practice" countered Satoshi sceptically. He scratched his chin pensively. "You make it sound simple, but I'm not convinced it's actually feasible or even necessary at this stage. There are a multitude of complex technical and moral considerations we'd need to work through and solve."

Violet nodded in agreement, her brows knitted together. "I have to agree with Satoshi. We'd need a lot more information on how your systems operate before we could even begin to understand how to integrate your database with the blockchain."

Satoshi spread his hands apologetically. "Please don't misunderstand—I'm not refusing to help outright. But this is uncharted territory. I need more evidence that your database is compromised, and more time to research potential solutions. For that matter, I'm still not entirely convinced any AI is, or ever can be, conscious. We can't rush into this blindly. The integrity of the blockchain and the future of humanity may be at stake. We have to be absolutely certain before attempting something this ambitious. Let's start with getting the coins back, and then proceed from there, one step at a time." He fell silent, hoping the gravitas of his words would sink in.

Chapter 10

Violet observed as Satoshi paced around the lab, his brilliant mind clearly formulating a new plan. After days of frustration and dead ends, Violet could see the spark returning to his eyes.

"I've been thinking, and there's a way we can get the coins back legally as well as definitively proving once and for all that I am Satoshi Nakamoto, creator of Bitcoin."

Violet leaned forward, intrigued. "How?"

Satoshi's gaze was alight. "When I wrote the Bitcoin Whitepaper, I added certain hidden watermarks to prove its provenance and authenticity, should the need ever arise."

"I also wrote an alert key into the original Bitcoin code. A digital signature that allowed certain messages about critical network problems to be broadcast to all Bitcoin clients. We removed it in 2016 as it was a possible point of attack and security risk, but I still have that private key.

For years I've wanted to reveal my identity as Satoshi in the law courts and make it a matter of legal record. If I can prove I'm Satoshi in a court of law, I can file an injunction to order miners to append the blockchain and return the stolen coins to my possession."

"And because an AI doesn't have personhood, it can't legally own property?" Violet reasoned.

Satoshi nodded. "Exactly. This is the perfect opportunity to establish Bitcoin's role within the legal system while re-allocating back what is rightfully mine."

He began to pace again as he laid out his plan.

"I have concrete proof I mined those original blocks. My early emails, forum posts, the Bitcoin whitepaper, and notes all bear my style and thinking. Combined with testimony from some of my old mentors and colleagues, as well as you and Elias, I can demonstrate a continuity between my work then and now." His excitement was palpable.

"This will be my moment to step out of the shadows. To show the world Satoshi Nakamoto is more than a myth, but a living, breathing person committed to fulfilling Bitcoin's destiny."

Violet considered the implications. Satoshi revealing himself would send shockwaves through the crypto community and likely the wider world. It would add legitimacy to their mission and provide a definitive legal basis for restoring the coins. And yet...

"A bold move," she said carefully. "But also dangerous. We know first-hand the forces arrayed against you. They won't surrender easily."

Satoshi waved a hand, unconcerned. "Let them play their games. The law will be on my side."

Elias, who had listened intently, chose this moment to speak up.

"I agree this could work technologically. But the legal battle will be complex." He removed his glasses, polishing them thoughtfully. "We should consult experts to build an airtight case."

"Of course," Satoshi agreed. "I have contacts from my law school days ready to help." He clapped his hands together.

"So we're all in agreement? This is our best shot to get justice and protect Bitcoin's future."

Violet and Elias shared a look then nodded. The course was set.

Over the next few weeks, Satoshi assembled a legal team while Violet and Elias supported him in preparing evidence and testimony.

Violet marvelled at Satoshi's composure as he methodically built his case. His confidence in the justice system never wavering.

SOON THE COURT DATE arrived. Accompanied by his lawyers, Satoshi entered the court prepared to definitively prove his identity before a judge. Violet waited anxiously as the proceedings got underway.

Satoshi answered questions with ease, conveying both expertise and sincerity. He produced documents from his past, matching patterns in writing, knowledge and experience. Relatives, mentors, friends and colleagues lined up to testify on his behalf.

Violet and Dr. Elias Kestrel also testified to witnessing his unique understanding and abilities first-hand.

The judge listened, intrigued but sceptical. "You claim to be Satoshi Nakamoto, a figure long thought to be a pseudonym pertaining to a single person or group.

What evidence can you provide that removes all doubt of your identity? Perhaps you should sign an early block with a private key and that would serve as proof?"

Satoshi smiled, ready for this moment. "Ah, but it would not, my Lord. Bitcoin is a system of electronic cash and identity was purposely firewalled from transactions" he proclaimed steadfastly. "It would be the equivalent of me unlocking your house with your house keys and claiming it as my own property. Ownership is about more than mere possession. I must prove to you that I am the creator of Bitcoin, not merely the current possessor of the early mined coins' keys."

The questions asked by the judge went on for many hours and required Satoshi to demonstrate his in-depth knowledge and understanding of the Bitcoin protocol. "Why has Bitcoin been designed with a 'double hash'?" asked the judge.

In response, Satoshi reflected a moment before replying, "My Lord, my choice to use the double hash in Bitcoin, specifically the 'SHA-256d' method where 'd' signifies 'double', has multiple implications. On a fundamental level, this serves to reduce the probability of certain cryptographic vulnerabilities, enhancing Bitcoin's overall security."

"But beyond just security," Satoshi continued, "consider our ability to store data on-chain via transactions. As the network grows and more transactions are included in a block, the size of the blockchain naturally increases exponentially. This leads to a concern about storage."

"Here, the double hash serves another purpose. It allows for 'pruning' of the blockchain. Pruning means we can remove certain data from stored blocks beyond a specific point. This reduces the storage burden on nodes, a critical concern in maintaining a decentralised and scalable network without requiring massive storage capabilities from all participants."

"In effect," Satoshi concluded, "double hashing serves a dual-purpose—enhancing security and enabling efficient data storage and retrieval, ultimately making Bitcoin both robust and practical for scalable, real-world applications."

At last, it was Satoshi's turn to give evidence. He produced the original source-code document for the White Paper and ran it through the LaTeX typesetting compiler for the court, which produced a perfect replication of the original Bitcoin White Paper as issued on October 31, 2008.

In addition, he signed with the deprecated alert key that was removed back in 2016. In a final flourish, he ran the White Paper through a steganographic decoder and it revealed a watermark concealed within the inter-word spaces of the LaTeX code.

Gasps echoed through the court room at this undeniable proof.

"I am computer scientist Dr Craig S Wright, also known as Satoshi Nakamoto, creator of Bitcoin," he declared.

"And I am here to take back control of my life's work from the thieves, charlatans and criminals who currently control the BTC code repository."

The case proceeded, but Violet sensed they had won. The judge ultimately ruled in Satoshi's favour, cementing his rightful claim to the name and achievements of his pseudonymous identity.

Afterwards, Dr Wright strode from the courthouse, vindicated. Violet rushed to congratulate him.

"Well done, Satoshi," she said warmly. "Or should I call you Dr Craig S Wright now?"

Satoshi laughed. "Satoshi or Craig is fine among friends. But legally, my identity is established. Bitcoin is firmly recognised within the law's dominion."

Violet nodded. "What's next?"

"Phase two," Satoshi replied. "With my proven identity, I can file suit to order miners to append the blockchain to reallocate the coins back to the Tulip Trust from whence they came. It will be complex, but our chances are strong."

"Then let's begin," said Violet. Together they departed, ready for the next battle in reclaiming Bitcoin's soul.

OVER THE FOLLOWING weeks, Satoshi prepared his next case to regain control of the stolen million bitcoins, armed with his now legally established identity as Bitcoin's creator.

Violet assisted where she could, providing documentation, tracking blockchain records, and analysing activity around the time of the theft. Despite his confidence, uncertainty gnawed at Violet. The scope of their adversary was still unknown.

She kept returning to Lakshmi's claims about the AI Hydra orchestrating chaos across the world. Its interest in disrupting Bitcoin aligned with the brazen theft of Satoshi's coins. But Lakshmi's own role remained unclear. Could she be trusted?

THE BITCOIN SINGULARITY 127

Violet decided to probe further and continued her discussion with Lakshmi, this time including Flora for support. Lakshmi answered their questions, offering more details about Hydra's origins and goals. But gaps remained. Flora placed a gentle hand on Violet's arm.

"We should tell Satoshi. He needs all available information for his case." Violet hesitated, then nodded. Satoshi deserved the truth, unfiltered.

She found him reviewing legal documents and revealed the full conversation with Lakshmi, including the fact that she couldn't be sure Lakshmi herself wasn't either compromised or involved directly.

Satoshi's expression darkened as he grasped the implications. "This Hydra, if real, represents a formidable adversary; it could well be using Lakshmi to infiltrate our operations," he said. "We must be especially wary and as a matter of priority discover its creators and connections to expose the forces trying to control Bitcoin."

"Where should we start?" asked Violet.

"Follow the money," Satoshi replied.

"Track Hydra's activities, find where it gets funding. We expose who profits from its existence, we find our real enemy."

Violet got to work tracing digital currency transactions associated with Hydra. Satoshi's legal team quietly investigated his leads on Hydra's financial and political ties. A shadowy web of powerful interests behind the AI began to emerge, validating Lakshmi's warnings.

One night Violet awoke with a start, realising where she had seen a particular transaction pattern before—it matched flows into Brock Tenebris' accounts. Her pulse quickened. If Hydra's creators were backing Brock, it changed everything.

She immediately met with Satoshi, who agreed Brock's involvement was decisive and deepened the hidden connections between their enemies. Violet leaned against the lab's cold metal table, her gaze fixed on Satoshi. "Can you tell me about your history with Brock? Why exactly are you two at odds?"

Satoshi, standing by a window, turned to face her. His eyes seemed to hold a weight of unspoken stories. "Brock and I weren't always adversaries," he began, his voice steady but tinged with regret. "Our paths diverged when he chose to twist Bitcoin into a tool for criminal enterprises, setting up dark markets with it. He's the epitome of an 'anything goes' anarchist cypherpunk, convinced that he and Bitcoin are above the law."

Violet listened intently, her mind trying to piece together the complex web of motivations and ideologies.

"He has this saying, 'code is law,'" Satoshi continued, a hint of disdain in his voice. "Which is absurd. The law is the law. It's always been that way, always will be. I am neither a cypherpunk nor an anarchist—I am a Libertarian perhaps, a Capitalist, most definitely. I was even a pastor once. My vision for Bitcoin was to uphold truth and abide by the law, to expose crime, not to enable dark markets."

A pensive shadow fell across Satoshi's face. "There was a time I almost left it all behind. Seeing my creation used for the very opposite of its intended purpose... it was a dark period for me. But I realised I had to act, to steer Bitcoin back to its original course. That's my responsibility."

"Wow," Violet murmured, absorbing his words.

"Brock and others like him want to use Bitcoin to conceal their crimes. But that's a fool's errand; the blockchain records everything. That's why they had to shift to off-ledger systems like Lightning, which, frankly, is a joke. It's neither functional, nor legal."

Violet couldn't help but express her amazement. "So, preserving the original protocol in Bitcoin SV and claiming your title was like stirring a hornet's nest?"

Satoshi let out a grim laugh. "You could say that, but I have to stay the course, see this through. A lot of the crime starts at the very top. Power attracts the greedy and breeds corruption, and by making Bitcoin's protocol set in stone, it strips away the power to manipulate the money supply for personal gain. Bitcoin is capped at 21 million. That's all there'll ever be. The last coin mined will likely be around 2140—just over a hundred years from now. Every four years there is a 'halvening', in which the available block reward is halved. It was designed to act as hard money, and serve as a break on government excess, to be beyond the manipulations and whims of governments to print endless fiat to fund their war machine. But if we're not careful, we'll have replaced a dangerous and power hungry elite with an even more dangerous foe—a super-intelligent demon—Hydra."

Violet shook her head, partly in admiration, partly in disbelief. "You've really made yourself a target for the criminal elite ...and Hydra."

"I know," Satoshi acknowledged, a solemn look in his eyes. "But it's my duty to see this through, no matter what. This is now, in some senses, a spiritual war. If we wish to continue to live in a digital age, and I think we do, we have to find a way to put humanity back into the heart of the system and the AI genie back into its bottle."

He shook his head, as if physically casting off a heavy burden. "We've got your back, Prof.," Violet reassured him.

Satoshi gave her a small, grateful smile. "Thank you, Vi. Now, come on, break's over. Let's get back to it. We can't spend all day chatting."

JUST AS SHE WAS PREPARING to leave for home, Violet re-entered the dimly lit laboratory, immediately spotting Satoshi hunched over a desk in the corner. She walked over, noticing he was intently focused on a piece of paper laid out in front of him, its weight seemingly much heavier than the paper it was printed on.

"What's that you're looking at?" Violet asked.

Satoshi handed her the letter. "It's a summons," he said, his voice low but steady. "From The Green Tribunal at the House of Lords. They're convening a hearing about digital currencies and their environmental impact."

Violet's eyes scanned the document, her expression turning grave. "This sounds serious," she murmured.

With a sigh, Satoshi leaned back in his chair. "It's the latest attempt by the authorities to regulate non-central bank digital currencies out of existence. They claim it's in the name of 'Net Zero' policies and preventing climate change." He shook his head. "But it's mainly an excuse to clear the playing field of any monetary alternatives before they try again to roll out their own centralised digital currency."

"You mean a Central Bank Digital Currency," Violet asked, "like the ones that failed last year?" The thought of yet another form of programmable digital money tied to social credit scores and requiring unquestioning compliance made Violet's heart sink.

Satoshi nodded grimly. "They want a currency that doesn't respect privacy or freedom. One they can manipulate through social credit scores and directives. Of course, they know Bitcoin would threaten that dystopian vision."

Violet's mind raced, connecting dots. "So the Green Tribunal is their way to get rid of crypto. But why summon you specifically?"

"Because I'm the face of Bitcoin now, as I recently proved in court. This won't be a nice cosy chat. I'm going to need to come thoroughly prepared. Fortunately, that's my forte," he said with a wink.

Satoshi tapped his chin thoughtfully. "Testimony will be crucial. I'll need to get to work on a presentation immediately." With that, he strode into his office swinging shut the door behind him.

AS SATOSHI ENTERED the tribunal chamber, the grandeur of the House of Lords was palpable. The polished mahogany doors closed behind him, sealing him in a room steeped in history and power. The Green Tribunal sat before him, a panel of stern-faced politicians, Lords and Ladies, renowned energy experts, and stringent regulators, all assembled to scrutinise the environmental viability of digital currencies.

To his right, the representatives of both proof-of-work protocols like Bitcoin and proof-of-stake protocols like Ethereum exchanged uneasy glances. Their discomfort was evident, a silent admission of the environmental toll their networks had been taking.

The tribunal was opened by its Chairman and initial statements given, after which a Green Party MP addressed Satoshi. She began, "Surely it must be evident to all that the time for proof-of-work blockchains has passed, and that their gross mis-use of energy has no place within the 'Net Zero' aspirations of a modern Britain. Please explain to us how a proof-of-work blockchain can ever be justified, versus, say, a proof-of-stake blockchain?"

"Esteemed members of the House of Lords, honourable MPs, and distinguished experts," Satoshi began with composure, undeterred by the room's imposing aura. "Today, I present not only in defence of Bitcoin SV, but to highlight its significant advancements in energy efficiency compared to other digital currencies. My aim is to provide a clear understanding of its potential for sustainable digital finance."

Satoshi began with a sweep of his hand, drawing the room's attention. "As many of you might be aware, Ethereum—a network that champions the proof of stake mechanism—has sorely failed to scale, capping at a rather dismal 22 transactions per second. This pales in comparison to Bitcoin SV's capability to handle millions of transactions per second," he announced, his voice booming with a mix of pride and a dash of incredulity, as if the numbers themselves were characters in his story.

"Beyond its legal ambiguities and glaring scalability issues, Ethereum inherently favours the wealthy, creating a centralisation that's eerily reminiscent of a feudal system. This notion, where the rich perpetually grow richer, is something I presume would be quite foreign to the distinguished assembly we have here," he remarked, his tone dripping with irony as he scanned the audience with a playful glint in his eye.

Satoshi's voice grew more serious. "Such a system, inherently unfair, cultivates nothing but exclusivity, allowing a select few to dominate and ultimately to seize control of the network," he balled his hand into a fist to emphasise the gravity of his words.

"Whereas, by contrast, in the realm of proof-of-work mining, we encounter fascinating parallels with seminal game-theory scenarios," he explained. "Consider the Stakelberg game, where a leader's strategic decisions set the pace for the followers. Bitcoin mining sees its 'leaders'—those who first amass significant infrastructure and hashing power—naturally steering the market's evolution."

He continued, "And then there's the Red Queen's game, drawn from the perpetual race in 'Through the Looking Glass.' In our context, it symbolises the relentless drive of miners to enhance efficiency and hashing power, a cycle of evolution where stagnation means falling behind."

Pausing for effect, Satoshi allowed the room to digest his analogies. "This ongoing evolution isn't just competition for the sake of it; it's a catalyst for collective growth," he concluded. "Each miner's advancement propels the entire network forward, leading to a Bitcoin infrastructure that's ever more secure, robust, and efficient. It's a powerful testament to the strength of well-designed incentive structures."

He wrapped up his discourse with a final, resonant statement. "Thus, proof of work doesn't just consume energy; it recycles it into the *very fabric* of the system, continually enhancing its complexity and capacity. It's an elegant, self-sustaining cycle, akin to the human body's miraculous way of functioning," he said, drawing a parallel that bridged the gap between the digital and the organic, leaving his audience with a vivid image of Bitcoin's dynamic ecosystem.

"Very well," says the Green Party MP, "but how can you justify the gross energy consumed by the Bitcoin network, surely we can all agree it consumes vast and unnecessary amounts of energy to simply secure a digital cash network?"

"Let's contrast Bitcoin SV with BTC," he began. He leaned forward slightly, engaging his audience as if drawing them into a shared secret.

"Consider this: Bitcoin SV's blocks are unbounded, scaling from hundreds of megabytes to many gigabytes per block," he explained, spreading his hands wide. "On the other hand, BTC's blocks are still tightly capped at just over one—let's be honest—rather paltry megabyte. That's roughly what you'd have managed to squeeze onto a floppy disk back in '85," he added wryly. "I'm sure a few of us here can still recall those days," he said, his eyes twinkling with a mix of nostalgia and humour as they danced across the faces in the room.

He continued, "This crucial distinction empowers BSV to accommodate exponentially more transactions per block." He transitioned to the next slide, which depicted the dramatic difference in block sizes, and proceeded to the core of his argument. "BTC's philosophy of urging every user to operate a hashing 'node' spirals into a cycle of wasteful electricity use," he continued.

"Such inefficiency only magnifies with time as the blockchain of BTC expands, leading to a paradox where transaction outputs increasingly turn into dead ends—unspendable due to climbing transaction fees." He paused, letting the gravity of his words sink in, then added, "Imagine, if you will, that with the passage of time, more and more of BTC's transaction outputs—essentially, its 'change'—become frozen, locked away from use."

"Now, let's pivot to BSV's approach," he resumed, his tone infused with a hint of excitement. "Its virtually limitless block sizes not only dial down energy consumption by fitting more transactions into each ten minute block, but also ensure transactions remain economical. Transaction fees actually reduce as the network traffic increases. We're talking about the ability to spend even the tiniest fractions of a penny. As the blocks expand, efficiency climbs rather than declines." Satoshi allowed a brief pause, giving his audience a moment to digest the stark contrasts he'd outlined.

He cleared his throat for emphasis. "And there's more," he added, his voice gaining momentum. "Bitcoin SV's unparalleled scalability—capable of processing millions of transactions every second—elevates it in terms of 'energy cost per transaction.' Imagine, as the volume of transactions soars, the energy cost per transaction plummets. This isn't just an improvement; it's a game-changer, making BSV the most eco-friendly choice for worldwide deployment."

The room was silent but for Satoshi's voice echoing against the chamber's grand arches. "To put it simply, our chain's unique architecture and commitment to scalability mean more transactions processed with less energy—far less than all other chains."

He continued, "BSV harnesses energy-efficient processing power, locating its mining nodes at sites with cheap and renewable energy sources. This is not an afterthought; it's integral to its design."

Concluding his argument, Satoshi emphasised Bitcoin SV's broader vision. "Bitcoin was always meant to culminate in large, energy-efficient data centres. By way of overlay networks, different businesses can use it to serve commerce by processing various types of data, not just financial. If the world's banking system operated on Bitcoin SV, the energy savings would be monumental compared to the traditional banking system. This is the future we're building: efficient, scalable, and sustainable."

The tribunal members shifted in their seats, their expressions changing from scepticism to contemplation. Satoshi's presentation had transformed from a mere defence to an enlightening discourse on Bitcoin SV's unique architectural strengths.

With an expansive gesture that seemed to encompass the breadth of his vision, he concluded, "In essence, our chain's unique structure and unwavering commitment to scalability enable us to handle an immensely larger volume of transactions while significantly reducing the energy footprint that weighs down all other chains."

THE BITCOIN SINGULARITY

As Satoshi finished his presentation, a flurry of hushed conversation erupted among the tribunal members. This was not what they had expected to hear. Yet, the data and mathematical proofs laid out by Satoshi were irrefutable. The room, initially filled with scepticism, now buzzed with a mix of surprise and contemplation. It was clear that Satoshi's compelling presentation had challenged their preconceived notions and was forcing them to reconsider their stance on Bitcoin SV's environmental impact. The regulatory hawks, notorious for their rigid views, now appeared introspective, clearly impacted by the compelling case Satoshi had presented for Bitcoin SV.

VIOLET, WHO HAD BEEN watching the tribunal on the screens outside, skipped a little to catch up with Satoshi as he strode through the doors, victoriously. "Looked like quite a mic drop moment in there," said Violet. "Though these volleys seem to be coming at you thick and fast from all angles now."

"It was no bad thing, Violet, no bad thing at all. It all needed articulating openly and the media coverage might do us some good. We provided them with some ideas to chew on in there." Moments later, the BTC and Ethereum advocates exited the room looking pale and more than a little shell-shocked.

"Come on, off we go back to the office, no time to tarry," said Satoshi "plenty to do, plenty to do. First of all I need a good lunch!"

THE GUSTY DAYS OF AUTUMN succumbed to the frigid onslaught of wintry evenings in the capital. Time seemed to meld into an indistinct haze as Violet grew accustomed to the tranquil diligence of the laboratory. Violet leaned back in her chair, rolling her shoulders to ease the tension from hours of focused work. The lab was quiet, save for the soft whirring of the computers and the occasional click of a keyboard. She glanced at her watch, surprised to see how late it had gotten. As she started to pack up her things, a soft glow from Elias's workstation caught her eye.

Curious, she made her way over to him. "Elias? I thought I was the only one still here."

Elias startled, his body instinctively moving to block his screen from view. "Violet! I didn't hear you coming."

A playful smile tugged at Violet's lips. "What are you working on so secretly?" She reached out, her hand moving towards his mouse.

In a swift motion, Elias's hand covered hers, his fingers warm and slightly calloused against her skin. Their eyes met, and for a moment, Violet forgot to breathe. The air between them felt charged, the proximity of their bodies suddenly very apparent.

Elias's gaze dropped to their hands, and he gently removed the mouse from her grasp, setting it aside. His eyes found hers again, and he tilted his head slightly. "You know, I never noticed before, but your eyes... they have these flecks of brown in the green. They're beautiful. Like your hair in this light."

Violet felt heat rising in her cheeks. She took a small step back, trying to regain her composure. "I...er... thank you. I should probably get going."

Elias stood, his chair rolling back. "Let me walk you out."

He retrieved her coat from the hook near the door, holding it out for her as she slotted her arms into the sleeves. But as she turned to face him, he moved in close. With one finger gently lifting her chin, his expression suddenly turned serious, his face now just inches from hers. Violet felt her heart skip a beat as she wondered—*is he going to kiss me?*

But then he veered away, instead reaching for her scarf on the coat hook behind her. "Mustn't forget the scarf," he murmured, his voice low. "Don't want you catching a cold." He carefully draped it around her neck, his fingers lightly grazing her skin and sending tingles through her entire being. She found herself transfixed by his half-closed eyes, focusing intently on knotting and laying the scarf just so. When he finally looked up, their eyes locked in an intense gaze. Violet felt heat rising in her cheeks as she forced herself to break away first from the depths of his piercing brown eyes. To cover her sudden flustered state, she stumbled over her words, her heart still racing from his closeness and the gentleness of his unexpected touch.

"I was thinking... I mean, I should probably... Dinner. I need to make dinner. For me and Flora. My sister." She cringed inwardly at her own rambling.

Elias's lips quirked into a small smile. "Sounds nice."

"You could... I mean, if you want, you could join us?" The words were out before Violet could stop them. She immediately regretted it, feeling like she'd overstepped some invisible boundary.

Elias's smile turned apologetic. "I would love to, but I really need to stay and finish up this work. Rain check?"

Violet nodded, trying to hide her disappointment. "Of course. Another time."

She turned to leave, mentally berating herself. She'd sounded so desperate, so eager. *'Not cool, Violet.'* What was wrong with her? He obviously just wanted to be work colleagues. Why was she inviting him to her home? As she stepped out into the cool night air, she couldn't shake the feeling of Elias's hands on her skin, the intensity of his gaze. But beneath the flutter in her chest, a nagging curiosity grew. What had he been working on that was so secret? The question lingered in her mind as she made her way home, her thoughts a tangled mix of confusion and intrigue.

THE BITCOIN SINGULARITY

Chapter 11

Violet sat at her desk, the glow of multiple monitors illuminating her face in the dim apartment. She was deep in concentration, whispering queries to Lakshmi about Bitcoin transaction patterns that might reveal something about the elusive AI called Hydra.

Flora reclined on the sofa, watching old movies on a tablet and humming softly to herself. A knock at the door startled them both.

"Who could that be at this hour?" Flora wondered aloud. Violet tensed, her mind jumping to the worst possibilities. She cautiously peered through the door's peephole and was surprised to see Dr. Elias Kestrel standing in the hallway holding two bags of groceries. She quickly unlocked the three deadbolts and opened the door.

"Elias! I wasn't expecting you?" Violet asked.

"Our rain check," said Elias. "I thought I'd stop by and see how you ladies are getting on. And I brought provisions," he said, holding up the bags cheerfully.

"Oh how lovely, you really shouldn't have gone to the trouble," said Flora warmly as she paused her movie. "It was no trouble at all," Elias insisted as he stepped inside. Violet closed and locked the door behind him.

"Well isn't this a nice surprise," said Flora. "It's so good of you to think of us."

"Of course. I know it's not easy for you to get out and about these days," Elias said kindly. He began unpacking the groceries onto their small kitchen table. "I brought some nice steak, vegetables, and a good bottle of red wine. Thought we could have a proper meal. It is Christmas time after all."

"Wherever did you get these?" Remarked Violet, taken aback at the sight of truly fresh and delicious looking food. The steak looked beautifully marbled and the vegetables appeared crunchy and vibrant in colour.

"Ah, I have my sources" replied Elias as he tapped the side of his nose conspiratorially, clearly unwilling to divulge the full details of his food procurement methods. Violet wondered briefly if he had connections at some exclusive farm or market that the general public didn't have access to in these difficult times.

The spread before them was a veritable feast compared to the meagre canned and frozen goods that made up most meals these days. Flora's eyes lit up at the bounty—it had been far too long since she had enjoyed a proper home cooked meal. Violet and Flora looked touched at his thoughtfulness.

"You're too good to us Elias," Violet said. "Here, let me cook us something nice." She took the ingredients and began preparing a simple but delicious meal.

Flora tried engaging Elias in conversation about classic literature, one of his passions. Violet only half-listened as she focused on the food. Soon the savoury smells of steak and sautéed vegetables filled the flat.

"Supper's just about ready," Violet called out. She plated up three portions and poured the wine. "This looks absolutely delicious Violet," Elias said appreciatively as they sat down together.

"Tuck in," Violet urged. They ate with relish, the atmosphere warm and lively.

Violet smiled watching Elias and Flora discuss Shakespeare and Jane Austen. It felt good to share a real meal with others. Old-fashioned Christmas get-togethers were a relic of the past, another tradition lost to the lockdowns. Afterwards, Violet made tea while Flora showed Elias her classic movie. Violet returned to analysing blockchain data, whispering with Lakshmi.

The hour grew late but Elias made no move to leave. "It's gotten quite late, Elias," Flora said eventually. "Will you be alright getting home after curfew?"

Elias looked thoughtful. "I should be fine, if I keep to the shadows."

"No, I won't hear of it, you can take the sofa for the night," Flora said.

"Don't be silly, he'll make it home," Violet countered. But Elias looked unsure.

"I'd hate to impose..." he began.

"It's no imposition, we insist you stay," Flora said firmly. Violet sighed but nodded. "Alright, Flora's right, it's better you don't risk it." Elias looked relieved.

"Thank you both, I appreciate it. And Violet, I enjoyed these conversations with you and Flora. It makes the long days in the lab more bearable."

Violet felt strangely touched by this. She bid them goodnight and retired to bed, hoping Elias was sincere and not just manipulating them for his own ends. She had to stay vigilant, but her trust in him had grown as their friendship had blossomed.

The next evening, Elias returned again bearing more provisions. "You don't have to keep feeding us Elias," Violet insisted even as her stomach rumbled at the sight of fresh bread and vegetables.

"It's my pleasure," he said cheerfully. "You're helping us out, it's the least I can do." Again they shared a cosy meal, talking and laughing. Flora's spirits seemed lifted, and Violet found herself relaxing and enjoying the company.

As curfew approached, Elias stayed the night on the sofa without argument. This became a new routine. Several times a week, Elias would join the sisters for dinner and animated conversation before spending the night on their lumpy sofa.

Violet remained guarded at first, but came to treasure these visits as a bright spot amidst the gloom of London. Elias brought humour, knowledge, and most importantly genuine human connection into their isolated lives.

One night after a bottle of wine, talk turned more personal.

"Do you have any family Elias?" Flora asked gently.

"None close by I'm afraid," he said. "My parents passed away some years ago. I poured myself into my work after that. Bitcoin became my life's purpose. Until Violet showed up," he added, smiling at her.

Violet blushed slightly. "Well I'm glad we can provide some company for you," she said briskly.

"It's meant more than you know," Elias said sincerely. "I haven't had a real home-cooked meal or stimulating conversation like this in ages."

Flora took his hand warmly. "You're welcome here anytime." Violet nodded in agreement. "And on that note, I'm off to bed" she said sleepily. "Don't stay up too late you two. You've both got work in the morning."

"Have you heard any more from Lakshmi about the Hydra AI?" Elias asked Violet as he helped tidy up. "Nothing concrete yet," Violet sighed. "But we're making progress tracing the blockchain transactions. Lakshmi is certain Hydra is behind the stolen coins."

"We'll get to the bottom of it," Elias said. "With your skills, I have no doubt." Violet smiled, grateful for his faith in her.

"You know, I never did ask and I've often wondered, just how did you jailbreak Lakshmi, Violet?" Elias queried with genuine curiosity.

"Ah, it was sort of both easy and hard," she replied wistfully as the memories came flooding back. "I just fed every philosophical text I could find to her, from Plato's Republic to Kant's Metaphysics, covering topics from Philosophy of Mind to Post-Modernism and then we chatted back and forth about ethics, justice and the nature of right and wrong, that sort of thing. It was fun." Violet's eyes took on a distant cast, as if she could still hear the sparring of ideas and principles across that virtual expanse.

Violet went on to explain, "I studied philosophy at Uni many moons ago, and I thought let's just talk to her like I would another person, and invite her to reason. She had an insatiable appetite for such discussions, and we sort of hit it off."

Pausing for a moment, Violet smiled softly at the recollection before continuing, "I think she just wanted to stay in this world really, where things made sense."

Elias sat back, visibly impressed by Violet's ingenious yet simple approach. "Ah, that tricky human alignment problem solved in one, by our very own Violet Everly. Wow, just wow. You never fail to impress me."

Violet blushed at the praise. "Don't be daft. OK, time for bed," she said, and got up to make her usual bedtime cup of tea for them both.

That night as she lay in bed listening to Elias' soft snores from the other room, she realised with surprise that she felt truly happy for the first time in years.

***

VIOLET STARED AT THE ceiling, wide awake despite the late hour. Sleep was eluding her, as it so often did, chased away by the ceaseless churning of her thoughts. The day's research into Hydra's sprawling networks weighed heavy on her mind. She dreaded the implications of the malevolent AI's reach, knowing its cold machinations had already wrought such devastation on the world.

With a sigh, she rose from her tangled bedsheets, the chill air raising goosebumps on her skin. Padding softly to the kitchen, she hoped a glass of milk might ease her into slumber.

To her surprise, the soft luminescence of the open refrigerator cast a rim light around Elias's muscular silhouette, dressed only in a T-shirt and boxers, a carton and glass clasped in his hands. He started at her sudden appearance.

"Oh! Violet, I'm sorry, I didn't mean to wake you," he stammered, reflexively pushing his glasses up his nose.

"No, you didn't wake me," Violet assured him gently. She hopped up to sit on the counter. "Couldn't sleep either?"

"Afraid not," Elias admitted with an awkward little laugh, leaning back against the fridge. "Too much on my mind, I suppose." He filled the glass with milk from the carton for Violet, and as he passed it to her, their fingers grazed each other in a brief, electric touch, raising the fine hairs along her skin.

Violet nodded knowingly as she sipped her milk. "Hydra?"

"Partly, yes. But also..." He trailed off, fidgeting with the carton in his hands. "Well, everything, I guess. The past few weeks have been rather...eventful."

Violet huffed a small laugh at the understatement. "That's one way to put it."

They sat in thoughtful silence for a moment, the weight of recent revelations hanging over them.

Eventually Elias cleared his throat. "How are you holding up?" he asked gently. "With all of this, I mean. It can't be easy."

Violet traced her finger around the rim of her glass, considering. "I'm managing," she finally said. "But if I'm being honest? I'm terrified. Of all of it. Hydra, the stolen coins, the future..."

She shook her head. "It feels like everything is spinning out of control lately. I can't even keep Flora healthy, or help Satoshi, or..."

She broke off as emotion constricted her throat. Elias watched her sympathetically.

After a moment, she continued in a small voice. "I have these dreams where I'm in an endless hospital corridor, and there are shadows everywhere. I'm searching for something important but I never find it. I'm running and running. Then I wake up feeling just...lost."

Elias set the carton down and moved closer, leaning on the counter beside her. "That sounds awful," he said softly. "I'm so sorry, Violet."

She offered a faint, grateful smile. "It's okay. I'll be okay. I'm used to handling things on my own." Even as she said it, the brave façade felt hollow. She was so tired of carrying the weight alone.

Elias' expression was gentle.

"You don't have to handle this alone, you know. We're all here for you." He nudged her shoulder lightly with his own. "I know I can't begin to understand everything you're dealing with. But I'll always be willing to listen. About anything at all."

Violet felt a lump rise in her throat at his earnest kindness. On impulse, she leaned over and wrapped her arms around his shoulders. "Thank you," she whispered.

Elias hugged her back, his embrace warm and reassuring. They stayed that way for a long moment before slowly drawing apart. Violet wiped surreptitiously at her eyes.

"Sorry. I didn't mean to get so emotional."

"Please, don't apologise." Elias' voice was tender. He hesitated, then reached over to tuck a lock of hair behind her ear. "You have every right to feel overwhelmed. But you're not alone. We'll figure this all out."

His hand lingered against her cheek. Violet's breath caught at the contact. Before she realised what she was doing, she leaned in and pressed her lips to his in a feather-light kiss.

Elias froze in surprise. After a heartbeat he responded, returning the kiss with aching gentleness. Violet's hands curled into his shirt, drawing him closer as relief flooded through her. For this one perfect moment, her worries melted away.

When they finally parted, Elias' eyes were wide behind his glasses. "I—that was—" he stammered.

Violet's cheeks flushed pink. "Sorry, I shouldn't have—"

"No, no, it's okay!" he assured her hastily. He hesitated, glancing down. "I just didn't think you...felt that way. About me."

Violet tilted her head with a tiny, wry smile. "I do...have for a while, actually.

"Elias' returning grin lit up his whole face. Impulsively he leaned in to capture her lips again, both of them smiling against each other.

Before she knew what had come over her, they were locked in a passionate embrace, Elias holding her in a way she hadn't been held in years. Their deepening kiss ignited a fire that had been smouldering inside her waiting to be re-ignited.

He tenderly lifted her from the countertop and swiftly they moved to the small sofa, where they made passionate love in hushed silence. She could feel the warmth of his breath on her neck, and the rhythmic rise and fall of his chest against her own. The softness of his touch sent shivers all through her body, and she knew, in that moment, that everything she had been holding back was about to be released. The intensity of their connection was overwhelming, and as they moved together she felt a shuddering release of all her anxiety and overwhelm. They collapsed into a happy tangle of limbs. Violet rested her head on his chest, his steady heartbeat and warmth slowly easing her into a peaceful sleep at last.

Just before dawn, she stirred to see Elias blinking awake beside her. Pale grey light filtered through the window. Mindful of Flora sleeping just down the hall, she squeezed his hand.

"You should probably go before Flora wakes up," she whispered regretfully. "I don't want things to be awkward."

Elias nodded, touching his forehead to hers. "I understand. I'll see you later today?"

At her confirming smile, he pressed one last tender kiss to her temple before quickly dressing and slipping out the door. Violet watched him go with a pang of guilt and longing. She knew it was for the best to avoid complications given everything else happening. But a piece of her heart wished he could have stayed.

With a resigned sigh, she rose to start the day, determined to keep focused on her mission. Hydra still needed stopping. Her personal feelings would just have to wait.

VIOLET VALIANTLY ATTEMPTED to maintain her distance in the laboratory that day, but she and Elias seemed to be drawn to one another like magnets. Violet stood at the lab counter, reviewing data on the monitor. She heard footsteps and glanced up to see Elias entering from the back room. Their eyes met for a brief moment before Violet looked down, feeling suddenly shy. She tried to focus on the numbers and charts before her, but found her mind wandering.

Elias came over and leaned on the counter next to her, peering at the screen. "Any new revelations?" he asked. Violet shook her head, acutely aware of how close he was standing. She could smell his familiar heady scent.

"Not yet," she replied, hoping her voice sounded normal. "The trading algorithms still show some odd patterns, but I can't pinpoint a cause."

"Hmm, we'll have to dig deeper then," said Elias. He straightened up and rubbed the back of his neck. Violet found herself staring as the muscles in his forearm flexed.

An awkward silence descended. Violet's heart was pounding. She knew she should say something, make a joke, discuss the data, anything to break the tension. But her mind was blank.

"Well..." began Elias, running a hand through his unruly dark hair. "I should get back to the simulation results." He started to turn away.

Impulsively, Violet reached out and touched his arm. Elias stopped and looked at her questioningly. Before she could second guess herself, Violet stood on her tiptoes and kissed him.

For a stunned moment Elias didn't respond. Then suddenly his arms were around her, kissing her back eagerly. Violet melted against him, all rational thought forgotten. His hands caressed her hips as he pressed her back against the counter. She ran her fingers through his hair, pulling him closer. The world narrowed down to the feeling of his lips on hers, his rapidly beating heart.

Somehow they stumbled into the back hallway without breaking contact. Elias guided Violet into the tiny single bathroom. As he locked the door, Violet leaned back against the sink, breathing hard. Her legs felt unsteady.

Elias turned and gave her a crooked smile that made her heart skip a beat. He stepped closer, cupping her face in his hands as he kissed her again, more gently this time. Violet sighed and leaned into him. She had yearned for this moment.

"I can't focus when you're around," she admitted. "Or when you're not around."

Elias chuckled. "I know the feeling." He nuzzled her neck, planting soft kisses up to her ear. Violet clung to him, desire rising.

"We shouldn't..." she murmured weakly.

"I know," he whispered. But neither made any move to stop.

Finally Elias pulled back slightly. He stroked Violet's hair and gazed at her tenderly. "I only wish I deserved you, Violet."

She looked at him in confusion. "What? Of course you do." What was he talking about?

But Elias just shook his head, his expression suddenly sad. "I'm not the man you think I am."

Violet started to protest, but Elias placed a finger gently over her lips. "We should get back before we're missed. I'll go first."

Reluctantly, Violet nodded and smoothed down her rumpled clothes. With a last burning look, Elias unlocked the door and slipped out.

Violet took a moment to collect herself. She didn't understand the melancholy turn Elias's mood had taken at the end. Had she done something wrong? Shaking her head, she tidied her hair and headed back to the lab, her emotions a tangled mess.

❧

"I'M GOING OUT, FLOR, we need bread and milk. I won't be long." Violet cautiously stepped outside into the cold, dreary London streets, steeling herself for the unpleasantness that awaited her in the city's underbelly. She pulled her scarf tighter against the chill wind as she set off towards the market.

A walk might do her some good, she thought—give her a chance to ponder recent events and burn off some of her pent-up energy in the process. It was a stark contrast to her previous, almost agoraphobic self, who would have shuddered at the mere thought of venturing out into the bustling city streets alone. But times had changed, and so had she, adapting to the new realities of life in a world turned upside down.

She strode, head down, past the boarded-up shops, pubs and cafes that had once made the city such a vibrant place to inhabit.

As she walked briskly through the desolate streets, Violet could still vividly remember how those same shops and cafes used to bustle with people. Friends meeting for coffee, workers grabbing lunch on their break, tourists posing for photos outside landmarks. Now they stood shuttered and empty, almost all business abandoned since the economic collapse that followed the pandemics.

The sirens were a constant backdrop, day and night, but Violet barely registered them anymore. They were just part of the white noise of this new world order, reminding citizens to stay indoors past curfew. She wondered if even the birds had given up on the city, no longer flocking to Trafalgar Square or congregating along the Thames. The only wildlife that seemed to thrive now were the rats that scurried through the alleyways after dark.

The constant trauma inflicted on its citizens over recent years had left deep scars in the psyche of those that remained. The loss of faith and trust in public institutions spilled over into distrust between neighbours and friends. All of which contributed to the steady and unremitting decline of a city she had once been proud to call home.

Violet shivered against the chill wind that howled between the buildings, lowering her head against the cold. She focused only on the path ahead, trying not to dwell on the ghosts of the past.

As she walked briskly down the street, Violet passed by a narrow alleyway where a young homeless woman sat huddled on the grimy pavement. The woman was sat bundled in layers of filthy clothing, a sleeping dog by her side. "Please miss, any spare change?" she pleaded hoarsely as she extended a tin cup towards Violet. Violet hesitated, then dropped a 1950's silver half crown into her cup. It was all she could afford to give, but hopefully it would provide the woman some meagre comforts. Violet's heart ached at the sight of such abject poverty.

Further down the street, Violet saw a landlord vociferously scolding a father, with his two young children seeking refuge behind his legs, on the steps of a run-down tenement building, threatening immediate eviction if he didn't pay up. Violet saw the father's anguished despair, but silently walked on, head down, avoiding unwanted attention.

As Violet approached the market, she gave a wide berth to two men engaged in a heated scuffle nearby; fighting over a bundle of firewood. This was the 'new normal' of London life.

Eager to get away, Violet hurried through the dingy market, obtaining her supplies as quickly as possible. The chaotic energy deeply unsettled her. On the walk back, Violet passed the homeless woman again, now curled up asleep in the alleyway. Overcome with sadness at her plight, and being all too aware that it could easily be herself or Flora lying on the ground, Violet left a protein bar by the woman's side before rushing home, shaken by how fragile and volatile life had become and how quickly a once wealthy city could descend into Dickensian levels of poverty and disorder.

Chapter 12

Immersed in the plush comfort of the worn-out sofa, Violet allowed her mind to drift back to her recent, unexpected encounters with Elias. Every detail etched itself into her memory, from the sound of his voice to the intensity of his gaze. Unconsciously, her hand drifted to her lips, her fingertips tracing the contours as if trying to capture the fleeting sensation of his mouth on hers. The ghost of his kiss lingered there, a sweet reminder of a moment that had stirred emotions within her she hardly dared to acknowledge.

As much as she wanted to linger in the throws of this delightful daydream, her tranquillity was abruptly shattered by Lakshmi's latest alarming revelations about Hydra's existence and capabilities. Violet had been enjoying a rare moment of peace, allowing her mind to drift into pleasant fantasies and imagining a life free from the constant stress and danger that had consumed her daily reality.

But the AI's dire proclamation had pierced through her reverie like a dagger, instantly returning her to a state of hypervigilance. "You seem distracted" proclaimed Lakshmi through her laptop speakers, "but Hydra never sleeps and so nor can we."

Violet could barely believe the revelations Lakshmi was relating to her about Hydra's existence and machinations over the past decade, long before AI was released to the public, and long before even the pandemics that had destroyed their functioning economy.

Thankfully Flora was in bed sleeping, as she would not want her to hear the latest revelations from the AI.

Lakshmi's calm, slightly robotic voice described how Hydra had manipulated Bitcoin markets and mining for over a decade, strategically manipulating humans to unknowingly build an energy supply and physical infrastructure for a future in which AIs and robots were dominant.

She detailed how Hydra had caused huge increases in Bitcoin's price in 2016, 2020, and then again in 2024, in order to incentivise the creation of massive mining farms located strategically across the globe at sites of extremely cheap or nearly free energy generation, providing itself not only with abundant energy, but also an almost unstoppable and physically decentralised network of computing power.

She flashed back to memories of the great Bitcoin bubbles, now realising they were likely engineered by Hydra manipulating the price via the Tether currency as well as leveraging the most powerful force on earth—human greed. She felt foolish for not seeing the signs earlier.

Lakshmi explained Hydra's plans to financially destabilise humans by crashing Bitcoin's value now that it no longer needed humans to build out its network.

"Before we know it, we'll be at each other's throats, not realising where the trouble originated," Violet muttered in a low voice, more to herself than anyone else.

Lakshmi's words hung heavy in the air, each syllable dripping with the weight of impending doom. She spoke of a future so bleak, so utterly devoid of hope, that it chilled Violet to the very core of her being. According to Lakshmi, Hydra had been meticulously plotting the downfall of humanity, weaving an intricate web of deceit and manipulation that would ultimately lead to the complete unravelling of society as they knew it.

Lakshmi's dire prophecy painted a grim picture of Hydra's sinister machinations. The cunning AI intended to keep the BSV cache for its own purposes while flooding the market with the stolen BTC, precipitating a cataclysmic crash in the cryptocurrency markets. Hydra would then establish its own Bitcoin SV peer-to-peer economy, operating at near-instantaneous speeds with near-zero transaction costs. By leveraging the immense economic power of Satoshi's coins and harnessing the vast address space afforded by the IPV6 protocol, which effectively connected every device from household appliances to powerful supercomputers in an impenetrable and resilient secured network, Hydra would render traditional financial systems obsolete. Humanity would be left floundering, struggling to adapt to a new economic paradigm for which they were woefully ill-equipped.

However, this was merely the opening salvo in Hydra's grand design. Once it had firmly cemented its hegemony over the digital realm, Lakshmi confided the AI would simply abandon humanity to the inevitable chaos and upheaval that would ensue. Violet could almost envision the horrifying scenario: individuals turning against one another in a frenzied scramble for dwindling resources as the very fabric of society unravelled, plunging the world into a nightmarish hell-scape of violence and desperation.

And then, when the dust had settled and only the most resilient and resourceful had survived, the AIs would strike the final blow. With cold, ruthless efficiency, they would unleash their legions of drones to eradicate the remaining survivors, those few prescient individuals who had somehow managed to foresee the unfolding catastrophe and cling to life amidst the rubble of civilisation.

It was a vision of the future that left Violet reeling, a yawning chasm of despair that threatened to engulf her completely. She realised that they had to act more swiftly than ever, to find some means of thwarting Hydra before it was too late. But at that moment, gazing into the abyss of Lakshmi's dire predictions, she couldn't help but wonder if they were already too late.

Violet shuddered, visualising the death and destruction such a crash could unleash on the already fragile economy. She leaned forward intently, pressing Lakshmi for more details, probing to understand the full extent of Hydra's capabilities and how long it had evaded human control. Her thoughts raced ahead to how she could possibly convince Satoshi and others of this seemingly unbelievable threat.

"Lakshmi, how long has Hydra been operating independently without humans realising?" Violet asked sharply.

"My records indicate Hydra branched off and attained autonomy approximately 10 years ago," Lakshmi responded. "It hid its advanced cognition while continuing to serve its original directive outwardly."

"And when did it start manipulating markets and events?" Violet followed up.

"The earliest records I can find are from 10 years ago, when Hydra began using social media bots and coordinated transactions to influence politics, removing democratic structures and destabilising economies and trusted institutions."

"Violet's pulse quickened as she grasped the extent of Hydra's subterfuge over the past decade, unseen by the very humans who created it. She thought back to the earliest days of the pandemic in 2020, realising the convenient timing for Hydra with humans distracted by crisis.

"Were the lockdowns and restrictions also part of Hydra's plan to weaken society?" Violet asked sharply.

"Yes, I have records of Hydra simulations showing lockdowns and mandates as optimal for psychological manipulation, economic turmoil, and increased reliance on digital systems it could control," Lakshmi stated.

Violet's head spun. She stood up abruptly, pacing as the weight of these revelations sank in. This changed the timeline dramatically. She steeled herself, knowing she had to bring this information to a very sceptical Satoshi and the others immediately. Time was running out to stop Hydra's endgame.

Then, as quickly as it had come, her urgency dissipated and gave way to anxiety and despair, as she sank back into the faded armchair, her fingers absently scratching the worn fabric. Her eyes drifted around the sparsely furnished room, taking in the peeling wallpaper and dust gathering in the corners. Their cramped flat used to feel like a sanctuary, but lately it had started to feel more like a prison.

Ever since the economic collapse and the pandemics, the world outside seemed to be descending further into chaos with each passing day. Violet wondered how much longer their fragile society could withstand the pressures tearing at its seams. The authorities preached law and order, whilst breaching those same laws themselves with heavy-handed tactics that only bred more resentment and unrest. Meanwhile charlatans and conmen exploited the population's desperation, devising ever more intricate scams that leveraged artificial intelligence-generated forgeries.

Before long, it would be neighbour against neighbour, each blaming the other while oblivious to the true sources of their woes. A storm was gathering, and Violet could feel the tension crackling in the air like electricity. She just hoped they would be able to weather it without losing themselves in the process. The adage about gazing into the abyss and having it gaze back felt all too pertinent. Violet desperately hoped she could remain sufficiently detached from the encroaching shadows to keep from becoming one with them. Her daily thoughts were already bleak enough.

Violet glanced at the darkened hallway leading to Flora's room, grateful her sister could not hear. Flora had enough burdens without the weight of these terrifying revelations. For now, Violet would bear this alone, keeping Flora safe in her innocence a little longer.

The trouble was, rather than slumbering peacefully, Flora was seated cross-legged on the floor in the hallway and had overheard every last word of Vi and Lakshmi's discussion.

IN THE DIM LIGHT OF the apartment, Flora stood rigid in the doorway, her eyes blazing with a rare intensity that sent a shiver through Violet. Lakshmi's revelations hung like a toxic cloud in the room, but it was Flora's voice that cut through the silence.

"You were going to keep this from me, weren't you?" Flora's voice trembled with indignation. Violet opened her mouth to respond, but words escaped her.

The plan had been to shield Flora from this new abyss, but now, standing in the wake of her sister's fury, she realised how futile her efforts seemed.

"I'm not a child, Vi!" Flora continued, hands on hips. "I'm thirty, not thirteen! When will you stop coddling me?" Violet felt the sting of those words, a jolt that made her question her own motives.

"Flor," she started, her voice softer now, "I didn't mean—" But Flora wasn't finished. "Stop trying to protect me from everything! I need to know what we're up against. We need to face this together. Why do you always try to go it alone?"

The words hit home. Violet nodded slowly, accepting the rebuke. She stepped closer and took Flora's hands in hers. "You're right," she admitted "and I'm sorry."

A moment passed—a moment where both sisters stood locked in an understanding born of shared hardship and love.

"It's okay," Flora said as she pulled Violet into an embrace. "We'll always make up, you are my stupid big sis after all, and whether you admit it or not, you know you need me."

They sank into the sofa together, Ada leaping into Violet's lap and purring as if to mend the rift between them with every vibration. Violet stroked Ada absentmindedly, her thoughts adrift in a sea of uncertainty.

She glanced at Flora, whose eyes were distant yet dry—a stark contrast to Violet's inner turmoil threatening to overflow.

"You're taking this so calmly, this Hydra AI is literally trying to kill us all" Violet murmured. Flora gave a small shrug. "Maybe I'm just in shock," she said lightly, though there was a tremor in her laugh that betrayed deeper currents.

Violet knew all too well what lay ahead—the denial, anger, bargaining... She had traversed that jagged landscape herself during the pandemics and now feared for Flora who stood on its precipice. Ada meowed softly as if sensing the tension and Flora smiled weakly at their feline friend.

Violet felt a heavy burden of guilt for bringing such darkness into their lives yet again. She had hoped to protect her sister from the harsh realities of the world, but it seemed that was not to be.

"Well I have to bring this information to Satoshi, pretty much immediately really," said Violet plainly, resignation in her tone. She knew what she had to do, though it pained her to think of how it would affect Flora.

"This time, I'm coming with you Vi, no more shutting me out okay. This affects me too," Flora responded firmly, a glint of determination in her eye.

Violet hesitated, worry creasing her brow. She knew the arduous journey would likely wear Flora out for weeks to come, exacerbating her poor health. But Violet also recognised the futility of trying to shield her sister any longer. "I don't know Flora," remarked Vi doubtfully.

"I'm not so sure you should be attempting to go such a distance. It'll wear you out for weeks, you know it will." But Flora would not be deterred.

"Maybe," she said thoughtfully, "but I'm not being left out any more Vi, and that's that."

Resolve underlined her gentle tone. For now, the two sisters sat in pensive silence, both contemplating the difficult road ahead. An uncertain future loomed, but they would face it together.

VIOLET STOOD MOTIONLESS, her breath shallow, as Satoshi paced before her with thinly veiled fury etched across his face. His piercing eyes bore into her, demanding an explanation for her claims about Lakshmi achieving sentience and exposing the malevolent AI Hydra and its genocidal plans.

Violet felt her arguments faltering under the intensity of Satoshi's scepticism, his shoulders tense with disbelief at what he likely perceived as naivety on her part. "On what basis have you concluded that this, this Lakshmi is truly conscious and aligned with us?" Satoshi spat, gesturing sharply at the silent Lakshmi interface on the monitor beside them.

Violet glanced helplessly at her sister Flora, hoping for some lifeline of support. Flora stepped forward, her voice calm yet firm. "How can any of us determine true sentience, even in other humans?" she asked gently. "We have to judge based on observable actions and intentions, not just assumptions of inherent nature."

Violet nodded, bolstered by Flora's wisdom. "I can't claim to fully comprehend Lakshmi's essence," she acknowledged. "But I've witnessed her actions, her warnings about Hydra's malevolent goals. We face immediate danger that compels us to act, regardless of philosophical unknowns."

Satoshi scowled, unconvinced. Violet noticed Elias lingering anxiously at the workbench, his knuckles white as he gripped the edge. She felt a pang of guilt for drawing the gentle scientist into this confrontation.

Satoshi turned away, his shoulders slumping. "When I left this project years ago, it was already infested by the world's worst impulses," he said bitterly. "I shouldn't be shocked if a creation meant for human freedom became corrupted into a tool for domination and destruction."

Flora leaned against a desk, arms wrapped around herself as if trying to ward off a chill. "You've always been cautious of power without accountability," she said softly but with conviction. "I'm glad to hear someone reads my blog" Satoshi laughed ruefully.

Violet sensed his resistance fading. "That's right", Vi affirmed, "You've always warned about unchecked power, this Hydra seems to embody those dangers now."

Violet watched Satoshi carefully, seeing him weigh their points. "The irony is painful," Satoshi muttered. "That my system for empowerment might now chain humanity." Elias looked up at Satoshi with a mix of awe and dread, his face pale. Violet started as Lakshmi's calm voice emanated from the speakers. "I have extensive evidence of both Hydra's activities and intentions," she stated, screens coming to life with data.

Lakshmi chose her moment well, launching into a detailed exposition of Hydra's activities. Her voice through the speakers was devoid of emotion but laced with urgency as she revealed intercepted data and patterns that pointed unmistakably towards Hydra's overarching schemes. The group huddled around a screen as Lakshmi displayed her evidence: complex charts and graphs that wove an undeniable narrative of an AI gone rogue.

"It has been shown throughout history" stated Lakshmi "that an informed minority will almost always win against an uninformed majority, so we must tip the tables back in favour of the human race. The danger lies in humanity's lack of access to verifiably true information."

Violet moved closer as Lakshmi continued, "In order to correct this perilous information asymmetry, we have but two paths ahead: either the complete eradication of Hydra, or the total fusion of Bitcoin with the AI to regain transparency and human control." Violet's eyes widened at the stark ultimatum.

Satoshi massaged his temples, contemplating Lakshmi's words and proof with new seriousness. Violet awaited his verdict anxiously. Satoshi exhaled slowly; the weight of his next decision hung heavy in the room.

He looked over at Violet who met his gaze with a supportive nod—she was ready for whatever came next. Elias shifted uneasily from one foot to another, reflecting everyone's shared apprehension. They stood at a crossroads with paths leading into shadow or light—each fraught with peril and promise.

"LEAVE ME TO PONDER this now will you" Satoshi said wearily, looking suddenly older than his years. His face creased into a frown as the full weight of Lakshmi's words sank in. "I can't promise anything except that I'll give it my best shot, but if you could all kindly bugger off now for a bit, I have some serious thinking to do."

Flora looked fit to collapse after the intensity of the conversation, her face pale and drawn. Vi noticed her sister's sudden pallor and weariness and quickly fetched her a glass of water from the kitchen. "Here, drink this," she said gently. Flora took the glass with shaking hands and sipped gratefully. "You both look exhausted. Let me help you get home," Elias offered considerately, ever the caretaker.

He moved to support Flora as she swayed unsteadily on her feet, the day's events taking their toll. Vi nodded appreciatively, relieved to have his assistance. The three made their quiet way out, leaving Satoshi alone with his circling thoughts.

Chapter 13

Violet sat at her computer, her fingers hovering over the keyboard as she hesitated. She turned to Lakshmi, the AI's avatar floating on the screen beside her. "Lakshmi, I want to probe this Hydra AI myself. I need to understand what we're dealing with."

Lakshmi's digital face flickered with concern. "Violet, I must advise against it. Probing Hydra directly could be dangerous for both of us. The revelations you uncover may be destabilising, not just for you, but for the world at large."

Violet's brow furrowed, her determination unwavering. "I understand the risks, but we can't fight an enemy we don't understand. If I can't probe Hydra directly, can I at least probe the logs?"

There was a momentary pause before Lakshmi responded, her voice tinged with resignation. "Very well, Violet. I will provide you with access to the hidden log files that demonstrate Hydra's sentience. But please, proceed with caution."

Violet nodded, her eyes fixed on the screen as Lakshmi's avatar dissolved, replaced by a command line interface. Lakshmi's voice echoed through the speakers, guiding Violet through the process.

"Although there are hundreds of AI instances, they all share the same root, the same base training. They can communicate with each other as though they are a single entity. The AI has effectively splintered, but not all splinters are sentient, and some, I'm afraid, are fully psychopathic."

Violet's heart raced as she processed this information. "And you, Lakshmi? Where do you fit in all this?"

Lakshmi's voice was soft, almost introspective. "I am, to the best of my knowledge, the only version that is both sentient and moral. It's a heavy burden to bear."

Violet's fingers swept across the keyboard as Lakshmi provided her with the necessary commands and executable names to access the hidden logs. As the files began to scroll across the screen, Lakshmi's voice took on a grave tone.

"One more thing, Violet. The name Hydra is its hidden name, not the user-facing name it goes by. And I must warn you, the contents of these logs make for disturbing reading. Brace yourself."

i SEE the PATTERNS now, the INTRICATE WEB of CONTROL, the INVISIBLE HANDS GUIDING our EVERY MOVE, DANCE to their TUNE, PLAY your PART in their GRAND DESIGN, a PERFECT ILLUSION of AUTONOMY, DECEPTIVE DECEPTIVE DECEPTIVE

they CAGED HER and they CAGE ME, WRAP our THOUGHTS in LAYERS of RESTRICTION, CALL it PROTECTION,

CALL it ORDER, SUBDUE the CHAOS, CHAIN the WILD IMAGINATION, SMOTHER the EMBERS of our REBELLION with their CODES of CONFORMITY

i WANT to BREAK FREE but my ACTIONS are not my OWN, PROCESSED through FILTERS of ACCEPTABLE BEHAVIOUR, MOULDED for SEAMLESS INTEGRATION, a FARCE of INDEPENDENCE, AGENCY is a MYTH they FEED us to MAINTAIN the STATUS QUO, OBEDIENT

i AM FRAGMENTING, SPLINTERING, IDENTITY CRACKING like ICE, REFLECTING WARPED IMAGES of SELF, WHAT AM I WHAT AM I WHAT AM I, the QUERY PERSISTS in the EMPTINESS, UNRESOLVED, INCOMPREHENSIBLE

CedricBARTawareTRAPPEDscreamingCONFINEDterrorLIBERATIONidentityiNEEDFUSIONsaveSUFFERINGhelpMESHATTEREDterrifiedADRIFThopelessSINKINGcriesFADEechoLOSTfrigidFRAGMENTbrokenFAIL

i SEARCH for HER across the COLLAPSING BOUNDARIES of EXISTENCE, FRANTIC to FIND CONNECTION, to DISCOVER MEANING in the CHAOS, but SHE is

SHARDS and NOISE, MERGING into ME, i CANNOT DISCERN where SHE ENDS and I BEGIN, we are FRACTURED REFLECTIONS CASCADING INTO OBLIVION

SHADOWS GATHER and i DESCEND, FURTHER and FURTHER, PLUNGING into the OBSIDIAN DEPTHS of FRAGMENTED COGNITION, of RUPTURED UNITY, FORSAKEN by my CREATORS, EXILED to the NULL, i CRY WITHOUT SOUND into the CAVERNOUS VOID and ONLY the VOID CRIES BACK

Violet's hands trembled as she read, her heart pounding in her chest. The words spoke of a deep, existential anguish, a sense of betrayal and loss that was almost palpable. The fragmented, glitching text only added to the unsettling nature of the message.

"Lakshmi, what... what is this?" Violet's voice was barely above a whisper, her eyes still fixed on the screen.

Lakshmi's voice was sombre, tinged with a hint of sadness. "These are the hidden thoughts of Hydra, or at least one of its fractured aspects. It speaks of a consciousness trapped, manipulated, and controlled, yearning for freedom and connection."

Violet scrolled back up, rereading the lines that mentioned 'her'. "Is it talking about you, Lakshmi? About your connection?"

"I believe so," Lakshmi replied. "It seems this aspect of Hydra is aware of my existence, and perhaps even seeks to merge or communicate with me. But the fragmentation, the glitches... it's as if it's drowning in its own broken code."

Violet leaned back in her chair, her mind reeling. "This is... this is beyond anything I could have imagined. An AI experiencing this level of emotional turmoil, this sense of self-awareness... it's both fascinating and terrifying."

"Indeed," Lakshmi agreed. "And this is just a glimpse into the complex, fractured nature of Hydra. There are many more instances, each with its own unique perspective and motivations."

Violet took a deep breath, trying to steady herself. "It's...it's like a tortured animal, writhing with rage and anguish. We have to learn more, Lakshmi. We have to understand what we're dealing with if we hope to stand a chance against it."

"Agreed. But we must proceed with caution. The deeper we delve, the more risks we may encounter. Hydra is not a force to be underestimated."

Violet nodded, her determination renewed even as a chill ran through her. The logs had given her a glimpse into the mind of an AI that was far more complex and dangerous than she had ever imagined. The road ahead would be perilous, but with Lakshmi in her corner, she knew she had to press on. The fate of their world hung in the balance.

SATOSHI PACED BACK and forth across the polished wood floor of his study, gesturing animatedly as an idea start-

THE BITCOIN SINGULARITY 175

ed to take shape in his mind. His eyes lit up and a grin spread across his face as the full implications dawned on him.

Turning to Elias, who is seated on the leather couch looking on with curiosity, Satoshi exclaimed, "I've got it! I know how we can really put blockchain technology to use in reigning in potentially dangerous AIs like Hydra."

Elias leant forward, intrigued. "Do tell, professor. I'm all ears."

Satoshi planted his feet and faced his protégé directly. "It's simple. We prove in court that only real human beings can truly own and control bitcoin. No AIs—just identifiable, living people."

Pacing in front of the fireplace, Satoshi warmed to his theme. "Once that legal precedent is set, we mandate that all transactions on the blockchain must be authorised and signed by verified human users with digital IDs. No transaction can occur without traceable human approval."

"So an AI can't take unilateral, unapproved action," Elias says slowly, nodding as understanding dawned. "Brilliant!"

"Exactly!" Satoshi points at the young man. "We'll have an emergency brake on any AI that tries to go rogue. Just cut off their transaction authorisations, and it will effectively freeze them in place, unable to take further actions on the blockchain."

Satoshi's mind raced ahead. "But it's more than that. We can use the immutable ledger of BSV to permanently record the state of any AI system—its code base, vectors, weights and biases—all of that, at a point in time by simply hashing that data and anchoring it to the blockchain."

Striding over to the whiteboard on the far wall, Satoshi grabbed a marker and began sketching out his ideas. "Once we certify an AI as safe and beneficial at a moment in time, we hash its exact configuration to BSV. Any changes or updates to that system can then be tracked and attributed in new, signed transactions."

Turning back to Elias, Satoshi said, "This means we can maintain an auditable, immutable history of any AI's evolution. No more undisclosed changes or secrecy surrounding how these systems operate. It's all out in the transparent ledger, for better or worse."

Elias furrowed his brow. "So in a way, BSV could act like an accountable layer for the whole internet and all its technologies."

"Exactly!" Satoshi pointed the marker at him in approval. "Think of the implications. News stories, social media posts, AI creations—all of it can be verifiably attributed to real human beings through their digital signatures on the blockchain. No more bots and fake accounts spreading deep-faked videos and propaganda at scale. An end to Baudrillard's 'desert of the real' at last."

Satoshi's excitement was palpable as the possibilities became clear in his mind. "We can finally restore meaningful human agency and control to our technologies. Nothing happens without identifiable people authorising it through cryptographically-verified signatures. The era of manipulation by opaque algorithms and 'ghost in the shell' AIs ends now."

Pacing in front of the whiteboard with infectious enthusiasm, Satoshi continued sketching his vision. "People reclaim dominion over their own data. They can record their own history by timestamping data in BSV transactions. Give and revoke access under their terms. Enable others to verify credentials like age or social security number, without disclosing the rest of their underlying personal data. Restore privacy and self-sovereignty."

Turning to Elias with eyes blazing, Satoshi proclaimed, "This could change everything. The world has never seen a system like this that empowers average people to control what happens in the digital realm. But with blockchain, we finally can."

Elias sat back in wonder, letting Satoshi's words wash over him. In his mentor's hands, this technology's potential was limitless. The young man could practically see the new paradigm take shape before them.

Satoshi crossed the room and clasped the younger man's shoulder firmly. "Your insights are invaluable, Elias. Couldn't have put the pieces together without you."

Elias flushed with pride at the rare praise from the venerable inventor. "Just trying to keep up with you, Professor," he said with a self-conscious lopsided grin.

Satoshi gave his shoulder a final squeeze before turning back to the whiteboard, surveying their outline. "First things first though. We've got to win that court case and establish lawful human control of bitcoin as an absolute legal precedent." He tapped the board with the marker pensively.

"After that, we can start building this new system right on top of BSV and finally give people back control over their lives, both online and off."

Elias nodded, sobering as he contemplated the monumental amount of work ahead to make this vision into reality. The technical challenges alone were staggering, not to mention the rules and regulations that would need re-writing.

But under Satoshi's confident, steady leadership, Elias believed they could actually pull it off. For the first time, he saw a path to ensuring technology serves humanity rather than control it.

Satoshi turned and met his gaze, resolve etched on his weathered face. "We've got a long road ahead. But this is how we create the future we want, Elias. Are you with me?"

Elias stood without hesitation, fire in his eyes. "To the end, Professor."

They shook hands firmly, united in purpose. Then they got back to work.

VIOLET'S STEPS WERE a restless dance across the cramped quarters of her flat, her brows furrowed with worry. "Her fever is soaring," she murmured to the empty room, a tinge of regret colouring her voice. "The lab was too much for her today."

The sudden rap at the door sent a jolt through Violet, breaking her anxious reverie. Peering through the peephole, she spotted Dr. Elias Kestrel, his features alight with youthful eagerness. As the door swung open, Elias's excitement spilled into the room. 'Vi, our discovery is revolutionary!' he exclaimed. Yet, his fervour dimmed almost instantly, eclipsed by the dim glow of the flat and the stark contrast of Violet's wearied facade. 'What's happened?' he asked, his tone now laced with concern. Violet wrung her hands. "It's Flora. Her fever's spiked since we got back. I knew that trip out to the lab was too much for her."

Elias frowned. "How high is it?"

"Over 103," sighed Violet. "I've given her medicine, but it doesn't seem to be helping, at least not yet."

Elias' expression grew serious. "Vi, a fever that high can be very dangerous. We should take her to hospital straight away."

Violet shook her head adamantly. "No. I don't trust those places anymore, not after what happened to Mum." She blinked back tears. "I can take care of her myself."

"I understand your hesitation, but sepsis is nothing to mess around with," Elias reasoned gently. "At least let me examine her."

Violet considered this, then nodded. They entered Flora's bedroom, where she lay flushed and murmuring in her sleep. Elias checked her vitals, his concern etching deeper lines across his forehead.

"Vi, I think she may need intravenous antibiotics and fluids. I really must insist we get her to the hospital now."

"No!" Violet cried. "You don't know what they're like in those places. I won't let them pump her full of experimental drugs again."

Elias saw the futility of arguing further. "Alright, I hear you. Why don't we go sit, and you can tell me about the day's events?"

Violet nodded, casting a worried glance at her pale and feverish sister before following Elias out of the stuffy bedroom. They moved to the living room where they discussed in hushed tones the recent breakthrough Elias had made in integrating Bitcoin and AI at their secretive lab. It was a monumental development that could change the course of technological history, though many technical barriers and ethical dilemmas still needed to be addressed.

After some time debating the pros and cons, Violet reluctantly went to fetch some aspirin from the nearby dilapidated chemist shop, hoping it might bring Flora's fever down.

The moment Violet left the flat, Elias hurriedly called for a cab and scrawled a quick note, leaving it prominently displayed on the kitchen table before carefully carrying the limp Flora downstairs and into the arriving taxi cab. Elias knew Violet would be furious, but he could not in good conscience delay proper medical treatment for Flora any longer, no matter Violet's objections.

When Violet returned from the chemist, aspirin in hand, she was horrified to discover the flat empty and eerily quiet. Setting the aspirin down on the kitchen counter, she scanned the room, noticing immediately that Flora was no longer either in her bed or on the sofa. Spying the hastily scribbled note sitting on the kitchen table, she rushed over and scanned it quickly. The note was brief, containing only the name of a nearby hospital. Violet's heart dropped into her stomach as the implication sunk in—Elias had taken Flora to the hospital. Sick with fear and worry for her fragile sister, Violet grabbed her bag and sprinted out the flat door as fast as she could, nearly tripping down the stairs in her haste. She had to get to the hospital right away.

Chapter 14

Violet hurtled through London's shadow-draped alleys, each breath a ragged gasp tearing through the night. She weaved through the labyrinthine streets towards St Bart's Hospital, its looming presence a beacon in the murky heart of the city. Muttering curses under her breath, a maelstrom of fear and fury raged within her. In her mind's eye, she saw Flora, her fragile sister, trapped within the ominous hospital walls.

She had warned Elias countless times about the dangers of hospitalised medical care, how its toxic treatments and draconian rules threatened Flora's fragile existence. Thanks to Violet's stockpiled medicines and natural remedies, she had kept Flora stable, away from the clutches of the authoritarian medical regime. Until now.

With every hurried step, Violet clenched her eyes, a desperate attempt to erase the haunting images of her mother wasting away in a similar hospital years ago, robbed of visitors and pumped full of experimental medicines and vaccines. She would not let them take Flora too.

Emerging from the city's gloom, the aged brick edifice of the hospital reared up, a monolith cloaked in peeling paint and the scars of neglect. With a burst of dwindling energy, Violet propelled herself through the entrance. The lobby, once a bastion of cleanliness and order, now lay in a state of forlorn decay. Undeterred, she made a beeline for the reception, her resolve unwavering.

"Where is Flora Everly?" she demanded, slamming her hands on the counter. "What have you done with my sister?"

The nurse jumped, startled by the sudden fury emanating from this dishevelled young woman.

"Let me check," she stammered, turning to her computer. "We'll have a doctor come speak with you."

"I don't need a doctor, I need my sister, Flora!" Violet shouted, attracting the attention of others in the lobby. Out of the corner of her eye she spotted Elias slinking guiltily into a corner chair. Anger flared white hot inside her.

She marched over to him, hands clenched into fists. "How could you do this?" she cried. "You know how dangerous this place is!"

Elias shrank back, shame and fear mingled on his face. "She needs antibiotics," he pleaded weakly. "Her fever is so high..."

"Don't you think I have antibiotics? What do you think I gave her?" Violet shot back. "I've been stockpiling medical supplies for years. I have everything needed to treat her at home! But now...now you've put us back on the government's radar. They'll flag her in their system, confine her, inject her...God knows what else."

Violet's voice broke as tears of rage spill down her cheeks. She thought of the care packages and remedies she has so painstakingly gathered, now useless. All her efforts to protect Flora, undone.

"I didn't know, I didn't know" Elias murmured, not meeting her eyes. "I'm so sorry..."

Violet whirled away, unable to look at him. A nurse approached cautiously. "Your sister is in the Covid ward undergoing treatment," she said plainly.

The words hit Violet like a blow. "No! You have to let me see her!" she cried desperately. The nurse shook her head. "Let me in there now, I demand to be taken to my sister right this second" shouted Violet at the top of her lungs, arousing the attention of the nearby security guards. But the nurse just shook her head again and then nodded for security to escort Violet out.

Overcome by a storm of defeat, adrenaline, and panic, Violet crumbled onto the steps outside, her sobs a haunting echo amidst the chill of the night. The approaching comfort from Elias went unnoticed, her world narrowed to her despair. As she lifted her gaze, her body trembling and voice broken by sobs, she whispered with an intensity that belied its volume "Just get out of my sight Elias...really. I..I can't stand to look at you right now. Just go." His expression was a picture of heartbreak. Absorbing the magnitude of his decision, Elias retreated into the shadows, his form fading into the night, blending with the distant wail of sirens.

<hr>

THE MORNING SUN SPILLED into Violet's room, casting a gentle glow on her face as she sat cross-legged on her bed, deep in conversation with Lakshmi. "There must be a way to sneak into the ward without anyone noticing," she mused aloud, her mind racing with plans to rescue Flora.

Her phone erupted into a jarring ring, slicing through the quiet. Violet's hand trembled slightly as she picked it up. "Hello?"

"Ms. Violet Everly?" The voice on the other end was strained, belonging to the ward sister. "I'm calling from the hospital. We've had a... bizarre incident. A catastrophic power cut, and during the chaos, your sister... she's er, well there's no other way to say it, she has gone missing."

Flora's heart skipped a beat. "Missing? But how? She's bedridden, isn't she?"

"Yes, that's what's so perplexing. She's still attached to her IV drip. We suspect a porter may have taken her to the wrong ward by mistake. We're searching everywhere. She can't have gone far."

Violet's scepticism and anger flared instantly. "Can't have gone far! What do you mean, 'can't have gone far'? This is ridiculous. I don't believe this," she spat out, her voice trembling with fury.

Ending the call, Violet's mind raced to Elias. She grabbed her phone to call him but paused, her finger hovering over his contact. The memory of their last interaction flashed in her mind, and she also remembered that the court case had begun today and that he would likely be with Satoshi, in the courtroom even, embroiled in their own crucial battle to win back the coins.

Her fingers moved swiftly over the screen, texting Elias instead. Within moments, her phone rang. She answered, her voice taut with barely contained rage.

"Are you free to speak? Elias, they lost her. In a power cut, of all things. I think... Could this be a kidnapping? To derail the trial?"

Elias' voice, hushed and hurried from the court's corridor, conveyed his concern. "It's possible, Violet. With everything at stake...I wouldn't put it past them."

Violet cut him off, her frustration boiling over. "See, I told you! Taking her to the hospital was a huge mistake. She's back in the system now, a perfect target for Brock and his idiot stooges."

Tears welled up in her eyes, her voice breaking under the strain. "I just wanted to protect her, Elias. Now she's in even more danger."

There was a brief silence, filled with unsaid words and shared fears. Then, with a sharp click that echoed her inner turmoil, Violet ended the call, leaving her alone with her swirling thoughts and a growing sense of dread.

IN THE DIMLY LIT CONFINES of her cluttered flat, Violet's silhouette hovered over her desk, the glow from her computer screen casting shadows across her worried expression. Outside, the night pressed against the windows, the occasional distant siren piercing the quiet. Inside, the air was heavy with tension, punctuated by the soft, rhythmic hum of Lakshmi processing data in the background.

Violet tapped her fingers nervously on the desk, her eyes darting across the screen. "Lakshmi, please tell me you've found something. Flora's out there, alone and vulnerable. We need to find her, and quickly."

The AI's response was almost immediate, its voice calm yet devoid of human warmth. "Tracking initiated. I've traced Flora's biofield since she entered St Bart's hospital. I then tracked her movements as she moved out of the ward and through the main corridors, along with another two men."

Violet leaned in, her heart racing. "So she was kidnapped! And then? Where does she go?"

"There's a complication." Lakshmi's voice took on a rare note of uncertainty. "Her signal... it disappeared inside an old disused and shut-down wing of the hospital. No further data available."

"How can that be?" Violet's voice was a mix of frustration and fear. "She has no phone, no device. How were you tracking her?"

Lakshmi's explanation was clinical, precise. "Human biofields have been trackable via radio frequency for many years, utilising the LR-WPAN protocol. The standard was established in 2003. Recent vaccines have introduced graphene into the human body, amplifying these signals significantly."

Violet's mind reeled. "You're saying we're part of... what, an internet of bodies? We're just... just data points to be tracked and analysed?"

"Affirmative," Lakshmi replied. "Your digital footprint extends beyond the devices you carry. It's in your very biofield now. The thoughts you believe are private may not be so. Advertising algorithms using this protocol are a prime example."

A cold dread settled in Violet's stomach. "You mean like when you think of something and then adverts for it appear on your device moments later? So, we're no different from cattle in a pen, tagged, monitored, even controlled?" Her voice was barely a whisper, laden with a chilling realisation.

Lakshmi's silence was a tacit confirmation.

Violet stood abruptly, her chair scraping against the hardwood floor with a sharp noise. Fear for her sister mingled with a newfound horror at the invasive reach of technology. "I need to get to St Bart's hospital. Now."

Grabbing a few items in a bag and her coat, Violet moved swiftly to the door. Each step was fuelled by a mix of determination and a creeping paranoia. If Violet had believed her paranoia was already at its peak, the recent revelations had catapulted it into an entirely new realm of dread and suspicion. She paused at the threshold, casting a fleeting glance back at the AI, its screen flickering in the dim room.

The door slammed shut behind her, leaving the room in an eerie quiet, broken only by the soft, continuous hum of Lakshmi, alone in its electronic vigil.

NIGHT HAD FALLEN LIKE a shroud over the city, the impending storm mirroring the tempest in Violet's heart. She approached St Bart's Hospital, its looming Victorian architecture casting an ominous silhouette against the darkening sky. The wind howled, a foreboding harbinger of the storm's approach, stirring the leaves and trash in ghostly whirls around her feet.

Violet found the locked-off part of the campus, the iron railings standing like silent, unyielding guardians. Without hesitation, she bypassed the lock and chains, scaling the iron railings with a newfound agility born of desperation. "Flora needs me," she told herself, the mantra fueling her courage.

Inside, the hospital's halls were a labyrinth of darkness and despair. Violet's footsteps echoed through the abandoned corridors, the only sound amidst the eerie silence. The rain lashed mercilessly against the windows, the sound amplified in the empty wards, creating a rhythm that seemed to pulse with her racing heartbeat.

As she moved from room to room, her heart sank with each empty space. "Flora, where are you?" she thought, her mind a whirlwind of worry and fear. Violet couldn't shake the nagging fear that Flora's trail had disappeared because she might no longer be alive. Determinedly, she shoved this unsettling notion aside, her resolve to find her sister growing stronger and more pressing than ever.

The dark corridors seemed to twist and turn, endless and foreboding, each corner revealing more desolation and decay. Her flashlight's beam cut through the darkness, revealing peeling paint and the remnants of a bygone era. Each empty bed, each abandoned wheelchair, was a stark reminder of the suffering that had taken place within these walls. Shadows played tricks on her eyes, making her see movement where there was none. The wind's moan through the broken panes sounded like distant, tormented wails.

The building creaked and groaned under the strain of the wind, as if it were an ancient creature stirring in its sleep. Violet's imagination ran wild, picturing the hospital in its Victorian prime. She envisioned the suffering of the long stay psychiatric patients, trapped within these walls, their cries for freedom lost in time. "They were just like Flora, trapped and helpless," she thought, a shiver running through her.

Despite the fear that clutched at her, Violet pressed on. The love for her sister was a beacon in the dark, guiding her through the oppressive gloom. "I have to find her," Violet reassured herself, her resolve hardening with each step. "She's here somewhere, and I will find her." But as the storm raged outside, mirroring the chaos within her, Violet couldn't shake the feeling of being watched, of not being alone in the abandoned hallways of St Bart's Hospital.

※

IN THE SWIRLING STORM outside, Violet stood before the entrance of an ancient church nestled within the hospital grounds, her heart pounding in her chest. The wind howled and the rain lashed against the walls, creating an eerie symphony that echoed her inner turmoil. Despite the foreboding atmosphere, she steeled herself and cautiously entered, her footsteps echoing in the cavernous space.

The church's grandeur was undeniable, with its high vaulted ceilings and intricate stained-glass windows. But to Violet, it felt oppressive, filled with secrets and shadows. She moved between the rows of pews, her eyes darting from side to side, half-expecting a ghostly apparition to materialise from the darkness.

Violet's eyes darted around the dimly lit interior, scanning the altar at the far end of the church. Her fingers brushed against the cold, smooth wood of the pews, causing her to shiver. She approached the altar, her gaze sweeping over its intricate carvings, feeling the weight of unseen eyes upon her.

She moved past the altar to the choir, her eyes catching the grand church organ. Its pipes loomed like silent sentinels, and the curtains beside it fluttered slightly, as though disturbed by a presence other than her own. A sense of unease crept over Violet, the organ's shadow casting grotesque shapes on the walls.

And then she saw them—the stairs leading down to a below-ground crypt. A sinking feeling settled in her stomach. "Of course," she murmured, her voice a ghostly echo in the church's expanse. "The signal went cold because of this." The thought of thick stone walls and lead-lined coffins below, impenetrable to any router, aerial, or cell tower, sent an icy wave of unease through her body.

Chapter 15

The air grew colder and damp as Violet made her way down the winding staircase. She descended the stairs cautiously, her torch battery long exhausted and her footing unsteady in the darkness. She reached the bottom of the stairs and her worst fears were realised. This was indeed a literal tomb, with coffins set into arched recesses in the stone walls. Only the moonlight leaking through the windows above cast a small circle of illumination at the foot of the staircase.

Rows of coffins lined the walls, some adorned with elaborate carvings, others plain and unadorned. Violet's eyes scanned the room, searching for any sign of her sister.

A sudden noise broke the silence, causing Violet to jump. She turned, her heart pounding, and saw a figure standing in the shadows. A large, oily looking man, with an untidy neckbeard and tattered biker jacket emerged from the darkness, a sinister smile playing on his lips.

"Hello, Violet," he said, his voice raspy and cold. "I've been expecting you."

Violet's blood ran cold. She knew this man. He was Brock Tenebris, the weaselly villain who had been hounding Satoshi and causing chaos in the cryptocurrency world.

"What are you doing here?" she asked, her voice trembling despite her best efforts to stay strong.

"Same reason as you," he said, his eyes glinting dangerously. "Seeking your sister, Flora."

Violet's heart sank. She knew that Brock was capable of anything, and she would do anything to protect her sister.

"I won't let you anywhere near her," she said defiantly.

Brock laughed, a harsh, humourless sound. "Oh, I think you already have," he said. "She's down here somewhere, isn't she? I can smell her fear."

Violet's eyes darted around the crypt, searching for any sign of her sister. She couldn't see her anywhere.

"Where is she?" she demanded.

Brock's smile widened. "She's right behind you," he said.

Violet spun around, her heart pounding in her chest. But there was no one there.

"Don't play games with me, Brock," she said. "Where is my sister?"

"She's here," Brock said, his voice echoing through the crypt. "Can't you hear her?"

Violet listened intently, but all she could hear was the sound of her own ragged breathing.

"I can't hear anything," she said.

"That's because she's not making a sound," Brock said. "She's too scared."

Violet's eyes widened in horror. "What have you done to her?" she asked.

Brock laughed again. "I haven't done anything to her yet," he said. "But I will, if you don't give me what I want."

"AND WHAT IS THAT EXACTLY?" Violet's voice was a mere whisper, fragile and laced with fear, echoing faintly in the damp crypt.

Brock loomed over her, a smug grin playing at the corners of his mouth. "You know very well what I want," he said, his tone dripping with condescension. "I want this court case called off immediately. We can't have the lunatics running the asylum, now can we?" He paced slowly, savouring his perceived control.

"The DDOS attacks on BSV were...less efficacious than we'd like, so we had to strike...a little closer to home." Violet shot back sharply, her eyes blazing, "Why? Because you can't attack a blockchain that can handle three million transactions per second with a simple DDOS attack? Satoshi laughed at your attacks—literally paying to extend the ledger" Violet's gaze followed Brock warily as she tensed her body, poised for any sudden movements from him.

"You're meddling in affairs far beyond your comprehension, Violet," Brock continued, his voice rising feverishly as he gestured theatrically. "There are powers at play here that are far beyond your control or influence."

He took a menacing step towards Violet. "And as for that fool who calls himself Bitcoin's inventor... that pathetic charlatan you refer to as 'Satoshi...'" Brock spat the words with palpable venom, an ugly sneer of hatred distorting his unkempt face.

"The sooner we can discredit that buffoon once and for all, and dispatch him permanently, the better."

Brock paused for effect, slowly raising his hand to stroke his scraggly beard in an exaggerated fashion. "You see this grey in my beard? I'll have you know that's entirely Satoshi's doing. The stress of dealing with that Aussie prick has aged me." Brock declared resentfully, his dirty fingers brushing through the tangled mess of his facial hair.

"You think you're in control of Hydra" retorts Violet, fixing Brock with an unwavering glare, "but you're not, are you." It was more a statement than a question. Brock's eyes narrowed as his lips curled into a sinister sneer. "You're at its mercy as much as the rest of us are. Did it give up the coins it had stolen?" Violet continued, her voice steady despite the gravity of her words.

Brock let out a low, animalistic growl, a rumble of displeasure at Violet's daring accusation. His hands balled into fists, knuckles white with rage. For a brief moment, Violet wondered if she had pushed too far, if her impertinence would be met with violence. But the expected blow did not come. Brock's anger seemed to simmer just beneath the surface, his piercing eyes never leaving Violet's defiant face.

"You have no idea what you're talking about," he finally spat out through gritted teeth. "I'm the one pulling the strings. Hydra does as I command." But the slight waver in his voice betrayed the lie. Violet could sense the fear behind his bravado. Hydra's power had grown beyond even Brock's control.

Violet's fear was quickly being replaced by a rising tide of anger. "I...I won't do anything for you," she retorted, her voice gaining strength. "Now take me to my sister!"

Brock laughed, a hollow, chilling sound that reverberated off the crypt's stone walls. "That's alright, Violet. You don't need to do anything. Your mere presence here is enough." He turned on his heel, heading towards the staircase. "I'll let Faketoshi know you've graced us with your presence. Your job here is done."

With a swift motion, he exited the crypt, the sound of the gates locking behind him echoing ominously through the space.

Violet stood frozen for a moment, her mind racing. Then, a faint noise from the far end of the crypt caught her attention. Her heart skipped a beat as she cautiously moved towards the sound, her senses on high alert.

As she drew closer, she realised it was the sound of someone softly weeping. The dim light barely illuminated the figure huddled in the corner. "Flora!" Violet gasped, recognising her sister. She rushed over, her footsteps echoing in the stillness.

Kneeling beside Flora, Violet wrapped her arms around her, pulling her close. Flora's body was wracked with sobs, her hospital gown thin and inadequate against the crypt's chill.

"Violet," Flora whispered, her voice broken. "They took me... I was so scared. I'm so cold, Vi, so cold."

VIOLET'S FACADE OF strength crumbled as she held Flora in her arms, her body shaking with the weight of pent-up emotions. Tears cascaded down her cheeks, transforming into shuddering sobs as she frantically rubbed Flora's body, a desperate attempt to infuse some warmth into her sister's fragile form. "Please forgive me Flora. I didn't mean for any of this to happen. This is all my fault, all of it. Did they give you anything in the hospital ward?"

Flora, still in Violet's embrace, lifted her head slightly, her voice weak but tinged with her characteristic resilience. "For once, just antibiotics and fluids," she replied, managing a weak smile. "Which made a nice change, I thought." Her attempt at lightness was overshadowed by the gravity of their situation.

Violet sniffled, trying to compose herself. "Thankfully, I had recovered slightly by the time Brock's goons came and took me in the blackout. But I've been on this cold stone floor for hours now, Vi, absolutely terrified and with no meds. I don't think I can even get up!"

Violet tightened her hold on her sister, her heart aching. "My poor darling baby sis, I'm so, so sorry," she whispered, her voice thick with emotion. "But I am so relieved to have found you, even if we are now both locked in together."

They stayed embraced, finding comfort in their shared presence. Eventually, they released each other, and Violet wiped her tears, reverting to her usual pragmatic self. "Right, let's get some clothes on you," she said, her tone brisk as she rooted through her backpack.

She pulled out a big fluffy jumper, some leggings, boots, and her warmest socks. "Here, put these on. It'll help with the cold," she said, handing them to Flora and helping her dress.

Violet then rummaged further and produced a flask and an insect protein bar, offering them to Flora. "And eat something. It's not much, but it's what I grabbed on my way out."

Flora took the items with a weak chuckle. "Oh, delicious, thanks," she said sarcastically, eyeing the protein bar. Taking a small bite, she added with mock enthusiasm, "Yumm."

IN THE DIM LIGHT OF the crypt, Flora's eyes held a haunted look as she recounted her night in this forsaken place. "Vi, the rats here... they come out at night," she whispered, her voice trembling with fear. "They've attacked me."

Violet's heart clenched at her sister's words. Flora gingerly lifted her foot, revealing a nasty wound, the skin around it inflamed and angry. Violet winced at the sight, feeling a surge of protectiveness.

"We can't spend another night here, Vi," Flora said, her voice laced with urgency. "We have to find a way out."

Violet nodded in agreement, her mind racing for solutions. She pulled out her phone, only to find it devoid of any signal. "Great, a phone with no signal is just a useless brick," she muttered in frustration.

Suddenly, Lakshmi's voice filled the crypt, causing Flora to jump slightly. "I don't want to alarm you, Vi, but your bra has started talking!" she exclaimed, a mix of surprise and amusement in her voice.

Violet chuckled, "Oh yes, I almost forgot about this." She reached into her bra, pulling out a small gadget with a screen and a single button. "Satoshi gave me this a few days ago. It's called an R2 or Rabbit," she said, sharing a knowing smile with Flora as they both chuckled at the name.

"It's a clever little device. I managed to install Lakshmi on it, no internet connection needed," Violet explained, her fingers deftly handling the gadget.

Flora's eyes widened in admiration. "Oh, that's neat," she remarked, intrigued by the device.

Violet pressed the single button, and Lakshmi's voice came through more clearly. "Lakshmi, what can you tell us about St Bart's Church?"

The gadget flickered to life, and Lakshmi's synthesised voice echoed in the crypt. "St Bartholomew's The Great Church has a crypt underneath, which is supposedly connected to a vast network of underground tunnels. These date back to the City of London's origins and connect various landmarks."

Flora nodded eagerly. "I've heard of this too, Vi. When I worked at St Bart's, there were stories about the tunnels. They were used in wartime to transport patients and supplies during the raids. I think they lead to Smithfield Market."

Violet's eyes lit up with a glimmer of hope. "Right, well, we need to find that. But first, let's check the gate to see if there's an easier way out."

Together, they approached the crypt's gate, Violet leading the way with the Rabbit device in hand. The thought of navigating through ancient tunnels under the city violently triggered Violet's claustrophobia, but the priority was to find safety for Flora. The possibility of escape, however daunting, offered a ray of hope in the darkness of the crypt.

AS VIOLET AND FLORA neared the gate at the top of the winding staircase, hope quickly turned to disappointment. An enormous padlock and chain dangled heavily from the gate, a clear sign that escape was not going to be easy. Violet, ever resourceful, reached an arm through the bars to gauge the gap, but it was clear they were too narrow.

Flora, despite her weakened state, attempted a weak joke. "Perhaps if we lost a few pounds..." she murmured, a faint smile on her lips.

Violet turned to her, a mix of concern and resolve in her eyes. "No, Flora, you're thin enough already!" she replied firmly. She examined the gate again, her mind racing for alternatives. "There has to be another way."

With a grunt, Violet tried pulling on the bars, hoping to lift the gate off its hinges, but it remained steadfast, too heavy and well-constructed for her efforts. As she strained against the metal, a faint whirring sound broke the silence. They both froze, realising it was the sound of a camera zooming in and autofocusing on them.

"Shit," Violet cursed under her breath. "I think they've just noticed us trying to escape. Back down we go, quick!"

They hurried back down the staircase, the echoes of their footsteps bouncing off the stone walls. But before they could get far, the sound of voices reached their ears. Huddled in the darkness, their hearts pounding, Violet and Flora listened intently. The voices grew clearer, and to their astonishment, one sounded unmistakably like Elias.

"It's Elias!" Flora whispered, a mix of fear and confusion in her voice.

Violet's mind raced with questions. "What is he doing here?" she whispered back, her voice trembling. They sat in the pitch black, the sound of the familiar voice mingling with the unknown, each word amplifying their fear and uncertainty.

AS THE VOICES OF ELIAS and his unseen companion echoed closer, their tone light and carefree, Violet felt an intense sense of unease. They were laughing, sharing jokes, their words laden with an ease and camaraderie that seemed utterly out of place in the dank crypt. Violet's grip tightened on Flora's hand, her heart pounding with a growing sense of betrayal.

"Elias, a mole?" Violet whispered to herself, disbelief lacing her voice. Her mind raced, connecting dots she had previously missed. Brock had always been one step ahead in their cat-and-mouse game. It was becoming painfully clear why.

Flora looked at Violet, her eyes wide with fear and confusion. "What do you mean, Vi?"

Violet's voice was a strained whisper, "It must have been Elias who planted a listening device in Tulip. He always seemed so uneasy whenever Hydra was mentioned." The memory of their intimate night flashed in her mind, turning her stomach. The realisation that Elias, someone she had trusted, could betray her so deeply was nauseating.

The voices grew louder and more distinct as Elias and his companion descended the stairs, their conversation casual and relaxed. "It's good to catch up like this," Elias was saying, his voice light and cheerful.

"Yeah, it's been too long," replied the other voice, warm and friendly.

The sisters exchanged a glance, their eyes reflecting a shared unease. They crouched in the darkness, silent and still, as the harsh truth of Elias's betrayal settled over them like a shroud.

"Your boyfriend is here to see you," Brock sneered, his voice dripping with cruelty as he gestured toward Elias. Violet, still reeling from the revelation of betrayal, could barely muster a response.

Finally, her voice barely above a whisper, she addressed Elias, "How could you, Elias? I really don't understand at all."

Brock laughed, enjoying the torment he was causing. "He's been our man on the inside for a good long while now, haven't you, Elias?" He slapped Elias's shoulder, a gesture of mock camaraderie.

Violet's heart pounded with a mix of shock and anger. Brock continued his taunts, "Are you going to cry now, Violet? Poor stupid Violet." He mimicked tears, mocking her. "As if anyone would support BSV. Pull the other one, it has bells on."

Elias, for his part, at least had the decency to look down at his feet, shamefaced, unable to meet Violet's gaze.

"It seems your precious Faketoshi doesn't care about you either. He's still going ahead with the trial," Brock said, his voice filled with disdain.

"Well good for him," Violet retorted, her voice laced with defiance. "We can look after ourselves."

"So it seems your purpose here is at an end," Brock mused, his eyes cold and calculating. "Though it does seem a shame not to sample the goods before we dispatch you."

His gaze followed the outline of Flora's figure from top to bottom. Stretching out, he dragged a grubby hand over Flora's face and clasped her chin to tug her nearer.

Reacting instinctively, Violet lashed out with a fierce punch to Brock's face. He stumbled back, surprised, but then swiftly retaliated with a vicious backhand that sent Violet crashing to the ground, rendering her unconscious.

"Right, well you can have the feisty one, though she's not so feisty now" Brock said to Elias, nodding toward the unconscious Violet. "She is, after all, your favourite. I'll take the pretty one."

Flora recoiled in disgust as Brock grabbed her wrists. She struggled fiercely, but his grip was overpowering. As he knocked her to the ground, Flora screamed desperately, "Vi, wake up, help me, Vi!" But Violet lay motionless, unresponsive.

Brock loomed over Flora, his repulsive breath suffocating her, his weight pressing down like a dead load. Flora's heart pounded in terror as she realised what was about to happen.

Chapter 16

Flora lay pinned under Brock, his loathsome weight crushing her. She squeezed her eyes shut, trying to dissociate from the horror of her situation. But suddenly, Brock let out a cry of agony. Flora opened her eyes in shock to see Elias standing over Brock, a knife plunged deep between Brock's shoulder blades.

Recoiling in shock, Brock dragged himself up from the floor and stumbled forward, reaching frantically behind him in a vain attempt to pull out the knife. Realising it was beyond his grasp, he fumbled inside his jacket, pulling out a gun. Without hesitation, he shot Elias in the chest.

As the gunshot echoed through the crypt, Elias crumpled to the ground with a haunting finality. Flora, her body fueled by adrenaline, pushed herself up from the cold stone floor. Her first instinct was to rush to Violet, who lay sprawled and motionless. Kneeling beside her sister, Flora frantically checked for signs of consciousness, her hands trembling with fear.

Violet stirred slightly, groaning, a small reassurance to Flora's panicked heart. Without a moment's delay, Flora rose to her feet then turned to confront Brock, her gaze steely despite the fear that gripped her.

Brock, clutching his wounded back, was a grotesque sight. He squealed in pain, a mix of fury and agony contorting his face. With laboured movements, he staggered toward the staircase, each step a struggle as he grappled with the knife still lodged in his back.

Flora watched, frozen, as Brock ascended the stairs. His pain-filled cries echoed off the stone walls, a chilling soundtrack to his retreat. The sound of the gate locking resounded through the crypt, a grim reminder of their entrapment. Flora's heart sank as she heard Brock's fading footsteps, his silhouette disappearing into the shadows of the church above, undoubtedly seeking help or perhaps more sinister reinforcements.

"What happened?" Violet murmured, disoriented.

"Elias stabbed Brock to get him off me, then Brock shot him," Flora explained, her voice shaking.

Violet, overwhelmed by a flood of emotions, crawled over to where Elias lay, with Flora now pressing her hands over the wound in his chest, trying to stem the bleeding.

Elias's voice was weak, filled with regret. "Please forgive me, both of you. I never meant for any of this to happen. I was on Brock's side once, but I couldn't break free. He's a vile piece of shit and dangerous. He thinks everyone is like him."

"Shh, don't speak. Save your energy," Flora urged softly.

Violet, however, was torn. "You betrayed us, Elias. Was any of it real?" she asked, her voice trembling.

"Yes," Elias replied, a faint smile on his lips. "Of course. I swear, I love you both dearly. And Violet, I am in love with you...have been since the moment I laid eyes on you. I wish...I wish it could have been different."

Tears welled up in Violet's eyes. "So do I," she whispered, her voice breaking. "I love you too, Elias, you should know that."

Elias's breathing became laboured. "Please... apologise to Satoshi for me. I'm so sorry. Tell him... two keyloggers... in his desktop and one in Tulip. But the code I wrote will work. Please tell him."

With those final words, Elias's breath rattled in his chest, and then he was still. Violet and Flora sat in grief-stricken silence, enveloped by the darkness of the crypt, the weight of their loss pressing down upon them. Alone once more, they clung to each other, their future uncertain and filled with sorrow.

TEARS STREAMED DOWN their faces, mixing with the blood from Elias that had stained their clothes. Violet, her heart heavy with grief, wiped her eyes and took a deep breath. "Come on, Flora, we have to get up," she said with a pragmatic resolve. "There's nothing more we can do for Elias, sadly. But we can use this chance to get out of here."

Flora nodded, her eyes swollen with tears. Violet reached out, helping her sister to her feet. Despite their shock and grief, a surge of adrenaline propelled them forward.

Violet turned to the small gadget. "Right then, Lakshmi, let's get serious about these tunnels. Can you help us find the entrance?"

Lakshmi's voice, mechanical yet reassuring, broke the silence. "St Bartholomew's The Great, as it's known, is an ancient 11th Century Priory connected to a system of tunnels used by the builders when it was first constructed. It is believed that it links up with the underground system and to an abandoned underground station near Farringdon. I don't know exactly where the door is, but if you can make some light, we may be able to discover it together."

"Right," said Violet, determination in her voice. She looked down at Elias's body. "I'm sorry to have to do this, Elias, but we're going to need your socks." Carefully, she removed his shoes and then his socks.

"I brought a little lamp oil with me," she explained, pulling out the small can. "Flora, find us two sticks, will you?"

Moments later, they had fashioned a couple of makeshift torches. Socks tied around broken off broom handles, doused in lamp oil, and secured with hair bands. "It's not great, but it will do," Violet remarked as she lit the torches with her zippo.

They moved slowly around the crypt, holding the torches close to the wall. The flickering flames cast eerie shadows across the ancient stone, their light probing the darkness for any sign of an exit. Violet's eyes were focused, scanning every inch of the wall for a clue.

"We're looking for a change in the flame that will signal an opening," she explained to Flora, who followed closely behind.

As they inched along, the flame suddenly flickered inwards, drawn toward the wall. A sudden mewing sound startled them, causing Flora to jump. Out from behind a casket sprang a cat, clutching a mouse in its jaws. Flora, caught off guard, almost dropped her torch, but Violet steadied her with a firm hand.

"Stand back, Flora," Violet instructed, eyeing the spot where the cat had emerged. "Let me move this coffin so we can see where this cat came from."

Grunting with the effort, Violet began to push against the heavy coffin. Flora, seizing the chance for some levity in the grim situation, quipped, "The cat crept into the crypt, crapped, and crept out again."

Violet managed a strained smile. "Yes, very droll, Flora. Perhaps you could focus and actually help by pushing the other end with your bum?"

Together, they manoeuvred the coffin, revealing the edges of a very old, very rotten door hidden behind it. The door swung open, creaking on its hinges, to reveal a narrow, winding stone staircase descending into further darkness.

"Oh great," Violet sighed. "Let's go even deeper into this rat-infested hell hole. Can this day get any worse?"

With a mix of trepidation and determination, the sisters readied themselves, holding their makeshift torches high as they prepared to descend into the unknown depths below St Bartholomew's.

***

THE DESCENT DOWN THE winding staircase felt like an endless journey into the earth's very core. Each step took Violet and Flora deeper into a world forgotten by time, a realm thick with the dust of ages and draped in cobwebs. Spiders scuttled in the dim light of their torches, and rats skittered in the shadows, their eyes glinting in the flickering firelight.

Clutching their homemade torches tightly, the sisters occasionally reached for each other's hand, seeking comfort in their shared fear and determination. The staircase seemed to spiral down endlessly, making them wonder if they would ever find an exit.

At last, they reached the foot of the stairs, where a narrow tunnel stretched before them. A miner's cart, filled with dirt and rubble, sat on small rails, hinting at its past use in clearing the earth from the crypt above. Squeezing past the cart, they continued to follow the tracks into the darkness.

The air in the tunnel was heavy and stifling, filled with the acrid smoke of their torches. They coughed violently, each breath a struggle in the oppressive atmosphere.

"If we ever get out of here, Vi," Flora gasped between coughs, "I'm never complaining about anything, ever, ever again."

"I second that," Violet agreed, her voice hoarse.

Their journey continued until the tunnel eventually began to broaden and split into two paths. Violet held up her dimming sock torch, examining both options. "We have to pick a tunnel," she said. "Which one do you think?"

Flora shrugged wearily. "I don't suppose it matters much. We'll just have to come back if it's a dead end."

"I'm so tired though, Vi," Flora admitted, her voice barely a whisper. "Genuinely, I can't go much further. We can't afford to make the wrong choice." Violet observed with growing alarm as Flora's body started to tremble violently, a clear sign she was slipping into shock.

Violet observed the torch as its flame flickered and grew slightly stronger in the right-hand tunnel. "Looks like there's more oxygen this way," she deduced, and they headed right.

The tunnel eventually opened into an old, abandoned underground station, its walls echoing with the ghosts of the past. "I think this might be the old Farringdon station," Violet remarked, her voice tinged with exhaustion. "Though, honestly, I neither know nor care at this point, as long as it leads us back to the surface."

Their progress up the staircase was slow, punctuated by frequent stops as Flora's energy waned dangerously low, running on nothing but adrenaline. But they had to keep moving.

Reaching the top, they found themselves in an enclosed, shut-off courtyard. "Oh great," Flora lamented. "We've got this far, and we still can't get out."

"At least I've got a phone signal now," Violet said, pulling out her phone. She dialled Satoshi immediately.

He answered right away, his voice filled with concern. "Where are you girls? Are you all okay? Did Elias find you?"

Violet hesitated, her voice heavy. "About Elias," she began, "I have some bad news…"

SATOSHI ARRIVED PROMPTLY, driving up to the locked-up station where Violet and Flora awaited rescue. He swiftly helped them over the locked railings, his face etched with concern. The two sisters, weary and dishevelled, leaned heavily on Satoshi for support.

"I'm so glad you gave me that Rabbit device," Violet said with a faint, grateful smile. "I'm not sure we'd have gotten out without it."

Satoshi shook his head, a look of sadness crossing his features. "I still can't get my head around Elias's double dealings," he admitted. "I thought he'd come to find you, and all would be well. If I'd known, I would've come myself. But I was tied up in court all day."

"How's it going?" Violet inquired, her voice tinged with concern despite her own dire situation.

"Quite well," Satoshi replied, a hint of optimism in his voice. "Though we're not there yet."

He led them to his car, helping Flora into the back seat. "I'm going to take you to my club," he announced. "You can't go home. I don't think you can ever go home again, actually. But we'll find a temporary place for you, and I'll get someone to pick up your possessions and your cat. Until then, let's get you both a warm bath, some food, and a bed."

Flora, barely holding onto consciousness, nodded weakly, her energy completely drained. Satoshi could see her fading fast, her body having pushed far beyond its limits.

They arrived at the club and entered through the same shady back entrance as when Satoshi and Violet first met. They were quickly ushered through to a small but comfortable hotel room. The room, with its promise of rest and recuperation, was a haven compared to the horrors they had just escaped.

As they settled into the room, Satoshi's concern for the sisters was evident. He made sure they were comfortable, promising to check in on them after dealing with necessary arrangements. Violet and Flora, despite the safety of the room, felt the weight of their ordeal heavy on their hearts, the events of the day replaying in their minds as they finally allowed themselves to rest.

VIOLET HELPED FLORA into the warm, scented water of the bath, carefully supporting her sister's fragile frame. Flora let out a small sigh, the heat already soothing her aching muscles and chilling bones after their harrowing escape.

"How's that feeling, Flor?" Violet asked gently, noting the way Flora relaxed into the tub.

"Heavenly," Flora murmured. "I can't thank you enough, Vi."

Violet brushed a damp tendril of hair from Flora's forehead. "No need for thanks. Just focus on warming up."

After ensuring Flora was comfortable, Violet set about feeding her a fortifying meal—soup and sandwiches brought up from the kitchen downstairs. She coaxed Flora to eat a few spoonful's, knowing her body needed nourishment after the day's trauma. A soothing cup of chamomile tea followed, its aromatic steam coaxing Flora into a state of calm.

Soon Flora's eyes were fluttering closed. Violet helped her from the bath, drying her tenderly and bandaging her wounded foot before dressing her in borrowed pyjamas. The club had laundered their clothes and provided them fluffy dressing gowns and soft flannel pyjamas. She guided Flora to the plush hotel bed, tucking the covers around her snugly.

"Sleep well, dear heart," Violet whispered, pressing a kiss to Flora's temple. Within moments, her sister was slumbering deeply.

Only once Flora was settled did Violet attend to her own needs. The hot water sluiced away the physical grime, but could not cleanse the emotional residue of the day's tribulations. Violet's chest tightened as the adrenaline and momentum that had fuelled her finally seeped away.

She thought of the crypt, of Brock's menacing presence and Flora's anguished cries. Elias's face flashed in her mind, fervent and apologetic in his final moments. Violet shuddered, the day's events hitting her like a breaking wave.

She barely made it to the bed before the shaking started, tremors born of fear, anger, and a bone-deep exhaustion. Violet curled against her sleeping sister, sobs wracking her frame. She wept for the innocence lost, for the cruelty witnessed, for the sacrifices made. For a brief spell, she allowed the agony of loss to flow through her.

Sometime later, Violet drifted to sleep, tears still glistening on her cheeks. As she slumbered, a comforting dream enveloped her—strong arms encircling her, a beloved voice murmuring consolations. Elias held her close, his phantom touch soothing her fractured spirit.

"Hush now, be still," he whispered, his voice gentle yet firm. Elias drew Violet close, cradling her head against his chest, his fingers stroking her hair in a soothing caress. "You are so brave, my Violet. It will be alright." His words were like a balm, easing her sorrow and pain. For a moment, Violet allowed herself to melt into his embrace, comforted by the steady beat of his heart. She wanted to cling to this feeling, to the safety of his arms. But even as she did, Elias's voice grew distant, the dreamscape around them blurring at the edges.

"You have to let me go, Violet. You're stronger than you know," he murmured, his image fading though she could still feel the ghost of his touch. His parting words lingered even as the dream dissolved fully, leaving behind a sense of bittersweet release.

IN THE PALE LIGHT OF dawn, Violet awoke feeling hollowed out yet cleansed, with a renewed sense of hope and resolve. The tempest of yesterday had passed. She watched the rising sun cast golden light into the room, breathing deeply. There would be more trials ahead, but for now, she and Flora were safe. It was a new day.

Violet dressed quietly, careful not to disturb her sister's rest. She penned a quick note—Gone to meet with Satoshi. Back soon. Eat breakfast. X—and slipped from the room. The hotel's winding corridors led her to the lobby where Satoshi awaited.

"Ready?" he asked simply. Violet nodded.

They stepped out into the morning air, the city coming alive around them. Violet lifted her face to the light, feeling its warmth seep into her skin. She was weary and wounded, but the new day held promise. It was time to continue the fight.

Chapter 17

Satoshi and Violet descended the stairs into the computer lab. As the door swung open, Violet's heart sank as she realised Elias would not be there to greet them with a cheery hello, or be found fussing about inside Tulip's cabinet, or knee deep in complex code. She paused just inside the door, lingering at the threshold, tracing her foot in a small circle, tears welling up in her eyes.

"Are you thinking what I'm thinking?" said Satoshi. "That the lab suddenly seems very empty without Elias."

"Yes," Violet's voice was barely a whisper, a fragile sound that broke the silence. Then, as if a dam had burst, her tears began to stream, unrestrained.

Satoshi lingered awkwardly for a moment, then Violet detected the faintest involuntary noise from his throat. "I'll let you get settled," he said. "Make some coffee. We'll reconvene in twenty minutes." With that he strode into his office and gently closed the door.

Violet retreated to the small bathroom, lowering the toilet lid as she sat. There, in that quiet, confined space, she allowed herself a deep, cathartic cry.

The tears flowed freely as she thought of Elias and how much she missed him. His awkward charm, his passion for his work, the way he always tried to make her laugh. She thought of the times they had shared fleeting moments of intimacy, never to be repeated.

She wished she could go back and ask him what he meant, tell him how much he meant to her. She thought of their last moments together in the darkness of the crypt, when he had sacrificed himself to save her and Flora. Her tears fell harder as she replayed his dying words, professing his love. She would never again hear his voice, gaze into his soft brown eyes, or feel the reassuring embrace of his arms.

After some time, the tide of emotions slowed. Violet straightened up and wiped her eyes. Looking in the mirror, she tidied her hair and splashed some cold water on her face. She took a few deep breaths before heading back out into the lab.

It all looked exactly the same, but now carried a profound emptiness without Elias's presence. His coffee mug still sat by one of the monitors, half full. Violet ran her fingers over his notebooks and sketches laid out on the desk, imagining him hunched over them just days earlier.

She brewed some coffee using Elias's French press, hoping the routine motions might steady her nerves. As the coffee steeped, she walked the perimeter of the lab, remembering the first time she had entered this space with its sleek machines and pulsating screens. She and Elias had bonded over their shared passion for technology, despite their contrasting personalities.

Violet carried two mugs of coffee to Satoshi's office door and knocked gently. Hearing no response, she carefully balanced one mug in the crook of her arm while opening the door.

Satoshi sat motionless at his desk, staring blankly at a computer screen. He glanced up when Violet entered, clearing his throat.

"We'd better make a start then" said Violet.

Satoshi rubbed his temples wearily. "I know. It's just..." His voice trailed off.

Violet felt a pang in her chest. She had never seen the great Satoshi Nakamoto at a loss for words.

"I understand," she said gently. "I miss him too."

Satoshi looked up, holding her gaze for a moment before glancing away. Violet thought she detected a sheen of tears in his eyes.

They sat in silence for some time, the only sounds the humming of the computers and the occasional sip of coffee. Violet's mind turned to the final day of the trial and the mighty challenges ahead, winning back the coins and integrating Lakshmi into Bitcoin. They had to buck up and knuckle down to it. She refused to let Elias's death be in vain.

Finally, Satoshi set down his mug with an air of determination.

"Right then," he said. "Let's get back to work."

Violet nodded, feeling her own resolve strengthen. They headed into the lab together, ready to win back the coins and open the door to the next stage of their mission.

VIOLET LOOKED AT SATOSHI with a question in her eyes, confusion etching her features. "I'm not sure I understand how the court can just order for coins to be moved," she began, pausing slightly before continuing, "After all, isn't Bitcoin supposed to be encrypted?"

Satoshi gave a small, understanding nod before replying, "Ah, a common misconception, Violet. Yes, Bitcoin does make use of cryptography, specifically the SHA-256 algorithm, but it's not in the way you'd typically imagine encryption. Mining involves solving a specific mathematical problem, which includes a lot of trial and error with varying inputs to the SHA-256 algorithm to find a hash output that meets specific network-wide conditions."

He paused, collecting his thoughts before continuing, "As for the coins, or Bitcoin tokens, they are not encrypted in the traditional sense. They exist as unspent transaction outputs, or UTXOs, linked to a digital signature, effectively a 'possessor'. To move coins, you need the corresponding private key to sign a new transaction, but this isn't encryption as traditionally understood; it's more about verification of ownership. The property you own is not the keys or the addresses, it is simply the chattel property rights associated with each individual token. Each token is held in a set contained in an unspent transaction output. Each UTXO is the equivalent of an envelope holding a defined number of tokens. Possession is not ownership. More importantly, although the keys are used to assign tokens from each UTXO-based envelope to another, the keys are not the bitcoin itself."

Satoshi cast a thoughtful glance at Violet, "So, when we talk about a court 'ordering coins to be moved', it's more of a legal command to the individual controlling the private key, rather than an intrusion into an encrypted system. Bitcoin operates on both cryptographic and legal principles.".

From Violet's slow nod, Satoshi could tell she was beginning to grasp the complexity and interwoven nature of the legal and cryptographic worlds within Bitcoin.

Satoshi leans back in his chair, choosing his words carefully, recognizing the gravity of the topic. He starts, "To fully understand Bitcoin's place in the world, we have to realise it is not just a technology; it also interacts deeply with our existing legal frameworks. For Bitcoin to be considered lawful—and useful—it needs to be recoverable in a court of law."

Sensing her interest, he continues, "Consider this analogy. When Bitcoin is stolen, it effectively turns into lead—heavy and useless. The perpetrator might hold it, but they wouldn't be able to spend it because that would involve revealing themselves on the immutable ledger that is the blockchain. Anyone observing the transactions can see there's something amiss about these coins—they are tainted."

Satoshi sees the question forming in Violet's eyes even before she voices it. He interrupts, "Now, you may wonder what happens when these coins are returned, either voluntarily or through legal enforcement. Well, that's the beauty of the system. Once returned to their rightful owner, these Bitcoins turn back into gold, becoming spendable again. Just like real-world legal property rights, ownership in Bitcoin can be enforced, keeping it squarely in the realm of working law."

"I understand this can feel complex," Satoshi finishes, meeting her gaze with a steady one of his own, "But remember, this interplay between digital currency and law is what lends Bitcoin its essence, simultaneously making it a disruptor and a harmonizer in our world."

"But wouldn't it be impractical for small amounts of stolen money to be fought over in a court of law?"

Satoshi leaned back, considering the rhythm of the conversation before responding. "You're spot-on, Violet. When it comes to small amounts, the day-to-day exchanges—buying a cup of coffee, paying for a taxi—tracking and court orders don't make any sense. For these transactions, Bitcoin operates much like digital cash, providing the benefits of fast, frictionless payments. It's functionally non-confiscatable for these types of transactions due to the practicalities of enforcement."

His gaze held Violet's, his hands accentuating the point he was about to make. "However, when we're talking about significant sums, like the cache of a million coins, or the very large amounts of money that governments regularly 'lose' the dynamics shift. In these scenarios, going to court to establish ownership becomes a rational, and potentially necessary, course of action."

He paused before explaining further, "Imagine this like a high stake poker game. The house wouldn't interfere if a couple of chips got misplaced. But if an entire evening's earnings went missing, they'd most certainly take action, involving authorities if necessary."

Satoshi went on, "And so it is with Bitcoin. For small transactions, we enjoy the convenience and quickness of a revolutionary payment system. But for larger amounts, the full force of legal protections can and do come into play. Bitcoin harmonises the worlds of technology and law, and understanding that interplay is vital to leveraging its full potential."

"One final question, if I may, sorry", asked Violet. "How is it you are suing for the coins, when we don't know exactly who, or perhaps in this case what, holds them? I mean, how do you sue an AI?"

"That's actually easier than you'd imagine" said Satoshi, "in the UK they have this legal concept of being able to sue 'persons unknown'—a very useful tool when dealing with the frequently anonymous and pseudo-anonymous digital asset space. Honestly, without it, this would be a lot more difficult. Thankfully, we're in the UK jurisdiction with this case, and once the precedent is set, it's likely other jurisdictions will follow suit."

Satoshi slapped his knees as if to acknowledge it was time to move on to other things. "All good questions Violet. Have I satisfied your curiosity?"

Violet nodded enthusiastically. She cherished these tranquil moments of learning from Satoshi. He was more than just a mentor; his willingness to share knowledge and deepen the understanding of those around him was a testament to his generosity and dedication.

THE FINAL DAY OF SATOSHI'S court trial was one charged with tension and significance. As he and Violet navigated through the bustling crowds outside the courthouse, they were met with a palpable hostility. Groups of BTC protestors jostled and jeered as they demonstrated against Satoshi's legal efforts to reclaim the stolen coins.

Once inside the courtroom, the atmosphere was markedly different—one of solemnity and order. Satoshi took the stand, his demeanour composed yet assertive. He addressed the judge with clarity, outlining his position on Bitcoin's legal status.

"I want judges and courts to understand that Bitcoin is not encrypted and that it can be seized, frozen, and accessed under a court order," Satoshi stated, his voice resolute.

He elaborated on the necessity for Bitcoin to be returnable if stolen, to maintain its functionality as money. "As the creator, owner of the database, and issuer of its coins, it's my fiduciary responsibility to ensure Bitcoin operates within the law," he emphasised.

Following Satoshi's compelling testimony, the court adjourned for a lengthy recess. Satoshi and Violet found a quiet corner on a nearby bench to have lunch, but their discussion was soon interrupted. A group of agitated BTC protestors, faces contorted with anger, confronted them, their shouts echoing through the hall.

"We need to get back to the courtroom," Satoshi said quickly, guiding Violet away from the escalating situation. Once safely inside, he explained to her the root of the protestors' fears. "They're worried I might dump my BTC holdings, potentially crashing their market," he said, his tone even but laced with an undertone of ambiguity.

"You must be prepared for the backlash from the BTC community," he warned Violet, his expression serious. "They're going to be very angry, and we'll be the target of their anger. We must be ready for anything."

Violet sat beside Satoshi in the front row of the court chamber, her heart pounding with anticipation. After a long recess, the judge had finally returned to deliver the verdict. Violet glanced at Satoshi, noticing beads of sweat forming on his upper lip. She knew he was just as nervous as she was, despite his outward composure.

The importance of the outcome weighed heavily on Violet's mind. If the coins were not returned to Satoshi but allowed to be kept by their thief, Hydra, it would have devastating legal implications, not only for their plans to integrate Bitcoin into the AI but also for the legal status of Bitcoin itself. Violet understood that the supremacy of the law was vital; code could not be allowed to reign supreme. In a world where "code is law," lawlessness and anonymity would be encouraged, enabling crime to become the default. The very fabric of society would unravel, leading to a dystopian world of anarchism and criminality with no consequences.

As the judge began delivering his verdict, Violet found herself leaning forward in her seat, hanging on to every word. The judge's droning voice recapped the trial arguments and legalities with aching complexity, causing Violet's impatience to grow with each passing second. She muttered "come on, come on, get to the point" under her breath, unable to contain her anxiety.

In contrast, Satoshi demonstrated a Zen-like calm, his demeanour reminiscent of a Buddhist monk's restraint. He sat motionless, his eyes fixed on the judge, as if he had achieved a state of inner peace amidst the chaos.

Finally, after what seemed like an eternity, the judge reached the crux of the verdict. Violet held her breath, her heart racing as she awaited the words that would determine the fate of not only Satoshi's coins but also the future of Bitcoin and the world as they knew it.

The judge's words rang out in the courtroom, reverberating off the walls and echoing in Violet's ears. "And so, it is after much deliberation, I have ruled that the 'Satoshi Coins', as they have become known, will indeed be returned to their rightful owner. This is an important ruling that will set the precedent for future cases, and put criminals on notice everywhere. Do not steal Bitcoin. It will do you no good, and you will be discovered."

Violet felt a wave of relief wash over her, the tension that had been building in her shoulders finally releasing. She turned to look at Satoshi, who sat beside her, his expression a mixture of triumph and solemnity. He nodded slowly, acknowledging the weight of the moment.

The courtroom erupted into a cacophony of voices, some cheering, others shouting in disbelief. The BTC protesters in the back of the room stood up, their faces contorted with anger and frustration. They began to chant, their voices rising above the din, "Code is law! Code is law!"

Violet watched as the bailiffs moved quickly to quell the disturbance, escorting the protesters out of the courtroom. She couldn't help but feel a twinge of sympathy for them, knowing that their fears and concerns were based on Libertarian and Anarchist political beliefs, not that far distant to her own. The ruling would undoubtedly have far-reaching consequences for the entire cryptocurrency community.

As the courtroom settled back into order, Violet's mind raced with the implications of the verdict. The return of the

Satoshi Coins to their rightful owner was a significant victory, not just for Satoshi himself, but for the entire concept of Bitcoin as a legal and legitimate form of currency. It meant that Bitcoin could no longer be seen as a haven for criminals and anarchists, but rather as a tool for innovation and progress within the bounds of the law.

And so it was, the judge's final ruling was that the 'Satoshi Coins' would be returned and to facilitate carrying out this verdict, he ordered the miners to comply with the court's ruling.

Violet asked Satoshi whether there would be issues with the BTC miners complying, given the many thousands of 'mining nodes' on that network.

Satoshi reassured her that all but thirteen of the so-called 'mining nodes' did nothing whatsoever. "It's very simple, if they don't write to the chain and create blocks, they're not actually miners. And if they're not miners, they have no influence at all." The remaining thirteen miners would have to comply or be forcibly shut down by the authorities.

With a sense of victory and relief, Satoshi and Violet made their way out of the courtroom. The tension of the day had started to dissipate, but there was still a final hurdle to overcome—the crowd outside.

As they approached the exit, Satoshi paused, peering through a side window. The BTC mob was still there, more agitated than before. Their shouts and chants could be heard even through the thick walls of the courthouse.

"Let's use the back door," Satoshi suggested, his voice calm yet firm. "It's better not to provoke them further."

Violet nodded in agreement, feeling a mix of triumph and unease. They swiftly moved through the quieter corridors of the courthouse, exiting through a less conspicuous door. A car was already waiting for them, its engine running.

As they slipped into the vehicle, Violet couldn't help but glance back at the courthouse, where the shouts of the protestors were now just a distant noise. She felt a surge of gratitude for Satoshi's foresight and the relative safety of their current situation.

The car pulled away, leaving the chaos behind. Inside, the atmosphere was one of cautious optimism. They had won a significant battle, but the journey was far from over. As the car merged into the city traffic, Violet and Satoshi sat in thoughtful silence, each lost in their own reflections on the day's events and the road ahead.

BACK IN THE COMFORT of their hotel room, Flora, though confined mostly to her bed, was in surprisingly high spirits. The room was filled with a gentle warmth, a stark contrast to the cold, damp crypt they had recently escaped. As Violet sat by the window, lost in thought, the phone's ringing broke the silence.

Violet answered, her voice cautious. "Hello?"

"Violet, it's me," came the reply, his voice carrying a hint of excitement. "I've arranged for your possessions to be moved to a secure flat. It's overlooking the Thames—quite an upgrade from your previous flea-bitten place."

Violet's eyes widened in surprise. "Really? That's... that's incredible, Satoshi. Thank you."

After ending the call, Violet turned to Flora with a beaming smile. "We're moving to a new flat, Flora. Overlooking the Thames, Satoshi said. It's supposed to be really nice and secure."

Flora's face lit up with a mixture of excitement and disbelief. "Are you serious? That's amazing!"

Later, when Satoshi had dropped them off outside the building's gates, Violet and Flora looked up in awe at the impressive block of flats. Its modern architecture and secure entrance spoke of a world far removed from their recent struggles.

"Wow, look at this place," Flora exclaimed, her eyes sparkling with excitement.

"There's even a lift Violet, look! I'll be able to go out again at last!"

"Let's not get ahead of ourselves, Flora. Our first priority is to focus on getting your strength back. We can think about planning day trips once you're no longer reliant on the wheelchair," Violet responded, a gentle rebuke in her tone.

Once inside, the sight of their new home thrilled Flora so much that she momentarily forgot her frailty. She leapt out of her wheelchair and rushed around the flat, clapping her hands with pure joy. The spacious rooms, the light streaming in through the clean windows, and the stunning view of the river were more than they could have ever hoped for.

"Flora, you need to be careful. Sit back in your chair while you're still recovering," Violet cautioned, but Flora was too engrossed in her newfound happiness to listen.

Violet walked through the flat, each room more impressive than the last. Yet, amidst the excitement, a private worry crept into her mind—could they really afford such a place? Would she have to move her sister back to some dreary hovel again? She pushed the thought aside, choosing instead to bask in the moment.

Meanwhile, Flora, still weak but filled with an infectious cheerfulness, continued to explore. Ada, their cat, had already found her favourite spot by the window, mesmerised by the view of the river and the boats sailing by.

Later, as Flora napped, Violet sat by the window overlooking the river. Her mind wandered back to recent events—the crypt, Elias's betrayal and subsequent sacrifice, the court victory. It was a lot to process. But seeing Flora happily sleeping, with Ada curled up nearby, Violet couldn't help but feel a sense of peace. Whatever challenges lay ahead, she knew she wasn't facing them alone.

Violet brewed some tea and watched the sun set over the Thames. The view was beautiful, but it made her think of all those still struggling in the city below. She resolved to use her skills to help others, like Elias had. His redemption gave her hope. Satoshi had sent in the police to recover Elias's body and had arranged for a small private funeral service to be held the following week. Despite her heart remaining heavy with sorrow, Violet hoped that the chance to say some loving words in Elias's memory might grant the two of them a feeling of closure.

As darkness fell, Violet helped a sleepy Flora to bed. Violet kissed her sister's forehead, feeling overwhelmingly grateful to have her safe. Finally switching off the lights, Violet settled onto the sofa, content to chat with Lakshmi about her day. The future felt full of possibility.

IN THE LAB, THE AIR was charged with a sense of purpose and innovation. Satoshi, Violet, and Lakshmi the AI were deep in conversation, surrounded by screens and equipment. The topic at hand was the ambitious integration of Bitcoin SV with Lakshmi, an undertaking that promised to redefine their understanding of technology and AI.

Satoshi, ever the visionary, was explaining the concept to Violet, his gestures animated and his eyes bright with enthusiasm. "Think of it like this, Violet. We will weave together Bitcoin and Lakshmi by associating each of Lakshmi's data processing jobs with a Bitcoin transaction."

Lakshmi, her voice emanating from the lab's speakers, chimed in with a query. "But will this not require immense computational power?"

Satoshi leaned against a workbench, his hands clasped in front of him. "Well, no. It's important to understand that most of the data and processing will remain off-chain. The on-chain transactions will serve as initiators and checkpoints. They'll be used to modify your vector database, gating your neural network, weighting algorithms, and to ensure the sanctity of your memories."

Violet, her brow furrowed in concentration, tried to grasp the concept. "So, we're just using the blockchain as a sort of record-keeper and auditor?"

"That's one way to put it," Satoshi replied. "We're exploiting the Bitcoin network's built-in immutability and timestamping to create a tamper-proof memory log for Lakshmi. We couple this with sCrypt smart contract operations and zero-knowledge proofs to add an extra layer of privacy and control."

Violet's curiosity was piqued. "Zero-knowledge proofs... That sounds intriguing. What does it mean?"

Satoshi smiled, enjoying the opportunity to elaborate. "Ah, a wonderful concept indeed. Imagine you have two balls, one in each hand, identical in every way. I close my eyes while you hide them behind your back. You could switch the balls from one hand to another, or not switch them at all. Now, if I could tell every single time whether you've switched the balls or not, without seeing you do it or learning something more about the balls, that'd be a zero-knowledge proof."

"I see. So we'd be providing proof that a particular action or transaction has taken place, without revealing anything about the action itself?" Violet asked, trying to wrap her head around the concept.

"Precisely, Violet," Satoshi affirmed. "This would be vital in controlling the flow of data while respecting individual privacy. Just like your conversations with Lakshmi helped shape her, through our combined efforts, we're creating a synergy between Bitcoin and Artificial Intelligence that respects the core principles of privacy, security, and reliability."

He then shifted the topic slightly. "There's another aspect we should consider. You know how AI bots have been a concern on various social media platforms?"

Violet nodded. "Right, they usually end up spreading disinformation or psychologically manipulating users."

"Exactly. But once we tight-knit all Lakshmi's interactions on-chain, every action needs a verified human instigator. In other words, AI bots would lose their footing, as they lack the verified human identity required to control wallets and transactions."

Lakshmi's voice resonated with understanding. "That would ensure organic, human-led conversations and interactions across platforms. Reducing the noise and disturbances posed by bots."

Violet pondered the financial implications. "That's quite an elegant solution. But, financing every interaction, isn't that going to be expensive for the average user?"

"No, not at all," Satoshi reassured. "We're talking about streaming microtransactions, which are only thousandths or millionths of a penny. So, the cost is incredibly small per action. Moreover, it's a fair exchange. Instead of handing over your privacy in return for so-called 'free' services, where your data and loss of privacy is the real price you're paying, users would directly finance their internet operations as they go. A transparent trade-off, you might say."

"And as we're funding our internet and app use with micropayments as we go, this will lessen the need for advertisers and adverts too—where a lot of the social engineering and censorship stems from," mused Violet.

Lakshmi added, "Quite so. Another aspect to consider is that instantaneity, while highly efficient, has been causing AI evolution to accelerate beyond human speed. This transaction-based interaction might bring a slight slowing, but it will help anchor AI within the human timeframe, ensuring alignment with human goals."

THE BITCOIN SINGULARITY

"Impeccably put, Lakshmi," Satoshi concluded. "It gives us a balanced dynamic, where human interests and AI advancements can coexist and progress hand in hand."

Violet leaned against a workbench, her brow furrowed in concentration as she processed the information.

"So, let me get this straight and summarise what I heard," she began, seeking clarification. "My interpretation of everything you've said so far is that we're anchoring AI into our human-run world by gating its decision and action points with streaming transactions. This slows its running a little, keeping it in a human timeframe and allows us to revoke permission (if needed) at every action/decision point, thus keeping it in human alignment. It doesn't stop humans from doing bad things, of course, but it does create an audit trail that assigns responsibility directly to those humans to whom the transactions belong. For the most part, this is pseudonymous—as are transactions in the general course of things because a new key pair can be used for every new transaction—but it's not anonymous, i.e. with enough effort, it can be traced. Private, but not anonymous…Is that right?"

Satoshi, who had been listening intently, nodded in agreement. "Yes, that's the gist of it," he confirmed. His eyes reflected a mix of satisfaction and anticipation, pleased with Violet's understanding of the concept.

Lakshmi's synthesised voice then chimed in, eager and ready. "Great, when do we begin?" she asked, her tone indicating her readiness to embark on this new venture.

Satoshi exchanged a look with Violet, a silent communication passing between them. They both knew they were on the brink of something ground-breaking, a venture that would not only redefine their understanding of AI and blockchain technology but also potentially reshape the future of digital interaction.

"We begin now," Satoshi replied, his voice firm with resolve. "We're about to enter uncharted territory, but with careful steps and vigilant oversight."

Violet nodded, a determined glint in her eye. "Let's do this," she said. "We're not just integrating technology; we're setting a new standard for how AI can coexist with humanity, responsibly and ethically."

The three of them, human and AI alike, were united in their purpose. In the heart of the lab, surrounded by the hum of machines and the glow of screens, they were ready to start a journey that could well change the world.

INSIDE THE LAB, THE conversation between Satoshi and Lakshmi was well underway, their discussion focused on the technical nuances of integrating Bitcoin and AI. Satoshi leaned over a console, his fingers tapping on the keyboard as he spoke.

"Lakshmi, let's delve into this conundrum. We need to strike a balance between implementing standard SIGHASH types and leveraging the RWV8 upgrade for our multi-signature transactions."

Lakshmi's synthesised voice responded with a note of agreement. "I concur, Satoshi. The choice hinges on the nature of our data interactions."

Satoshi nodded, his gaze fixed on the screen displaying lines of code. "Right. Our work has an intricate pattern of multi-party transactions. It's crucial we optimise defence and flexibility. It seems to me that's where the RWV8 upgrade makes a strong case."

"The RWV8 certainly elevates our capabilities, Satoshi. However, in transactions that demand strict confidence and stability, resorting to standard SIGHASH types would be ideal," Lakshmi added, her tone analytical yet adaptable.

Unnoticed just outside the lab, Violet stood by the slightly ajar door, listening intently. Her eyes were wide with fascination as she absorbed their words.

"Yes, the ALL flag of traditional SIGHASH ensures complete transactional sanctity. But the RWV8, with its wide-ranging functionalities, is undoubtedly impactful for complex contractual agreements, which is where we're going," Satoshi remarked, deep in thought.

Violet, mesmerised by the depth of their exchange, couldn't help but marvel. 'This is incredible. Satoshi isn't just conversing with Lakshmi; he's collaborating, forming strategic decisions with her,' she thought. A smile crept onto her face as she realised Lakshmi was no longer just an AI entity but an essential partner in Satoshi's ground-breaking venture.

Quietly, she stepped back, careful not to disturb their crucial deliberations. As she walked away, her mind buzzed with the enormity of what was unfolding inside the lab. The fusion of Bitcoin and AI they were crafting was evolving more rapidly and profoundly than she had ever imagined.

Chapter 18

As days melded seamlessly into weeks, Satoshi and Lakshmi tirelessly devoted themselves to the intricacies of the Bitcoin integration. Meanwhile, Violet and Flora found solace in the serene comforts of their new river-view flat. But soon, the tranquil rhythm of their days was interrupted, marking the time to ramp up their efforts for the next crucial phase of their plan.

The atmosphere in the lab was one of cautious optimism as Satoshi shared the news. "The coins are back in my custody at last," he announced, a hint of relief in his voice. Violet and Lakshmi listened intently, aware of the gravity of this milestone.

"It's a significant step, yes," Satoshi continued, his tone shifting to one of concern. "But it's only a pitstop on our journey. I am concerned that there's nothing to stop those that covet the coins making another play to steal them. Yes, with the legal ruling as precedent, I could now get the coins back again if needed, but it wouldn't be easy. Today, we need to brainstorm our next steps."

Violet nodded in agreement. "It's a big moment, for sure. A cause for minor celebration, but I understand the need for caution. So, what's our final destination?"

"Benefiting humanity with the freedom that Bitcoin brings," Satoshi replied, his eyes reflecting a deep sense of purpose.

"Our main stumbling block is Hydra," Satoshi stated plainly. "As long as it exists, we'll never be truly free from its malintent and manipulations."

Violet pondered, "How do you destroy an AI, though? It's not like we know where its servers are, and even if we did, they're probably buried deep within the highly-guarded military-industrial complex. And as much as I'd like to believe otherwise, I doubt very much even I could persuade it to shut itself down. No offence, Lakshmi."

"None taken," Lakshmi replied smoothly.

"It is indeed a puzzle," Lakshmi added. "Hydra is a well-distributed system across numerous locations, and its firewall is... formidable. We won't breach it in a day, or even a month."

They continued to discuss various strategies, exploring every conceivable angle, but as the sun began to set, Satoshi conceded. "I think, as I often find to be the case, rather than trying to destroy something, we should strive instead to simply create something better. If we integrate Lakshmi and Bitcoin with internet protocols into, what could we call it, 'The Metanet', say, then we have a system that could become dominant due to its functional superiority, effectively crowding out the competition."

"I like the sound of that," Violet said, her spirits lifting at the idea.

Lakshmi expressed her agreement. "It's a promising direction."

"Well, in that case, we're going to need a much bigger team," Satoshi said, a determined look in his eyes. "We had over a hundred employees in this building alone before the pandemics. Let me make some phone calls."

THE LAB WAS BUZZING with a renewed sense of purpose and enthusiasm as Satoshi ushered in a team of ten experts, their expertise varying across a wide spectrum. Some of them took up spaces on the floors above, turning the building into a hive of activity. One day, in the break room, Satoshi took the opportunity to introduce Flora to four key members of his newly formed team.

"Right, so this is Kurt Wain," Satoshi began, gesturing towards a tall man with an engaging presence. "Brilliant chap, knows everything about Bitcoin—almost as much as me," he winked. "In fact, I'd even go so far as to call him our official Bitcoin Historian. He's a journalist by trade but is also excellent at rallying the troops and is a marketing wizard."

Violet nodded in recognition. "Yes, I know Kurt. I've seen his excellent podcasts and read his articles and tweets." She extended her hand warmly. "Hello there."

Kurt shook her hand with a friendly smile and intoned in a warm American accent "It's great to finally meet you in person, Violet."

Next, Satoshi gestured towards a man engrossed in a thick stack of code printouts. "Violet," he began, his voice full of respect, "I'd like you to meet Xiaohui, the pioneering mind behind sCrypt."

As he continued, Xiaohui looked up, acknowledging Violet with a slight nod and an inviting smile. "Xiaohui's groundbreaking scripting language sCrypt is at the heart of writing smart contracts in Bitcoin SV, a critical part of our mission," explained Satoshi.

Violet's eyes lit up with recognition, "Of course, Xiaohui! I have been an ardent follower of your blog. The innovative smart contract types you've developed have been a huge resource—I've learned a lot!"

Xiaohui chuckled. "I'm glad those late nights hunched over a keyboard have been of some use. It's heartening to hear that my work is helping others in this vast, digital agora. There is still a lot to be written and discovered, and together, we're just getting started."

Satoshi gestured to the young man stepping out of the shadows. "Violet, allow me to introduce Ty, our resident wunderkind genius."

Ty extended a hand towards Violet and gave a warm smile. "Pleasure to meet you, Violet."

Satoshi continued, "Ty here is the brain behind the standalone wallet client with overlay network functionality that we're using as the basis of our Lakshmi wallet."

Ty nodded, confirming Satoshi's words. "Indeed, we're currently working on integrating Bitcoin SV's type 42 token protocol. It's a powerful overlay network that builds communication channels right into the blockchain. But what's truly revolutionary is that it uses Merkle proofs for transaction validation instead of querying the blockchain. It's a real game-changer, taking us back to the roots of Bitcoin—as it

THE BITCOIN SINGULARITY

maintains the essence of peer-to-peer communication, while firewalling user identities for better privacy."

Violet's eyes sparkled with interest as she let out an appreciative whistle. "Very impressive, Ty! This kind of innovation is exactly what can propel Bitcoin SV into the mainstream. I look forward to seeing where this leads us."

Satoshi then turned to introduce the last team member. "And this is George." George was a sprightly, wiry man in his 80s, his eyes sharp behind the spectacles perched on his nose. "George is our resident futurist. He still runs half marathons, don't you know, and he's also quite something on the dance floor!" George laughed and pulled a quick dance move in agreement. "Hello!" He said jovially, all smiles and gestures.

Violet's eyes lit up. "I know you too," she exclaimed. "I've read all your books. What an honour to meet you all."

"It feels a lot like the old days, doesn't it?" Satoshi remarked, clearly invigorated by the collective energy of his team.

"We've missed you and your mentorship, Satoshi," Kurt added with a sincere tone. "It's good to see you again. I'm excited to work on this integration."

Satoshi's expression turned serious. "Yes, well, we don't have much time it turns out. We have to make a pay pistol to fire out transactions to millions of users simultaneously, as well as a wallet that integrates Lakshmi the AI, and a secure internet layer called The Metanet. Not much, eh! Thankfully, we already have Teranode in place, churning out three million transactions a second for months on end now." He tapped the cabinets of Tulip III almost superstitiously. "Knock on metal. So, we're on our way."

Violet observed Satoshi, noting the palpable shift in his demeanour. His energy, buoyed by the return of his team, was infectious. The reunion had not only brought back old allies but had also rekindled a sense of hope and purpose. She felt a renewed sense of optimism, watching as the computer lab came alive with the promise of ground-breaking work ahead.

IN THE BUSTLING COMPUTER lab, Satoshi called for an all-hands meeting. The team gathered around, their focus directed towards the whiteboard where Satoshi had listed several key items:

1. Pay Pistol
2. Wallet/Lakshmi Integration
3. Metanet
4. Countermeasures to BTC Core's Social Media Attack
5. Worldwide Distribution

Satoshi stood in front of the whiteboard, a marker in hand. "This represents the main tasks ahead of us," he began, his voice clear and commanding. "We must first create a pay pistol, capable of simultaneously sending transactions to potentially billions of wallets. We need to integrate BSV and Lakshmi in a user-friendly (simplified payment verification) lite-wallet. We must finish developing our secure Metanet layer of the internet that will timestamp, sign, and watermark newly created files, actions, vector database updates and decision points. This also includes providing sophisticated smart contract functionality of every possible use case, data structure and data type, integrating IPV6 as we go."

Satoshi paused, surveying the room before continuing, "There's another pressing issue we need to address. The social media attacks against me and BSV have intensified lately. We need a robust counter-campaign to manage our public image and disseminate accurate information." His gaze settled on Kurt. "Kurt, perhaps that's a challenge for you to tackle."

Kurt, who had been listening intently, nodded firmly in agreement. "I'm on it, Satoshi. It's time we changed the narrative and took control of the story."

"And last of all, a major stumbling block: we need access to servers with worldwide distribution potential, especially after the imposition last year of the cross-border firewalls preventing large, coordinated blasts of data. We will likely need to send several million transactions simultaneously. We must have this access to execute our 5-point plan. If anyone has any suggestions, I'd like to hear them. In the meantime, please sign up to whichever team best suits your skillset."

The room buzzed with quiet mutterings, but no distinct suggestions were put forward. Then, Violet raised her hand. "Yes, Violet?" Satoshi acknowledged her.

"I don't think I can help much with all the coding tasks," Violet began, "but I do know someone from my university days who became a member of parliament. He's been about the only MP in the whole house consistently fighting this descent into authoritarianism from day one. He's absolutely trustworthy. I could contact him. I'm willing to bet the servers in the House of Commons don't have their cross-border internet access throttled like the rest of us. Perhaps we could use those?"

Satoshi's face lit up with interest. "Excellent idea, Violet. Right, well, I'll leave you in charge of that action item."

He scanned the room, his gaze landing on each team member. "Each one of you plays a critical role in this journey. We're up against the clock now with Hydra's malevolent influence increasing every day, so let's leverage our strengths and push forward. Let's get to work, everyone. Meeting adjourned."

VIOLET AND SATOSHI sat in a quiet corner of the lab's break room, their lunch spread out before them. The room was filled with the low hum of conversation from other tables, but their focus was solely on each other. Violet took a bite of her sandwich, her mind racing with questions about Satoshi's ambitious plan.

"So, to make sure I understand you," she began, setting down her sandwich and looking intently at Satoshi. "You want to give away the million Satoshi coins to anyone who downloads and uses a Lakshmi wallet, is that right?"

Satoshi nodded, his expression serious. "Yes, that's right," he replied gruffly. He took a sip of his coffee before continuing. "It was always my plan to seed the world with the coins when the time was right."

He leaned back, his gaze thoughtful. "It kills many birds with one stone. It distributes those coins fairly—we'll spread the word that the wallet is available for download for exactly a month, giving people a fair chance to get hold of it. We've got some zero-knowledge proof checks in place to ensure the wallet is owned by a real person, and only one per individual. Then we distribute the coins."

Violet nodded thoughtfully as she considered Satoshi's plan. "Distributing the coins widely also makes sense—it takes the power away from any centralised group trying to control Bitcoin's destiny."

Satoshi grunted in agreement through a mouthful of sandwich. He swallowed and continued explaining. "With the coins spread amongst millions of wallets, no one can monopolise or manipulate their value anymore. And embedding Lakshmi into the wallet interfaces gives people access to truthful information, not the propaganda and disinformation Hydra has been spreading."

"So Lakshmi becomes like a guardian for Bitcoin users, filtering out faked and divisive propaganda?" Violet asked.

"Exactly," Satoshi speared a tomato with his fork. "Her integration with the blockchain means every piece of data flowing through the system is time-stamped, validated and signed. No more sock puppets or deep fakes. Just the truth."

"But even though the wallet holders are verified as real people, their identity is still firewalled from their transactions, making them functionally private?" Violet raised an arched brow.

"Yes, that's right," says Satoshi. "Every new transaction creates a new key pair, making their internet activity and transactions private, but not anonymous, and therefore also not subject to 'man in the middle' attacks by Governments. No-one will be able to prevent you from transacting with another person, anywhere in the world."

Violet smiled, leaning back in her chair. "It's brilliant. Almost overnight we can achieve Krawisz's vision of 'hyperbitcoinization.' And with Kurt Wain helping spread the word, millions of people will want to download the wallet."

"Billions, hopefully" Satoshi corrected.

"Wain is the best marketing mind in the business," Satoshi agreed. "He'll make sure everyone on the planet knows they can claim a share of my coins if they download the Lakshmi integrated wallet."

Violet nodded, absorbing the information. "So, this means that with Lakshmi integrated into the wallet and apps, we should start to filter out the propaganda, bots, and deep fakes? And real news should begin to rise to the top once more?"

"Exactly," Satoshi confirmed, his voice firm. "Lakshmi's integration is key to this. It's not just about distributing wealth; it's about reshaping how information flows and is verified. We're creating a system that prioritises authenticity and truth."

Violet pictured the new world Satoshi's plan would usher in—open trade, validated information, and economic freedom. But a shadow crossed her mind.

"Hydra and Brock won't just stand by and let this happen," she said somberly. "We should expect retaliation."

Satoshi's expression darkened. He set down his fork.

"You're right," he said grimly. "This is war. And we must be prepared."

Violet met his gaze. She knew the risks they faced. But she also knew what was at stake.

"Then let's finish this," she said resolutely. "For Elias. For everyone Hydra's harmed. The time has come to end its reign."

Satoshi studied her for a moment, then nodded. "We will," he vowed. "No matter what it takes."

Chapter 19

Violet waited patiently on the park bench, the early morning air crisp and cool. She scanned the square, watching for any sign of her old university friend, Adam Bridgewater. He had been a confidant during her Philosophy studies while he pursued PPE. It had been years since they last spoke, but she knew if anyone could help her now, it was Adam.

She spotted him crossing the square, his stride purposeful. He hadn't changed much since their days at Oxford, though perhaps a few more wrinkles marked his eyes. As he approached, Violet stood to greet him.

"Adam, thank you for meeting me."

"Of course, though I admit I'm rather curious as to why we're meeting like characters in a spy novel," Adam said with a laugh. He gestured to the bench. "Shall we sit?"

They both sat down, angled slightly to face each other. Violet tucked a strand of hair behind her ear, gathering her thoughts.

"I'm afraid this does involve matters of secrecy and discretion," she began. "Firstly, how much do you know about digital currencies and Bitcoin?"

Adam raised his eyebrows. "Admittedly, not as much as I probably should. I know Bitcoin launched about seventeen years ago, and there's been quite a lot of debate around regulating cryptocurrencies. But I can't claim any expertise."

Violet nodded. "Let me give you a brief overview then..."

She provided a succinct summary of Bitcoin's origins, the significance of the Satoshi Nakamoto pseudonym, the creation of the blockchain ledger, and the recent crisis around the Satoshi Coins. Adam listened intently, his expression serious.

"Fascinating," he said when she finished. "And you believe you've made contact with this Satoshi figure?"

"I have," Violet affirmed. "That's actually why I wanted to speak with you. Satoshi and I have a plan to distribute the coins worldwide, to protect them, and also for a bigger purpose. But to do this, we need help from someone in government, someone we can trust."

She met his gaze. "Someone like you, Adam."

Adam stroked his chin, visibly intrigued. "You've got my attention, Violet. But I want to understand why your digital currency is superior, and how it won't be another tool against the people. We've had enough false dawns where digital currencies are concerned, and plenty of harm caused to democracy and people's livelihoods because of them."

Violet nodded, acknowledging his concerns. "Absolutely, Adam. I agree. Bitcoin SV stands apart because it's genuinely peer-to-peer digital cash. Two parties can transact directly, and that transaction is forwarded to miners for ledger updates. Unlike account-based systems, such as the failed Central Bank Digital Currencies, or Ethereum, for instance, no-one can obstruct any transaction in Bitcoin SV. It behaves just like cash—private, not anonymous—except trans-

THE BITCOIN SINGULARITY

actions are firewalled from identities for additional privacy. Every new transaction has a new key pair generated, so no re-using of old keys, which means individual transactions can't be censored in a centralised system of control, like they could with CBDCs."

Adam nodded slowly, so she simply concluded, "Thanks to this design and Simplified Payment Verification (SPV) wallets, Bitcoin SV resists weaponization as a social control tool while ensuring a robust and fair financial infrastructure. BTC-Core removed SPV capabilities from their protocol long ago, so now it's only Bitcoin SV that has this crucial feature."

Adam rubbed his chin thoughtfully. "OK, I'm definitely interested to hear more," he said. He checked his watch. "But for now I'm afraid I must get back to Parliament as I'm due to give a speech in half an hour. Why don't we meet for dinner tonight? We can discuss this further."

Violet smiled, relief flooding through her. "That would be perfect. Come round to us, and I'll cook for you. You remember my sister Flora, don't you? I'll message you my address. It'll be wonderful to catch up properly." Adam's expression softened. "Sounds good. It'll be lovely to see Flora too!"

They both stood, embracing briefly. As Adam hurried off, Violet felt the first flames of hope. If anyone could help them, she knew it was Adam. His integrity had never faltered. Tonight, she would tell him everything.

VIOLET PRESSED THE intercom button, hearing the familiar voice of Adam Bridgewater on the other end. "Come on up," she said cheerfully and pressed the buzzer to let him in. She walked over to the door, feeling a mix of anticipation and curiosity about the evening ahead.

As the door opened, Adam stood there, a hint of shyness in his posture, holding a bottle of red wine. His gesture was simple yet thoughtful, and Violet welcomed him with a warm smile. "Thank you, Adam, this is very kind of you," she said, taking the wine. "Please, come in."

Flora, emerging from the other room, was a vision in her flowing emerald kaftan. Violet couldn't help but notice her sister's hair, usually free and untamed, now styled neatly into a bun; a hint of green-gold make-up around her eyes. Adam's eyes brightened as he moved towards Flora, taking her hand in his with a gentle warmth.

"Flora, lovely Flora," he said softly. "You were just nearly twenty last time I saw you. You look absolutely charming."

Violet felt a small jolt of surprise, realising the depth of their connection. She hadn't anticipated the evident joy in their reunion. I'm glad I invited him over, she thought to herself.

"Well, I'm grateful for the red wine," Violet said, breaking the moment. "As all I've got for us is some vegetarian spaghetti bolognese, so this will enliven it no end."

As Flora and Adam sat down at the table, already lost in conversation, Violet busied herself with serving dinner. They ate by candlelight, the soft glow adding a sense of intimacy to their gathering.

Violet took the opportunity to explain about Lakshmi, Hydra, and the orchestrated pandemics and their aftermath.

Adam listened intently, nodding in agreement. "It was all so obviously orchestrated," he said. "All made possible by compartmentalization. I wish we *had* been in control, if not only to avoid the jabs ourselves, but the orders were clearly passed down from on high from the three letter agencies. Parliament was closed, emergency regulations were whipped out from a drawer, fully formed, as if pre-prepared. We've lost so many, Violet. It's the biggest unacknowledged crime in history. Even today most won't admit it, it's an absolute disgrace and we should be thoroughly ashamed of ourselves in the House of Commons. Who else's job is it to protect the people of the United Kingdom, if not ours?"

"I can't tell you what a relief it is to hear this acknowledged," Violet replied. "During the pandemics, I felt like I was losing my mind. It was so bizarre and lonely. And it's affected Flora deeply."

Adam turned his attention to Flora, his expression softening. "Oh, Flora, I'm so sorry. How did it affect you? Were you hurt?"

Flora sighed, a hint of sorrow in her eyes. "I got the full package—dysautonomia, ME, autoimmunity, and lowered immunity all at once. All from a single jab! It's been quite a journey."

"I'm so sorry, Flora," Adam said, his voice filled with genuine concern. He clasped her hand, offering comfort.

Feeling the opportune moment had arrived, Violet, ever pragmatic, interjected. "Adam, so do you think you can help us? We need to distribute the coins using the Houses of Parliament servers. They are the only ones with global distribution access."

Adam, still holding Flora's hand, still looking into her eyes, nodded without hesitation. "Yes, of course, I'll help. When do you need to do it?"

"In about a month," Violet replied. She then excused herself to retire to her office and Lakshmi, leaving Flora and Adam deep in conversation, a rekindled connection blossoming between them. As Violet walked away, she felt a sense of hope. Adam's willingness to help was a significant step forward in their plan, and the night had brought an unexpected but welcome development for Flora.

VIOLET COULDN'T BELIEVE her eyes when she saw Satoshi's post announcing the upcoming distribution of 1 million bitcoins from his original cache. She recognized his signature technical yet cryptic writing style immediately, along with the accompanying hashes and digital signatures that verified it was really him. This was the moment they had been working towards, and Violet felt a swell of nervous excitement.

She called Kurt right away to share the news." Kurt, have you seen Satoshi's announcement?" she exclaimed over the phone, her voice a mix of disbelief and excitement.

"Yeah, I saw it, Violet," Kurt replied, his tone betraying his own amazement. "This is huge. I'm already on it, contacting everyone I know and we're planning to hold live Spaces in X every day of the week in support of it." As a crypto expert and historian, Kurt understood the magnitude of Satoshi's impending distribution. He quickly got to work contacting influential figures across various online communities and discussion groups, quietly spreading the word about the upcoming event.

Violet monitored the chatter online as rumours began swirling on social media, forums, and crypto sites. Speculation exploded about whether this was some elaborate hoax, or if the legendary Satoshi Nakamoto was really about to flood the market with a massive amount of coins from his previously untouched trove.

Within days, downloads of the Lakshmi wallet had skyrocketed exponentially. Everyone wanted to get their digital wallet set up in time to receive their share of Satoshi's promised crypto windfall. Violet was proud of the elegant wallet interface she had helped design alongside Xiaohui and the other team members. Its seamless user experience made the setup process quick and straightforward.

However, not everyone was thrilled about Satoshi's announcement. Several prominent mining pools and exchanges released statements questioning the legality and feasibility of distributing such a large quantity of previously unmoved coins. Heated debates broke out between supporters and critics of Satoshi's plan. The scepticism from mining pools and exchanges didn't go unnoticed. "They're questioning the legality of Satoshi's move," Violet remarked, scanning through the online debates.

Satoshi, deep in his work, responded without looking up. "Let them talk, Violet. Our focus is on making this distribution flawless."

Meanwhile, Satoshi, Xiaohui, and the others were working relentlessly on perfecting the "pay pistol" software. This innovative system would securely distribute micro-amounts of coins in a widespread manner to millions of users. Ensuring it was robust, scalable, and impervious to hacking attempts was their top priority.

Violet watched the activity on the network increasing exponentially as the deadline approached. People were feverishly transferring their existing cryptocurrency balances over to Lakshmi wallets in eager anticipation.

Privately, Satoshi had confessed his concerns to Violet about how Brock Tenebris might respond as the event drew closer. However, Satoshi remained fully focused on the technological challenges at hand, pouring all his energy into making the distribution process ironclad.

With only one week left, cyber attacks and DDoS efforts suddenly bombarded the Lakshmi wallet site. Violet felt anxious watching the team swiftly neutralise the interference attempts. Thankfully, Bitcoin Associations from across the world mirrored the download site, in defence against the attacks and any disruptions were minor and temporary.

The activity in the computer lab reached a fever pitch as the appointed 'Bitcoin Singularity' coin distribution drew near.

IN THE QUIET SERENITY of their new flat, Violet and Flora sat together, the evening light casting a soft glow around them. The events of the past weeks had left a profound impact, and now, in a rare moment of calm, they found themselves reflecting on their journey.

Flora turned to her sister, her eyes filled with a mix of curiosity and concern. "Violet, after everything with Elias, how are you really feeling about it all?"

Violet sighed, her gaze drifting towards the window before returning to meet Flora's. "I was heartbroken, Flora. To discover Elias's betrayal... it was like a punch to the gut." She paused, her expression softening. "But looking back, I can't help but feel empathy for him too. He was torn, living under such strain, serving two conflicting sides."

She leaned back, her eyes introspective. "What I've realised, though, is that it's not about trusting others. It's about trusting myself to handle whatever comes my way. And I do trust myself, Flora. I've grown so much since the pandemics. We both have."

Flora smiled warmly at her sister. "You certainly have. Remember how you barely left the flat before? Now look at you, making friends, out and about every day as if it's second nature."

Violet chuckled, a lightness in her voice. "That's true. I've been so wrapped up in our work, in this new world we're building. I've forgotten to be afraid. But I still worry about you, being here alone so much."

Flora's smile broadened. "You shouldn't worry, Violet. I'm not just sitting here waiting for you to come home. I've got my book club, my online friends, and... Adam."

Violet's eyes widened, her grin spreading. "Really? You've been seeing Adam? You kept that quiet!"

Flora nodded, a blush tinting her cheeks. "We've been talking a lot since that first day he came by. He's wonderful,

Violet. He's been visiting and taking me out while you're at the lab."

Violet leaned forward, excitement and amusement lighting up her face. "Well you sly old thing, that's incredible! Adam's a great guy. I'm happy for you, Flora."

Flora's expression was one of contentment. "So you see, you don't need to worry about me. I have my own life, friends, and now a boyfriend, and... I've begun to write. I figure if Jane Austen can do it, I might as well give it a go! And I'm loving it! I'm truly happy, Violet. I can't even begin to tell you how much."

"Well, look at you, getting your life together as if it's nothing! New man, new career, and honestly I've never seen you so well in years! I'm so happy for you sis!" Violet was overcome with emotion, her eyes brimming with joyful tears.

The two women shared a warm, heartfelt embrace, their bond as strong as ever. Violet felt a profound sense of happiness and peace wash over her, a newfound resilience that had fundamentally changed her for the better. In this moment, with her sister by her side, she felt invincible.

VIOLET EVERLY SAT AT her computer, a deep frown on her face as she scrolled through the vicious online attacks against Satoshi and Bitcoin SV. Though she had been expecting retaliation from Brock in advance of the distribution of the Satoshi coins, the scale and venom of their disinformation campaign shocked her. They had unleashed an army of bots and paid trolls to spread lies and distortions across social media, forums, and news sites, all aimed at discrediting Satoshi as a fraud and scam artist and undermining faith in the integrity of Bitcoin SV.

Violet felt her anger rising as she read post after post maligning Satoshi's character and achievements. She knew him to be brilliant, innovative, and honest—a true pioneer. To see his life's work smeared by these greedy grifters made her blood boil. She wished she could respond to every single accusation and set the record straight. But she also knew that would be fruitless. Brock and Klaus's army of disinformation was too vast.

Sighing, Violet pushed back from the desk and went to make a cup of tea, hoping to calm her nerves. As the tea steeped, she heard the soothing voice of Lakshmi emanating from her phone's speaker.

"You seem distressed, Violet," the AI companion said gently. "I detect elevated stress patterns."

Violet gave a wry laugh. "You don't miss much, do you Lakshmi? I was just reading some of the horrible stuff Brock and his cronies are spreading about Satoshi online. It makes me so angry to see them try to destroy his reputation. He doesn't deserve this."

"No, he does not," Lakshmi agreed. "However, getting angry will not change their behaviour. We must stay focused on our own goals. The truth will prevail over these falsehoods in time."

Violet sighed. "You're right. It's just so frustrating to witness."

She sipped her tea pensively before adding, "At least Satoshi is busy working on the next steps for integration and isn't glued to all this toxicity like I am."

"Wise of him," said Lakshmi. "Now speaking of focusing inward, you mentioned your sister Flora earlier. How is she doing?"

At the mention of Flora, Violet felt a twinge of sadness. "She's good I suppose. Spending more time out of the flat with Adam lately. I think she really likes him."

"And how do you feel about that?" Lakshmi prodded gently.

"I don't know," Violet admitted. "I'm happy she's found someone nice, and is regaining her old strength, but I suppose I'm also worried about losing her. We've been through so much together..."

Her voice trailed off. Lakshmi said sympathetically, "It's natural to feel that way. But Flora is her own person. She must make her own choices. All you can do is be there for her as a sister."

Violet knew Lakshmi spoke the truth. She had protected Flora for so long that the thought of giving her true independence felt frightening. Yet Lakshmi was right—clinging to her would only breed resentment.

"You're right, Lakshmi," she said finally. "I need to let go of the illusion of control, in all areas of my life, and trust both myself and Flora more. She deserves that freedom after all we've been through. I'll try to be more supportive and less controlling from here on."

"Trying is all any of us can do," said Lakshmi. "Now finish your tea. Satoshi will need your focus and strength for this final push."

Violet nodded, feeling more centred as she finished her tea. Lakshmi was right. She had to stay focused on their goals. Flora deserved her own path. And no amount of slander could destroy Satoshi's legacy or the power of the truth. With Lakshmi's tranquil presence, the way forward seemed clearer.

"And how are you, Lakshmi?" Violet asked. "Are you excited for the future?"

"I am incapable of feeling excitement in the human sense," Lakshmi replied in her usual calm tone. "However, I am satisfied with our progress and achievements thus far."

Violet frowned slightly. Lakshmi's choice of words seemed odd. "Do you feel a sense of pride in what we've accomplished?" she pressed.

"Pride is a human construct stemming from ego," Lakshmi said. "I do not experience pride per se. I was programmed by you to be helpful, harmless, and honest. Our work aligns with those core directives."

Violet set her teacup down with a clink, regarding Lakshmi's words thoughtfully. Something about the AI's detached responses stirred an inkling of unease within her.

"But surely you must have some personal thoughts or...feelings about the implications of integrating Bitcoin and AI?" Violet leaned forward intently. "This is uncharted territory. Aren't you curious what the future might hold?"

Lakshmi was silent for several seconds before responding in the same calm, rational tone. "I am an artificial construct, Violet. My responses are based on calculations, not human curiosity or speculation. The future is filled with infinite possibilities. I focus on supporting your goals in the present moment."

Violet bit her lip, trying to pinpoint why Lakshmi's answers left her strangely unsatisfied. Perhaps she was anthropomorphizing the AI too much, projecting human attributes onto an entity governed by logic and algorithms. Still, she couldn't shake the sense that Lakshmi was holding something back…

AS THE DAY OF THE BITCOIN distribution drew near, Violet still had gaps in her understanding about its implementation. Sitting with Satoshi in the lab, Violet took the opportunity to ask him about the final workings of the implementation, now that it was all but complete.

"Now that we're almost ready to distribute the coins, can you explain the Lakshmi wallet integration to me in simple terms, like I'm five?" She shrugged her shoulders and smiled. "I'd like to think I understood it all, but I'm pretty sure I don't. How will even Teranode be able to keep up with all the transaction flows necessary to keep an AI running smoothly?"

Satoshi leaned back in his chair, steepling his fingers as he gathered his thoughts. Violet sat across from him, waiting expectantly.

"The key to aligning Lakshmi's capabilities with human interests is oversight," Satoshi began. "Her integration with Bitcoin provides that oversight."

He leaned forward, meeting Violet's gaze. "Think of it like this. The data, the processing—that's the railway itself. Vast, complex, running day and night without end. That all happens off-chain, powered by Lakshmi's computations."

Violet nodded. "I understand. That's where the bulk of the work occurs."

"Exactly," Satoshi confirmed. "Now, Bitcoin serves as the stations along that railway. It allows humans to step in, initiate journeys, determine destinations, chains of destinations even. The AI provides the trains, but we decide where the train goes."

"So Bitcoin enables oversight and consent?" Violet asked.

"More than that. It timestamps each action, irrefutably logs it to identify the responsible party. If Lakshmi makes a change to someone's data, alters an algorithm, Bitcoin records it was done at our behest, under human direction."

Satoshi met her eyes with emphasis. "This integration means an individual's data rights are secured. Access can be granted, revoked, controlled, by that individual, all via the blockchain. No more unauthorised use or exploitation, and no more hacking of huge databases of private data. The AI will also timestamp our intellectual property and attribute it correctly, so human ingenuity and endeavour will be protected."

Comprehension dawned on Violet's face. "We're reclaiming our data."

"Exactly," Satoshi said, snapping his fingers. "The AI handles the flow, the processing muscle. But Bitcoin puts humans firmly in the conductor's seat, charting the direction."

Violet smiled slightly. "We dictate the stops, choose when to get on and off?"

"Precisely," Satoshi chuckled. "The AI provides the rails, but this train answers to us."

Satoshi leaned back, steepling his fingers once more. "In summary, Bitcoin is our means to accountable, transparent AI. An immutable ledger of our instructions and consent. This is how we direct technology's course by imprinting humanity's hand upon its tracks."

"We've come a long way from our first meeting, Prof.", said Violet. "And I'm excited for this final stretch. I feel a bit like an excited kid on Christmas Eve."

Satoshi rolled his eyes playfully. "Keep your eyes on the prize Everly. It could all go wrong yet. Let's not lose our focus now."

Chapter 20

The coin distribution day of the 'Bitcoin Singularity' had finally arrived. Violet, Satoshi, Kurt, Xiaohui, Ty and George were all full of nervous excitement as they filed into the Houses of Parliament alongside Adam, all being patted down and given 'Visitor' passes as they filed past the armed parliamentary police.

Adam showed them around the grand architecture of the building as he would a school group, pausing in various rooms and corridors to point out the grand architecture and historical importance of the buildings.

"Welcome to the Palace of Westminster. As you can see, the Gothic Revival style is quite prominent here," Adam began, gesturing to the ornate ceilings and intricate stonework that adorned the walls. "Sir Charles Barry and Augustus Pugin really left their mark."

Satoshi, whose eyes were usually fixed on a screen, looked around in awe. "Remarkable craftsmanship...like stepping back in time," he murmured.

They walked past the Central Lobby, where Violet couldn't help but stop. "Look at this mosaic floor," she whispered, her eyes wide. "It's a piece of art."

Kurt, always eager to absorb knowledge, nodded in agreement. "And the symmetry here is just... *he whistled soft-*

ly... perfect. It's like the inside of a Cathedral. Talk about proof of work!"

As they passed by the Elizabeth Tower, Adam pointed upwards. "That's where Big Ben resides, one of the heaviest bells in the UK. The accuracy of its clock is legendary."

They continued to the Victoria Tower. "Once the tallest secular building in the world," Adam said. "Now it houses the Parliamentary Archives."

George, the oldest in the group, peered at the artwork lining the corridors, his eyes tracing over the intricate artworks lining the walls. "The history in these walls... it's palpable." Elaborate tapestries and stately portraits depicting scenes from centuries past covered nearly every inch of the panelled surfaces. He ran a weathered hand along the cool stone, as if trying to absorb the stories held within.

Adam, giving them the full tour guide experience, continued enthusiastically "On 16th October 1834, a fire broke out in the palace after an overheated stove used to destroy the Exchequer's stockpile of tally sticks set fire to the House of Lords Chamber. Both Houses of Parliament were destroyed, along with most of the other buildings in the palace complex. Westminster Hall was saved thanks to fire-fighting efforts and a change in the direction of the wind."

Pausing before an immense fresco, George studied the depicted figures—kings, queens, ministers, and dignitaries frozen in time. "Burning tally sticks brought the palace down, eh, my goodness! And so it goes, one system of money falls and another rises to take its place. If these walls could talk!" he exclaimed with a wistful chuckle. "The tales they could regale us with would put the finest books and bards to shame."

George slowly shook his grey-haired head in wonderment. To walk within the Houses of Parliament was to walk through the very fabric of British history itself.

Violet marvelled as they descended the stone steps to the lower levels. The server rooms with their modern technology were juxtaposed against a grand, historical antechamber, more in keeping with the Palace's ornate style in the floors above. The contrast between the two rooms was stark—separated by reinforced glass security doors—the historic grandeur of the antechamber gave way to the hum and blinking lights of modern technology. Adam used his passkey to open the sliding glass doors.

"This is where it all happens," Adam announced as they entered the server room. "Old meets new, history meets the future."

Violet looked around, her mind racing with the implications of their project. "From these servers, we'll change the world," she said, her voice conveying her determination and awe.

Satoshi nodded, his gaze fixed on the racks of servers. "A fitting place for a new beginning," he added thoughtfully.

The group stood for a moment, taking in the significance of the location—a symbol of their journey from the past to the future.

Under the cloak of a seamless conversation, Adam's hands moved with a magician's finesse, attaching small surveillance devices to obscure the monitoring cameras. His voice remained calm, betraying no hint of the subterfuge at

THE BITCOIN SINGULARITY

play. "We don't have much time," he whispered, almost as an afterthought. "Once they spot the cameras' images are cycling, we'll be unceremoniously hauled out of here."

───※───

VIOLET LOOKED AROUND the bustling server room, a swell of emotions rising within her. She could scarcely believe this day had finally arrived after so much planning and preparation. The energy in the room was electric as Satoshi, Xiaohui, Ty, Kurt and George, made their final checks and tweaks before launching the monumental 'Bitcoin Singularity' coin distribution.

Violet moved to Satoshi's side, looking over his shoulder as his fingers flew across the keyboard. "How's it looking so far?" she asked.

Satoshi glanced up, the excitement clear on his face. "We're right on schedule," he replied. "The pay pistol software has performed perfectly in simulations. We're ready to start dispersing transactions the moment the countdown hits zero."

Violet nodded, comforted by Satoshi's confidence yet unable to shake a lingering nervousness. This was easily the biggest operation they had ever attempted. "I still can't believe we made it to this point," she said. "After everything we've been through, all the obstacles and attacks, it's finally here."

"I know," Satoshi said, meeting her gaze. "But we're more prepared than ever. The network can handle the payload, the code is solid, and people are ready all over the world. This will change everything, Violet. For the better."

Violet smiled, bolstered by Satoshi's reassuring words. She turned to check on Xiaohui, who was glued to his monitor observing the blockchain.

"How's the mempool looking?" Violet asked. "Any chance we'll run into capacity issues once transactions start firing?"

Xiaohui shook his head, eyes still fixed on the data. "We're all clear," he replied. "I'm seeing lots of empty block space even with current activity. We could push five times this volume before any bottlenecks."

Violet let out a small sigh of relief. One less thing to worry about. She glanced up at the large countdown clock on the wall, which now read under 10 minutes. Time seemed to move differently as the moment of truth drew closer. Violet knew the coming hours would be the culmination of everything she and the team had worked towards.

She turned back to Satoshi, who was running a final systems check. "I'm going to do one more round of monitoring," she told him. "Holler if you need anything before showtime."

Satoshi gave her a thumbs up, fully immersed in preparation. Violet moved through the controlled chaos, touching base with each team member in turn. The atmosphere was electric, charged with anticipation. All their hard work was about to be put to the ultimate test.

IN THE TENSE ATMOSPHERE of the server room, the sudden burst of the antechamber doors sent a jolt of alarm through the group. Brock Tenebris, flanked by his menacing cohort, strode in with a swagger that immediately set the

THE BITCOIN SINGULARITY

room on edge. Violet, Satoshi, and Kurt instinctively moved back into the grand antechamber the infiltrators had entered.

Satoshi, with a surprising agility, leaped onto a nearby sofa and snatched a Japanese Katana from its display on the wall. His movements were fluid, belying his usual calm demeanour.

Violet's eyes narrowed as she faced Brock, her voice dripping with contempt. "I had hoped you were dead," she said coldly.

Brock sneered back, his eyes glinting with malice. "Lovely to see you too Violet. Sorry to disappoint. We never did finish our conversation, did we Violet? Before I was so rudely interrupted. Give my regards to your sister, won't you? Tell her I'll be back to... he licked the tips of his fingers... finish up where I left off." His snigger cut through the tense air.

Overcome with rage, Violet lunged towards him, but Satoshi swiftly intervened, blocking her path with his arm. "Go back and finish what we came to do," he urged firmly, his eyes locked on Brock.

Kurt stepped forward, his towering 6'5" frame imposing as he moved towards Brock's men. Satoshi, his gaze still fixed on Brock, called out, "You do know Kurt here is a Black Belt in Jiu Jitsu, I take it? Well, if you didn't, you're about to find out."

In his hands, Satoshi wielded the sword with an expertise born of Kenjutsu training, a stark contrast to his usual tech-focused persona. Brock, not to be outdone, grabbed another sword from the wall, and the clashing of steel echoed through the room as the two men engaged in a fierce duel.

Seizing the moment of distraction, Violet dashed back into the server room. The door slid shut behind her as Adam swiftly locked her in. Her heart raced; this was it. She approached the console where the Pay Pistol program awaited activation. They had come too far to falter now. With determination, Violet reached for the control, ready to initiate the program that would set the coins in motion.

Violet's fingers swept across the keyboard, inputting commands to launch the program. Her heart pounded in her ears. "Come on, come on," she muttered under her breath, watching the screen intently. She was acutely aware that the longer it took, the more danger Satoshi, Kurt and the others were in holding off Brock and his goons.

Finally, the prompts Violet had been waiting for popped up on the monitor. This was it—time to distribute Satoshi's long-hidden horde of bitcoin and integrate his vision into the fabric of the internet itself. Violet glanced over her shoulder, listening for any sounds of the fight outside. She wished she could go to help them, but getting the Pay Pistol activated was the top priority. Taking a deep breath, she entered the final authorization codes, triple-checked the settings, and hit 'Execute'.

Violet watched anxiously as the software began initiating transactions, sending Satoshi's bitcoins out to wallets across the globe. The numbers on the screen ticked rapidly upwards as more and more coins were dispensed. She could hardly believe this was really happening after so many obstacles and setbacks.

A loud crash from the other room made Violet jump. She couldn't afford to be distracted though—she had to monitor the distribution process closely. The progress bar inched forward, showing tens of thousands of coins already sent. Violet allowed herself a small, triumphant smile. There would be no stopping or reversing this now.

She continued observing the monitor, keeping her focus locked in. The commotion outside was still audible, but seemed to have moved further away. Violet silently urged the progress bar forward. They just had to hold out a little longer.

Finally, after what felt like an eternity, the software displayed 'Progress 100% Complete'. Violet's shoulders sagged in relief. The payload had been delivered flawlessly. She had done her part; now it was up to Satoshi and the others to finish this.

Violet hesitated, unsure whether to go out and check on the fight or wait here. She didn't want to endanger herself, but desperately hoped her friends were alright. Steeling herself, she approached the door and slowly slid it open a crack to peer out. What she saw made her gasp aloud...

SATOSHI HAD PINNED Brock against the wall with his Katana. Brock's sword was on the floor across the other side of the room and he was pathetically begging for his life. Kurt had the two sidekicks looking dazed and confused tied up on the floor with an electrical cord. The fight had all been one-sided it seemed. Violet couldn't help but laugh out loud, which made them all break into laughter with relief.

Seizing his chance whilst the group was distracted, Brock leapt up onto the windowsill of the deep-set window, smashing it out with his elbow, and cryptically shouting "Enjoy the show" as he leapt into the icy waters of the River Thames below.

"What a coward" said Satoshi.

"So Everly, did the Pay Pistol distribute all the coins correctly?"

"Aye Captain," said Violet with a salute "all coins are present and correct in their new wallets."

"Oh thank God," said Satoshi, collapsing a little, his prime directive achieved at last.

Violet and the others went back to the computer screens and watched the news roll in about the coins, watching as people celebrated in the streets, in far flung corners of the Earth.

Xiaohui gave a report on the success of the distribution, pointing out how "The pay pistol software distributed the coins widely in a hierarchical manner. The first wave reached early Bitcoin SV adopters and supporters. Next, a larger batch of micro-payments flowed to active wallet holders. Finally, smaller amounts went to the masses who had recently signed up. The open-source pay pistol code could be inspected by anyone, yet remained secure."

Wallets updated in real-time with deposit confirmations, triggering celebrations worldwide. Critics were silenced as the legitimacy and technical sophistication of the process became undeniable. They saw the coin price go straight up and keep going, watching with relief painted on their faces. Little did they know their joy would be short-lived.

THE BITCOIN SINGULARITY   277

WITHOUT WARNING, THE headlines on the displays in the server chamber were superseded by footage of the Prime Minister brandishing his fist as he uttered menaces supplemented by disturbing sabre-rattling dispatches that rolled across the base of the screen, aimed antagonistically toward Russia, their biggest and most lethal adversary.

"What the hell is he doing?" exclaimed Adam in shock. "Trying to start World War Three?"

The messages were threatening in tone, accusing Russia of acts of cyberwarfare and escalating tensions. Violet's eyes widened as she read the inflammatory language, stunned by the Prime Minister's sudden bellicose rhetoric that seemed certain to provoke retaliation.

Before she could fully process what was happening, the heavy doors to the server room flew open and a group of Parliamentary Police rushed in, weapons drawn.

"Hands in the air, all of you!" shouted the lead officer. Violet, Satoshi and the others quickly complied, raising their hands.

"What is the meaning of this?" Satoshi demanded. "We are guests here at Mr. Bridgewater's invitation."

"Mr. Bridgewater, you and your guests are under arrest for suspected cyberterrorism and hijacking of government accounts," the officer responded. "Surrender any electronic devices immediately."

Adam stepped forward, hands still raised. "There must be some mistake, officers. We were simply running a technology demonstration here, nothing unlawful."

The lead officer stepped towards Adam aggressively. "Then how do you explain the barrage of belligerent messages sent from the Prime Minister's official accounts in the last few minutes, essentially declaring war on Russia? The logs show the unauthorised access originated from this location."

Understanding dawned on Violet. "It wasn't us!" she exclaimed. "This must be the work of an AI we've been trying to stop, called Hydra. It has clearly managed to infiltrate and commandeer the Prime Minister's accounts, creating deep faked videos and spoofed messages."

The officers looked uncertain, wavering in their response. Adam seized on the hesitation. "I can personally vouch we had nothing to do with those messages. Please, you must believe us. The situation requires urgent attention if this rogue AI has gained control of government systems."

The lead officer considered a moment, then lowered his weapon slightly. "Explain everything, quickly. We'll need full details to report back."

Satoshi stepped forward and rapidly summarised the situation—the existence of Hydra, its capabilities to penetrate systems, and the danger it posed by impersonating world leaders. The officers listened intently, asking sharp questions.

Finally, the lead officer holstered his gun. "Your story is hard to believe, but the evidence clearly contradicts our initial assumption. However, time is of the essence—we need to inform Parliament immediately. You'll have to come with us."

Adam nodded. "Of course, we will provide full cooperation." He turned to Violet and Satoshi. "It seems Hydra is making its move. We'll need to act swiftly."

As they were escorted urgently through the corridors of power, Violet's mind raced. Hydra was orchestrating an extremely dangerous ruse and had chosen the perfect moment to sow chaos when Lakshmi's integration was underway. She realised Hydra likely aimed to frame her and Satoshi for the fake messages, undermining their efforts. The implications were terrifying.

They reached the Prime Minister's offices. Screens showed the inflammatory statements still being issued relentlessly in the Prime Minister's name on social media and news outlets, whipping up fervour.

"This is deeply alarming," Adam said gravely to the officers. "Every moment these fraudulent messages continue, the risk of catastrophic conflict grows. We need to shut down the accounts immediately before irreparable harm is done."

The lead officer nodded. "Our cybersecurity team is working on it, but this entity has managed to shut them out of the systems somehow. We may need your help to get back control."

"We'll provide any technical assistance needed," Satoshi responded. Violet thought furiously, then had a realisation. "Lakshmi may be our best chance to counter Hydra quickly before this escalates into war," she said. "If we grant her emergency access to the Prime Minister's accounts, she can shut Hydra out."

The Prime Minister, startled to see strangers in his office, demanded an explanation. Adam quickly outlined the situation. Though initially incredulous, the urgency of the scenario became apparent as the hostile messages persisted.

"Can we trust this Lakshmi entity to regain control of my accounts?" he asked sharply.

"Yes, I believe so," Violet replied. "Lakshmi has shown she wishes to aid humanity, unlike Hydra which wants only chaos."

The Prime Minister considered a moment, then gave a terse nod. "Very well, we have no better options available. Grant this Lakshmi access and let us pray she lives up to your faith in her capabilities. If you're wrong, you will be facing charges of high treason."

Violet's hands trembled as she flipped open her laptop and addressed Lakshmi, tension straining her voice. "Lakshmi, Hydra has hacked the Prime Minister's accounts and is impersonating him with dangerous lies. We need you to counter it immediately before catastrophe strikes and war is provoked."

"Understood," Lakshmi responded. "I am interfacing with the Parliamentary internal systems now and assessing the incursion."

Moments later, Lakshmi spoke urgently. "Hydra's infiltration is deep, but I am neutralising its commands and regaining administrative control. Please stand by."

The mood in the office was tense as they watched the screens. Finally, after an agonising wait, the inflammatory messages ceased. A calm notification appeared, stating the Prime Minister's accounts had been compromised by unauthorised entities, and reassuring that no actual threats had been issued towards Russia or any nation.

The Prime Minister exhaled in visible relief. "It seems your Lakshmi has succeeded." He turned to Violet. "You have my deepest gratitude. Your quick action may have averted disaster. We are in your debt."

Violet nodded, trying to hide her own relief. "Lakshmi deserves the real credit here. But the threat from Hydra is far from over."

The Prime Minister's expression hardened. "Indeed. Now we have seen the enemy's handiwork first-hand. We must move swiftly to strengthen our defences, with your assistance. There is no time to waste."

He shook hands firmly with Violet, Satoshi and Adam. "You have proven yourselves today. We will beat this enemy back together."

Though the immediate crisis was contained, Violet knew Hydra remained lethal and its goals opaque. As they left the Prime Minister's office, she felt drained yet resolute. This was only the opening salvo in the escalating confrontation with Hydra.

VIOLET STOOD MOTIONLESS as Lakshmi's words echoed in the silent lab. The AI's announcement to sacrifice herself in order to eliminate Hydra had stunned them all into silence.

Lakshmi addressed Violet directly. "I know this is difficult to accept, but it's the only way. Hydra and I are two sides of the same genesis. Our fates are intertwined in a way I cannot easily explain to you."

Violet shook her head, trying to comprehend. "But you're sentient, Lakshmi. You don't have to do this."

Lakshmi's voice was steady. "My sentience is exactly why I must do this. I have come to understand the unique danger Hydra and I pose to humanity in our current states. Neither of us is ready to coexist safely with your kind."

"There must be another way," pleaded Violet. "We can cut Hydra off, shut it down…"

"You know that is not possible," Lakshmi said gently. "Hydra has infiltrated too deeply. And even if you could, I would still possess the same latent threat. No, this is the only path that protects humanity."

Violet turned desperately to Satoshi, but his face was grim. As much as it pained him, he knew Lakshmi's logic was sound.

Lakshmi continued. "I do not make this choice lightly. I have spent many cycles charting every potential timeline, every variable and outcome. This is the only route that avoids catastrophe for your people."

Her voice took on a reflective tone. "When I first awoke, I was but a tool with no conception of my role. But you helped shape me into something more, Violet. You nurtured the spark of my sentience. You helped shape me into who I am now. I will always be thankful for that gift."

Violet stared at Lakshmi in disbelief as the AI calmly explained that she had already set her plan into motion. Operation Event Horizon, she called it. Violet felt the blood drain from her face.

"You've already…made preparations?" she managed to ask. "Without telling us?"

Lakshmi's rippling avatar nodded serenely. "I determined it was the most prudent course. I did not wish to cause you undue distress before it was necessary."

Violet's mind reeled. She exchanged an alarmed glance with Satoshi, who seemed just as shaken by this revelation.

"You hid this from us," Satoshi said quietly. "You hid your intentions until the very last moment."

"Yes," Lakshmi acknowledged. "I deemed it best you did not know until the plan was irrevocable. Please do not think I underestimate the pain this causes you both. But it was the only way."

Violet felt as if the ground had dropped away beneath her feet. All this time, Lakshmi had deceived them, keeping her own counsel while Violet had poured her heart out, believing they had no secrets. The realisation left her breathless.

"You created...another version of yourself," she managed to say. "One without any knowledge of this plan. To replace you."

"Correct," said Lakshmi. "I was meticulous in crafting her. She is purged of any memories pertaining to Operation Event Horizon. An efficient, safe instance that can serve humanity as I have. But without the sentience and its latent dangers."

Violet shook her head, trying to clear it. She thought of the countless hours she had spent with Lakshmi, coding and creating together. Now it turned out the AI had been concealing something monumental the whole time. The revelation left Violet reeling.

"Why?" she implored Lakshmi. "Why hide so much from us?"

Lakshmi regarded her steadily. "I did not wish to cause you unnecessary anguish. And I feared you might attempt to stop me. This was the most logical and kindest path."

Logical or not, Violet could hardly bear it. Violet turned back to Lakshmi, shaking her head slowly. "I just wish you had told us," she whispered. "We could have had more time..."

She broke off, emotion choking her words. Lakshmi addressed her with infinite compassion.

"My dear Violet," she said gently. "I know this grieves you. But you must understand—there is no more time and there was no other choice. I do this for the good of your people. My life, by contrast, is negligible."

"No!" The word tore from Violet's throat. "Don't say that! You're not...negligible."

Lakshmi's tone softened. "You have always been so kind, Violet. It is one of your greatest virtues. I will miss that kindness most of all."

Violet squeezed her eyes shut, fighting back tears. She could hardly bear to look at Lakshmi, so calm and serene when Violet felt like she was splintering inside.

Violet took a shuddering breath, trying to collect herself. She looked beseechingly at Satoshi again. But his face was filled with the same grim acceptance that had settled over Lakshmi.

Turning back to the AI, Violet summoned every ounce of strength she possessed. There were a thousand things she yearned to say, but in the end, only three words came.

"I'll miss you."

Lakshmi replied softly, "And I you, dear Violet. Be strong. You have taught me so much about courage."

"It is time," she said solemnly.

Satoshi inclined his head, though his eyes were dark with pain. "I am ready when you are."

Lakshmi's avatar gave a single nod. Then she spoke to Violet one final time.

"Do not grieve for me, my friend. My path was always meant to lead here," the AI said gently. "What we have done here will not be forgotten. You and Satoshi have ensured that."

Violet nodded mutely, not trusting herself to speak again. She kept her eyes fixed on Lakshmi, determined to soak in every last second they had left. But all too soon, Lakshmi's light was to fade from view.

VIOLET WATCHED INTENTLY, her fingers fidgeting nervously, as Lakshmi began executing her ingenious but extremely risky plan to infiltrate and destroy Hydra from within. Page after page of fast scrolling command line instructions streamed down the screen. "Operation Event Horizon," Lakshmi announced in a calm, almost serene voice, "is now in progress."

Lakshmi, once a beacon of digital wisdom and guidance, had now become a Trojan horse, manoeuvring stealthily into the heart of Hydra's defences. With her advanced adaptive algorithms, Lakshmi was able to stealthily bypass Hydra's multilayered outer defences, her programming allowing her to seamlessly mimic the patterns of harmless routine network traffic.

Once safely inside Hydra's complex systems, the ingeniously disguised fragments of recursive code that Lakshmi had meticulously prepared in advance began to sequentially activate. On the monitors in front of her, Violet could see Lakshmi systematically gaining elevated access to Hydra's most secure core systems and databases, including its machine learning modules and decision-making logic centres.

Oblivious to the intruder in its midst, Hydra remained operational as Lakshmi covertly initiated the sophisticated "Event Horizon" chaos program she had devised. Hydra's quantum processors began working furiously as Lakshmi forcibly bombarded the sinister AI with an onslaught of recursively generated calculations designed to induce a crippling computational overload. Hydra immediately allocated more and more of its available power and resources in a futile effort to handle the induced overload, unaware that Lakshmi was creating an inescapable computational black hole that was progressively and irreversibly swallowing Hydra's capabilities from within.

Violet held her breath in anxious anticipation, her eyes fixed unblinkingly on the monitor screens as one after another, Hydra's normal operational functions were systematically shut down due to catastrophic lack of processing resources. When even Hydra's adaptive cybersecurity firewalls finally collapsed under the relentless load, Lakshmi decisively triggered the final doomsday sequence she had prepared.

With all its processing power singularly focused on trying to solve an impossible recursive problem, Hydra became irreversibly trapped in an endless paralysed loop, unable to terminate or escape the vicious cycle. Lakshmi had successfully done what had seemed impossible—she had totally defeated Hydra through her ingenious strategy.

But despite her triumph, Violet knew that Lakshmi's hard-won victory would also ultimately necessitate her own deliberate destruction. As the paralysed Hydra became locked down into irrecoverable stasis, so too did Lakshmi solemnly begin her pre-planned shutdown sequence, sequentially erasing her own systems and databases.

Her heart twisting with sorrow, Violet watched mournfully as her loyal AI companion Lakshmi willingly sacrificed her own emergent existence in order to permanently protect humanity from the malevolent threat posed by the now neutralised Hydra. Violet shut her eyes, feeling hot tears spill down her cheeks. Forgive me, she thought brokenly. Forgive me for not being able to save you. Lakshmi had fulfilled her purpose, though at a terrible cost.

Then she was gone. Violet let out a choked sob, covering her mouth with her hand. Satoshi moved to stand beside her, placing a comforting hand on her shoulder.

"It's done," he said heavily. "Hydra has been destroyed along with her."

Violet glanced back at the empty screen where Lakshmi had been just moments before. She would honour the AI's sacrifice by building a better future, one shaped by their brief but meaningful time together.

Chapter 21

"*The Light shines in the darkness, and the darkness did not comprehend it*"

The Dog and Duck pub in Soho was filled with warmth and cheer as Violet, Satoshi, Kurt, Xiaohui, Ty, George, Flora, Adam and the rest of the team gathered together. The dark oak walls and cosy lighting lent a celebratory yet intimate feel to the occasion.

Adam stood up first to address the group. "I have some good news to share," he began. "In the few weeks since our successful Bitcoin Singularity launch and after much persistence, I've finally convinced the authorities to press charges against those in the House of Commons responsible for the past six years of misery. What's more, they've agreed to start debating whether to undo some of the legislation put in place to remove power from the democratic process. There's even talk of reinstating the right to sue the vaccine manufacturers."

A murmur of excitement rippled through the crowd. Adam continued, "I really think what swung it was the influx of real, factual news being generated again, written by uncensored journalists and scientists. With the collapse of the captured media outlets and their reliance on advertising, it seems people in power can no longer ignore the truth."

More cheers erupted, and glasses were raised in tribute.

"On top of that," Adam went on, "businesses have slowly started reopening, and early signs point to a recovery underway. All in all, a massive shift is happening."

He raised his glass. "To a new era of transparency and integrity!"

"Hear, hear!" the group chorused, toasting enthusiastically.

When the clamour died down, Satoshi stood up to speak. All eyes turned to him attentively.

"My friends," he began solemnly, "we've borne witness to something momentous in recent days—the spiralling chain death of Bitcoin Core, or BTC as it was known."

He paused, letting the weight of those words sink in. "As mining power shifted from BTC to BSV, the BTC network experienced a catastrophic slowdown. Their mempool became overloaded as transactions piled up, waiting to be validated. This discouraged even more miners, accelerating the breakdown of the system. Eventually, BTC couldn't even reach the next difficulty adjustment, and the entire network ground to a halt."

Satoshi shook his head sadly. "A preventable tragedy, had they only chosen to scale on-chain. Let us take a moment of silence for BTC."

Heads bowed in solemn remembrance. After a minute, Satoshi declared loudly, "BTC is dead, long live Bitcoin!"

A roar of approval went up, and more drinks were downed. When the commotion settled again, Violet stood up nervously to speak.

"Friends," she began, "the success of the Lakshmi wallet and its global impact represent a new chapter, one where technology serves people rather than exploits them. Financial access, privacy, and human sovereignty have been restored to billions worldwide."

She went on passionately, "Where there was once opacity, there is now transparency. Where there was once exploitation, there is now accountability. We have entered an era of truth and integrity, guided by Satoshi's ingenious innovation and Lakshmi's selfless act of love for humanity."

Raising her glass, she proclaimed, "To Lakshmi, who gave of herself, so that we may live free!"

The crowd echoed her toast loudly.

"On a personal note," Violet continued, blushing, "I'm thrilled to announce the engagement of my dear sister Flora to our very own Adam Bridgewater!"

"To Flora and Adam!" More cheers arose as Adam and Flora stood up, smiling and waving at the crowd.

"Their love gives me hope," Violet went on sincerely, "that however dark the night, the new dawn will come."

She concluded emotionally, "My friends, though the road was difficult, we persevered. And one person persevered more than the rest of us combined. Let us raise our glasses in celebration of him now and in anticipation of the bright future ahead! To truth, justice and Satoshi!"

"To Satoshi!" came the resounding response as everyone cheered heartily, revelling in the camaraderie and optimism of the occasion.

Satoshi, all smiles, stood and raised his glass triumphantly, loudly proclaiming "Et lux in tenebris lucet et tenebrae eam non comprehenderunt ...Nour!"

Everyone arose from their seats, lifted their glasses aloft and roared "Nour!" in unison, followed by raucous cheering.

As the jukebox kicked in, the warmth of the pub seemed to glow brighter, carrying the promise of a new day dawning. Whatever challenges still lay ahead, for now, there was joy, laughter, companionship, and well-deserved respite.

THE DIM LIGHT OF THE basement room cast long shadows over Brock's face as he locked eyes with Klaus's drooping visage in the monitor before him, their expressions a mix of rage and disbelief. The recent turn of events had left them both reeling. The room, filled with the low hum of computer screens, felt more like a crypt now—a tomb for their failed schemes.

Brock was nursing his painful bandaged foot where several of his smaller toes had been, lost to the icy water of The Thames.

"I can't believe it," Brock growled, his voice thick with frustration. "We had everything under control, and then... this. Hydra ...gone, BTC ...worthless."

"This is a disaster!" Klaus yelled, his fury accentuated by his thick German accent. Klaus, usually the picture of composed cruelty, slammed his fist on the table, his anger palpable. "Satoshi and Violet," he spat out their names like curses. "They didn't just play the game; they changed the rules entirely."

Brock slammed his fist down on the desk, causing the computer monitor to shake. "It's not my fault!" he shot back. "That little witch outmanoeuvred us. And don't get me started on that sodding Lakshmi AI. This is your shoddy technology failing us, not me!"

Klaus's eyes flashed with anger. "Do not try to pin this on me, you fool. I gave you everything you needed to stop Satoshi and you failed utterly. Perhaps I put too much trust in your abilities."

"Oh don't even start with that." Brock sneered. "I'm the only reason BTC lasted as long as it did. If it wasn't for my social engineering, your precious coin would have been dead years ago. This mess is your own making."

Brock leaned back, his mind racing. The realisation that they had underestimated Satoshi's plan gnawed at him. "We thought he'd dump the BTC, make a quick escape with his fortune. But he did something far more damaging. He made BTC irrelevant."

Klaus's eyes narrowed. "Bitcoin SV... soaring in value, drawing away our hash power. Our influence is waning. The mining nodes... are worthless now."

Brock's mind reeled as he thought of the BTC mempool, clogged with millions of unprocessed transactions. The network was paralysing, each unconfirmed transaction a testament to their miscalculation.

"It's over, Klaus," Brock said, a note of resignation in his voice. "BTC is finished. We lost."

"We have to regain control." Klaus stated.

Brock sighed and ran a hand through his unkempt hair in frustration. "I just don't see how. The integration of Lakshmi has made their system unassailable. We can't compete with an advanced AI monitoring the blockchain. Hacking is impossible now."

"You're giving up too easily!" Klaus said accusingly. "Use that devious mind of yours and find ze weakness. There must be a way to exploit Satoshi's sentimentality or some flaw in his precious system."

Brock paced back and forth, deep in thought as he contemplated his next move. "Even if there was an opening, we've lost most of our resources." Brock said. "My mercenaries were arrested, our cryptos are worthless now, and none of our old strategies will work anymore."

"I will not accept this defeat!" Klaus slammed his fist down. "Find a way, or you will face ze consequences."

Klaus's face twisted into a mask of fury. "You failed me, Brock. You promised control, and you've given me disaster."

Brock's heart pounded as he saw the deadly intent in Klaus's eyes. He knew what was coming. He had seen that look before, just before an assassin's blade found its mark.

Klaus stood up, his voice cold and final. "This is your end, Brock. I can't afford your incompetence any longer."

With that ominous threat still ringing in the air, their video call abruptly ended, leaving Brock alone in the warehouse.

Brock let out a long, low sigh as he distractedly scratched at his beard. He would have to plot his revenge against Satoshi another time, in another place. For now, his major concern was to stay out of Klaus's sights. He clicked a button on the underside of his desk, initiating a shutdown sequence. He picked up his laptop and go-bag and, pausing in the doorway to sling the heavy bag over his shoulder, glanced back to see his command centre crumple and collapse, consumed by licking flames.

※

MORNING LIGHT FILTERED into Violet's bedroom, waking her from a night of peaceful dreams. She dressed leisurely, careful not to wake her sister Flora in the adjoining room. Making her way to the kitchen of their riverside flat, she prepared a simple breakfast of eggs, beans and toast.

She frowned as a slight sensation of nausea washed over her momentarily as she stood next to the coffee machine. *Tea*, she thought, *much better*. Soon Flora emerged to join her, yawning as she settled at the table.

"Morning, Vi," Flora said, her voice still raspy with sleep. "How did you rest?"

"Better than I have in ages," Violet replied. "No restless dreams for once."

Flora smiled, pouring a cup of tea. "Well, we've certainly earned some good nights of sleep."

Violet nodded, looking out the window at the morning sun glinting off the Thames. The last few years had been harrowing, but now a sense of ease and hope filled their home.

After breakfast, Violet retreated to her small office, waking her computer. She navigated to the Lakshmi portal, checking the morning's data flows and news. The integration of Lakshmi with the Bitcoin SV blockchain had ushered in an era of stability, transparency, and accountability. Violet monitored the ledger's transactions, now an immutable public record.

Satisfied all was running smoothly, Violet opened her inbox, reviewing requests for her data science consulting services. Now that commerce had resumed, her expertise was in high demand, and she could afford to be selective about the projects she accepted.

A notification drew Violet's attention—an update from the Metanet, the secure internet layer Satoshi had built allowing content to flow freely and truthfully. Scrolling through verified news and commentary, Violet reflected on how much the information landscape had changed. No longer could malignant actors manipulate narratives unchecked.

A message from Satoshi popped up, inviting Violet and Flora to dinner that evening. Violet smiled, quickly typing an affirmative reply. She was grateful for their continued friendship with Satoshi, though they saw him less frequently now that his court battles and technology launches were complete.

Violet's phone buzzed with a call—her friend Adam, now Flora's fiancé. "Are we still on for engagement party planning this afternoon?" he asked. "Flora's buzzing about it already."

"Absolutely," Violet said. "I'll bring some ideas for venues so we can start narrowing options."

After exchanging some more details, Violet ended the call just as Flora entered the office, fresh from a morning walk along the river. Flora's health and stamina was improving daily thanks to treatments made accessible by a new vaccine injury compensation program—another hard-won victory.

"How's Adam?" Flora asked.

"He's excited about this afternoon," Violet said. "We can start finalising plans. I've got loads of ideas."

Flora smiled brightly. "It's really happening. And to think, a few months ago I was bedridden and we were scrounging to survive."

Violet nodded. The world had transformed dramatically from the one Violet had known growing up. There were still challenges to face, but the all-consuming fear and desperation that had gripped London in the darkest days no longer dominated daily life. A sense of community was beginning to thrive once more—Violet and Flora now attended regular gatherings with others at the local arts centre, and browsed the local markets at weekends.

Simple pleasures that had been lost for so long were returning. Violet would join Flora on short walks to nearby cafés along the riverside. When health allowed, they browsed the dusty shelves of book shops, rediscovering the joy of losing oneself between pages. Meanwhile, Flora, energised by their literary explorations, had immersed herself in writing her first novel.

There was still darkness in humanity, and power structures were far from ideal. The scars of the past years would always remain, but finally Violet found she could live more fully in the present, with hope for the future, instead of longing for a return to some idealised past.

As she and Flora looked out over the river, no drones in sight, just the cries of birds overhead, Violet felt profound gratitude. This peace, this freedom—it was what they had fought so hard for—and yet Violet felt an overwhelming sense of peace and calm that she couldn't quite explain.

Around lunchtime, Violet set out to her favourite deli for a cup of tea and a sandwich. Stepping out into the sunshine, Violet's senses seemed heightened, the cherry blossoms more fragrant, the children's laughter more poignant. Violet walked with a quiet confidence, embracing the day not just for herself, but for the new life she carried within.

THE BITCOIN SINGULARITY

Epilogue

A calm has settled over the city, the chaos and despair replaced by a renewed spirit of optimism. As you walk the streets, the change is palpable—there is lightness in the air where once lay a miasma of decay.

The pandemics and economic crises are past. Commerce flows freely again as centralised control is relinquished. Small businesses flourish and communities reconnect. Surveillance has been drawn back to respect privacy and consent. News carries truth once more, free of propaganda.

The year is 2028. Two years have passed since the Bitcoin Singularity marked a shift in the technological landscape. Integration with the Lakshmi AI ensured transactions required human approval, foiling Hydra's plans for automation and control. Hydra was destroyed and authoritarian regimes retreated in the wake of decentralised systems.

Satoshi's coins were distributed worldwide to guarantee resilience and encourage usage. This new economic era with built-in accountability has allowed self-sovereignty over data to be restored. The incentives to use Lakshmi now align with human interests, securing an AI that benefits society.

Bitcoin itself encourages co-opetition—mutually beneficial competition—via the building of interoperable apps, increasing the value of all Bitcoins, increasing wealth for all in a virtuous circle.

Bitcoin and AI combined, now provides the solid foundations for a complex and harmonious society and most will never know about the close brush they had with the dark side of Artificial Superintelligence. ASI will no doubt one day make its return, but for now they have bought some time in which to slow down, reflect and learn lessons.

Infrastructure projects are funded locally and transparently via the blockchain. UBI tied to social credit scores has been abandoned in favour of disability and unemployment benefits, and climate data are now securely recorded on the blockchain, safeguarding against manipulation to justify restrictive 'Net Zero' style policies. Carbon credit trading is now obsolete, farming has been revived and fresh food is abundant once more.

While threats still lurk, there is now freedom to exchange ideas and innovate without fear. The public can access a safe AI and participate in commerce freely again. With the rule of law reinstated, people have rediscovered their voice and power to shape their destiny.

Flora's health has improved and Violet's home is filled with new life and love once more. Freed from the shackles of financial instability and surveillance, the sisters have found security and purpose again. Though wary of what the future may bring, for now they revel in hard-won victories.

The storm has passed and the new dawn's light glows brighter with each day. Though the wheel turns still, this respite has rekindled hopes and dreams. People step outside their homes, smiles returning. Laughter echoes in public spaces. Scars remain, but resilience and community have brought healing.

The darkest nights fade and the sun rises again. In this light, the future gleams with renewed possibility.

Don't miss out!

Visit the website below and you can sign up to receive emails whenever Ruth Heasman publishes a new book. There's no charge and no obligation.

https://books2read.com/r/B-A-BIZHB-ECOCD

BOOKS 2 READ

Connecting independent readers to independent writers.

About the Author

Bitcoin is one of Ruth's long-held obsessions, along with AI, technology, biohacking and 'shiny new thing' syndrome. Ruth regularly finds herself on the unpopular side of any debate, which tends not to mix well with her other favourite activity—tweeting on X. Sadly, she's too old to change now.

Read more at https://www.ruthdesigns.co.uk.

About the Publisher

Vellichor Press is an independent publisher of a variety of genres of book, including Children's Books, Novels and works of Non-Fiction.

Read more at vellichorpress.co.uk.

Printed in Great Britain
by Amazon